My Husband

Dacia Maraini

Translated by

Vera F. Golini

Wilfrid Laurier University Press

We acknowledge the financial support of the Government of Canada through the Book Publishing Industry Development Program for our publishing activities. We acknowledge the Government of Ontario through the Ontario Media Development Corporation's Ontario Book Initiative.

National Library of Canada Cataloguing in Publication Data

Maraini, Dacia
    My husband / Dacia Maraini ; translated by Vera F. Golini.

Translation of: Mio marito.
Includes bibliographical references.
ISBN 978-0-88920-432-4

    I. Golini, Vera. II. Title.

PQ4873.A69M513 2004   853'.914   C2004-900453-0

Italian Edition, *Mio marito*
© 1968
Casa Ed. Valentino Bompiani
Milan
CL 04-0197-8

English Translation
© 2004 Wilfrid Laurier University Press
Waterloo, Ontario, Canada N2L 3C5
www.wlupress.wlu.ca

This printing 2010

Cover design by Leslie Macredie. Cover artwork by David Hockney, *Two Deck Chairs, Calvi*, 1972. Acrylic on canvas 60" x 48". © David Hockney. Text design by PJ Woodland.

Printed in Canada

Mixed Sources
Product group from well-managed forests, controlled sources and recycled wood or fibre
www.fsc.org Cert no. SW-COC-003049
© 1996 Forest Stewardship Council
FSC

Clothed in flames and rolling through the sky is
      how I felt the night he told me
he had a mistress and with shy pride
slid out a photograph.

    ...

If it is true we are witnessing the agony of
      sexual reasoning in our age
then this man was one of "those original machines"
that pulls libidinal devices into a new transparence.

    ...

To stay human is to break a limitation.
Like it if you can. Like it if you dare.
                      —Anne Carson, *The Beauty of the Husband*

Contents

Acknowledgements VII

A Note on the Translation IX

Introduction 1

My Husband 15

Dazed 22

Mother and Son 27

The Wolf and the Lamb 32

The Two Angelas 39

The Other Family 45

Diary of a Telephone Operator 54

Beloved Death 67

The Red Notebook 71

Suffering 76

The Linen Sheets 81

Marco 86

The Blond Wig 94

Diary of a Married Couple 100

Plato's Tree 109

Maria 115

These Hands 121

The Life and Prose Works of
    Dacia Maraini: An Afterword 145

Appendixes
    Interviews with Dacia Maraini 169
    Bibliography of Maraini's Writings 170
    Maraini's Filmography 173
    Awards and Translations of
        Maraini's Prose Works 173

Critical Bibliography of Maraini's
    Prose Works 177

～

Acknowledgements

The idea of this translation owes its origin to an annual congress held in the mid-1990s by the American Association of Italian Studies, with participation by members of the Canadian Society for Italian Studies. At that time, a group of academic women realized that there were very few collections of short stories written by Italian women, and almost no translations. We also sensed the need for more monographic studies on Italian women writers, especially of the twentieth century, as a new millennium approached. Our wish for more monographs is well on its way to being realized, since the nineties have seen the publication of three monographs on Dacia Maraini alone. Translations of works by Italian women writers are also multiplying in time, as evidenced by the rich list of translations of Maraini's prose works appended at the conclusion of *My Husband*, the first English translation of *Mio marito*.

My great thanks are owed to Dr. Walter Martin, professor of English, and distinguished professor emeritus of the University of Waterloo, who became involved thanks to his great love of Italian language and culture. His several and meticulous examinations of the manuscript, his ·vigilance and resourcefulness certainly have contributed accuracy and freshness to this translation. I sincerely thank my family for their patience, and Dacia Maraini herself, for her constant interest in this work. I owe an expression of gratitude to the WLU Press team of editors, especially Carroll Klein for her interest and invaluable guidance. My sincere thanks are given to St. Jerome's University for the sabbatical leave granted me, which has made this publication possible.

$\mathcal{A}$ Note on the Translation

$\mathcal{T}$*he act of translation is a process of shaping and* transformation, a creative activity invested with much responsibility owed to the original writer, to the work of art itself, and to the potential reader. Access to today's infinite resources in the areas of language studies greatly facilitates the work of translation and lends it renewed vigour, as is evidenced by the large number of translations of Maraini's popular prose works, a list of which is appended to the conclusion of this book. Today, the Italian phrase "traduttore, traditore" (translator, traitor), no longer need be true as it may have been in past times.

As a student of Maraini's writings for the past two decades, I have approached this translation with curiosity and with pleasure, wishing to give the reading public the flavour of the language, the irony, and the social perspectives of this extraordinary living writer. Dacia Maraini published this collection of short stories at the age of thirty-two, following her first three novels. Maraini combines a deep insight into human emotions and motivations with a passionate concern for the retrieval of women's unwritten history. Such themes give rise to a rich vocabulary that draws the reader into intimate Italian ambiances and distances the reader in order to frame wider vistas of landscapes, cityscapes, and interiors, which can be both alienating and welcoming. I have come to view Maraini's writing as a metaphor for both microscopic and macroscopic study; that is, she is able to perceive the human condition through the lens of both the microscope and the telescope, focusing on detail, but also providing wide panoramic perspectives—a technique that proves exciting for the translator and useful for the film director.

This translation seeks to be faithful to the word and the spirit of the original text, employing, however, the idiomatic English widely used in

Canada today by the young generation, since this is the age group most frequently presented in the stories. In addition, a deliberate effort has been made to convey the veracity of the original text even when it reveals some oversights by the young Maraini, as in the instance of the last story, "These Hands" (Le mani). The diary through which the protagonist tells her story inaccurately records the passing of time between November and March: December has thirteen weeks, and February has nine!...The stream-of-consciousness narration and the monotony of the life of the protagonist are such that the reader, like the narrator, is easily made numb to time. To date no critic has drawn attention to this—so naturally and automatically flows the (inaccurately marked) passing of time within the fiction. Therefore I have chosen to preserve in the translation the incorrect temporal sequence just as it is present in Maraini's story in Italian.

The work of translation demands meticulous attention to detail, as the translator attempts to reproduce the sense and semblance of the original. Natalia Ginzburg, an author greatly admired by Maraini, stated in an interview: "What a job of ants and horses translation is....One has to be as exact and industrious as an ant and have the impetus, the strength, of a horse to pull ahead."[1] Ginzburg was alluding to her translations of Proust and Flaubert, whose works she loved and rendered into Italian. Her sincere love for these authors and her wish to share their works with other Italians nourished her through the ravages of the war years. It is my hope that this first translation of *My Husband* into English may inspire in the reader of stories, in the students of women's studies and cultural studies, and in the research scholar alike a similar love for the writings of Dacia Maraini.

VFG, 2004

ote

1 Peg Boyers, "An Interview with Natalia Ginzburg," *Natalia Ginzburg: A Voice of the Twentieth Century,* ed. A.M. Jeannet and G. Sanguinetti Katz (Toronto: U Toronto P, 2000) 29.

$\mathcal{I}$ntroduction

$\mathcal{T}$*he short story has been a staple in Italian litera-*
ture from Boccaccio's *Decameron* in the mid-fourteenth century to Verga
and D'Annunzio in the late nineteenth century. Pirandello's collection,
Novelle per un anno (Short Stories for One Year), published at the turn of
the twentieth century, and later, Alberto Moravia's *Racconti romani* (1954,
Roman Tales) as well as *Nuovi racconti romani* (1959, *New Roman Tales*)
infuse refreshingly new life in this genre with some of Moravia's best
sketches of working-class characters in everyday situations. However,
collections of short stories by Italian women writers have been rather rare,
perhaps because in past centuries women communicated most often
through letters and journals, by which they also kept records and edu-
cated themselves and others. The first appearance of the novel in Italy, just
before the middle of the nineteenth century, provided the stylistic and lin-
guistic vehicle that enabled narration to be shifted from serials in the public pages of newspapers to the more private exercise of creating books. As
a result, women writers were able to participate in the vast flourishing of
the Italian novel in the late nineteenth century. This continues to be for
women, the most popular and successful of the genres; Sardinian Grazia
Deledda, its most celebrated exponent, was awarded the Nobel Prize for
literature in 1926.

Dacia Maraini has been publishing novels since 1962, to national and
international acclaim;[1] in addition, she has published over forty plays,
and has produced a large number for the Italian theatre, which today are
performed on stages around the world. Her collection of short stories,
Buio (1999, *Darkness*, 2002), was awarded the prestigious Italian prize, the
Strega, for literature. The stories are centred on violence against children—a global concern in the 1990s and today.

Violence is also the overarching theme of her seventeen stories in *Mio marito*—violence against women, physical, emotional, and mental violence, as well as violence in the form of abuses by social institutions in need of reform.

The 1968 publication of *Mio marito* coincided with the beginning of intense social questioning and change in Western cultures. In the two decades following World War Two there was in Italy a preoccupation about the widening gap between the upper and lower classes. Social infrastructures such as labour laws, medical benefits, unemployment insurance, and other public services were almost non-existent. The economic gap between North and South Italy was alarming. The 1960s brought mass education beyond the primary level for the first time, and the number of students spiralled beyond what could be accommodated at universities, which were in great need of reform. In the area of labour, federal and local administrations failed to take effective action. As a result, Italy was plagued by workers' and student strikes throughout the 1960s and later: "The 1970s, in particular, were years of increasing liberalization and secularization of Italian society, with new social and pressure groups demanding greater civil liberties and new rights for women."[2]

Through these decades Italian women participated fully in public displays of social unrest, voicing concerns on feminist issues. Attitudes that called for radical changes challenged every area of society and politics, obliging Italians to rethink their cultural life in terms of gender—something completely new in the country's history. Women's movements in Italy had been significant in the late nineteenth and the early decades of the twentieth century, but the massive participation and the wide-ranging effects that characterized the feminist movement of the late 1960s were unprecedented.[3] In the period between 1970 to 1985 there were visible signs of change as "divorce and abortion were legalized and new laws relating to the family were passed."[4] In 1970 the divorce law passed and was upheld overwhelmingly by a national referendum in 1974; the ban against advertising contraception was lifted in 1971, and in 1975 a reform of family law gave equal rights to both parents. In 1977 women were finally granted improved rights in the workplace, including equal pay for work of equal value. Paternity and five-month maternity leaves became law as well, while abortion was finally legalized in 1978.

The publication by the Committee for Equality, titled *Le donne italiane in cifre* (1986, Statistics on Italian Women), presents data on various facets of private and public life for the two decades following the publication of *Mio marito*. They show that, unlike the strides taken with respect to abortion, divorce, and contraception, reforms in education and work opportunities in the 1970s still lagged behind. For example, while the percentage of the female population receiving a high school education between 1972 and 1983 improved from 42.5 to 49.3 percent, with respect to a university education only 2.1 percent of women held a degree, compared with 3.6 percent of men.[5] Statistics related to employment are also of interest. In *Mio marito* men and women lacking a university degree are often portrayed as unemployed or seeking work in vain. Women made up 52 percent of the population in 1985; 35 percent of these, fourteen years old and over, were part of the workforce. Of the 35 percent comprising the female workforce, 32.4 percent were employed, while 58.1 percent were looking for work. The difficulty of finding gainful employment discouraged many from searching for work outside the home. Data recorded for 1980 and 1985 indicate that 41 percent of women reported home and family as their occupation.[6] Maraini herself provides some data in her 1987 essay, "Reflections on the Logical and Illogical Bodies of My Sexual Compatriots," where she states, "There are twelve million full-time housewives in Italy still. It's hard to forget this. Twelve million women who do heavy labour, without schedules, without salary, without insurance, and, above all, without the respect of those who demand this work and who make use of it."[7]

Dacia Maraini has been actively involved with the Italian feminist movement since its inception in the 1960s. She helped found and fund theatre groups for women so that feminist issues and ideas could have a voice. She also campaigned successfully to bring reform to prisons for women.[8] As a writer, political activist, and TV commentator, she joined a number of national movements such as "Rivolta femminile" and "Movimento femminista romano," openly campaigning for abortion laws, contraception, and divorce. Her personal engagement with social issues continues to provide much material for her creative works, which are considered, in diverse ways, a reflection of the national social condition. *Mio marito* can be regarded as a microcosm, containing the seeds of works published since 1968 that focused on concerns involving identity, family, memory, violence, and enclosure.

The short stories contained in *Mio marito*, translated for the first time in English in *My Husband*, provide a fascinating glance going back nearly four decades, and so they enable readers to measure the gains Italian women have made in terms of parity, autonomy, education, and human rights. In this respect, these stories of Italian women may also reflect the condition of middle-class women throughout post-war Europe.

At the same time, *My Husband*, as a work of fiction, provides examples of deliberately exaggerated personalities. The men and women in these stories are at times caricatures, but at times we see portraits of reasonable people resembling those with whom we work and live. As such, they arouse our sympathy, because they are trapped within the confines of an urban society on the eve of what was to become Italy's economic and social transformation.

From *L'età del malessere* (1963, *The Age of Discontent*, 1963), her first international best seller, to her blockbuster, *La lunga vita di Marianna Ucrìa* (1990, *The Silent Duchess*, 1992), which established her as Italy's foremost writer, Maraini's art is committed to a critique of social structures and values, especially as they affect women. The stories in *My Husband* address fundamental issues of feminism, including homosexual relations, a "hot" and taboo topic in Italian Catholic society of the 1960s. When first published, these stories seem to have had a clear resonance with the times; inhumane living and working conditions often form the frame within which female characters exist and suffer. The poverty and deplorable lives of female narrators and male partners are recurring motifs, as is the helplessness of workers in the absence of proper labour laws. "Diary of a Telephone Operator" was turned into a film in 1969, the year after publication, and the celebrated actress Claudia Cardinale played the leading role. In "These Hands" the supervisor publicly reprimands workers who, despite protests and demonstrations, are obliged to breathe poisonous factory fumes and work on inefficient assembly lines. When the narrator loses a finger on the machine she operates, her misery becomes so evident to her that she tires of life altogether; her mangled hand becomes a symbol of her physical mutilation and continued suffering.

Maraini's female characters in heterosexual relationships illustrate numerous predicaments that persisted till the mid- to late 1970s: lack of access to contraception, unwanted pregnancies, the impossibility of divorce and abusive husbands who were neither reported nor punished. In some stories, husbands take other partners, sometimes with the wife's knowledge and helpless approval, as in "The Linen Sheets" and "The Wolf and the Lamb." The lack of divorce laws led to ménages-à-trois, threesomes cohabiting under the same roof. But this living arrangement is introduced also to draw attention to the still existing need for adequate housing throughout the Italian peninsula. The situation of the man with two women in the house is, in addition, a humorous criticism of wives' tolerant attitudes toward husbands with mistresses. Both stories outline the progressive exploitation of the wife by the husband and his lover. In the latter story, Elisa is encouraged by her mother to leave her wastrel husband, whom she does not need because it is her money he spends. Elisa is unable to accept her mother's advice, so complete is her self-effacement: "My husband is a rather handsome man. I can't imagine why he married an ugly face like me. 'To get at your money,' says my mother who's got no brains and can't see farther than her nose." When the mistress becomes pregnant, the mother's fears are realized. The story ends with a macabre choice for Elisa: "As I put down the cup and looked at them, their eyes filled with curiosity. I smiled and they responded with a grin. They both looked as if they would never smile again." Elisa lethargically—and with drastic consequences—accepts whatever human relations bring, remaining naive about men and life's possibilities.

Memory is another of Maraini's central concerns in *My Husband*, as well as in several novels she has published since 1968. A humorous treatment of this theme is given in "Plato's Tree," illustrating Socrates' idea of the nature of memory as described by Plato in his dialogues. According to Socrates, memory is of two kinds: "like a stone that always keeps the information carved in it, or like a tree full of birds that at the first gust of wind fly off, leaving the tree empty." When she cannot explain to herself why in her daily diary two pages have remained blank, the protagonist decides that her memory is of the latter kind. Those pages coincide with her husband's unexplained absence. Has he gone away forever? Is she the cause of his absence? Has her memory, like Plato's birds, "flown away" from fear? To the unnamed narrator it is clear that Carmelo is torn between his two lives: not free with her after a civil marriage, but obliged to support a wife and children by his first, Catholic marriage. Underpaid and unable to divorce, Carmelo is at his wits' end, at times abusive to the narrator. The mystery of his absence is answered by a shocking discovery: "I passed out. I lay there on the floor in shock....Try as hard as I might...I was unable, totally incapable, of remembering anything." The narrator is like Maraini's many protagonists who suffer from a lack of personal and social memory, as in "Dazed" and "Suffering." In prose works that followed *My Husband*, Maraini sought to create female characters more awake to personal and social problems, more capable of finding and confronting choices as a way out of life's predicaments.

Closeted gay and lesbian relations are portrayed in two interesting stories, one somewhat humorous, the other tragic. Centuries of religious dominance have created homophobic attitudes in Italian culture that were particularly apparent in the 1960s and '70s. In these stories, human involvements outside of heterosexual relations are therefore portrayed as dysfunctional, superficial, and traumatic. "The Two Angelas" shows the impossibility of realizing, in private life, fantasies and aspirations that do not conform to social norms. The narrator, an elementary schoolteacher, painfully realizes that as an adult she cannot give life to the fantasy for a lesbian love she entertained when a teenager:

> I haven't seen Angela since the morning when, faint with pas-
> sion, I kissed and gently nibbled her ear. Angela, contrary to what
> I had imagined, burst out laughing. She said she knew I was in love
> with her and would return my love out of curiosity and fun. Let's try
> to love each other, she said at one point, taking her clothes off in a
> hurry and throwing them all over the room. A minute later, she
> stood naked in front of me, wearing only her red bootees and a
> mocking, provocative smirk on her small, fat lips.
>
> At that precise moment all my love vanished, disappeared,
> evaporated like water on fire.

Having failed to realize her deepest desire for human contact, the narrator resolves to live with memories, the only things that can awaken in her the joy of living. The story "Maria" is told by the less dominant partner; she recounts Maria's sufferings, caused by her parents who are unable to accept her homosexuality. The narrator is accepting of existence; she works to support the cerebral and questioning Maria. Although these two women live in a manner very similar to that of an exploitative, heterosexual husband-wife relationship, there is love between them, and a comfortable acceptance of one another. But Maria's parents, unable to accept her lifestyle, have her forcibly committed to a mental hospital. Maria takes her own life when she realizes that her life is impossible on the outside and absurd in the asylum run by strict Catholic nuns. It is possible to read between the lines the blame that is assigned to institutions that do not provide adequate assistance, and to parents, who lack understanding and tolerance for their children's life choices. In fact, the disruptive influence of parents in children's lives is a frequently recurring theme in *My Husband.* In "Dazed," "Suffering," "Mother and Son," "Marco," and "Diary of a Married Couple," oppressive or uncaring parents have a destructive influence on the lives of children of both sexes.

The stories "Dazed" and "Suffering" show in humorous but poignant images how oppressive parental pressure causes withdrawal and alienation from reality in female protagonists, whose desire for anonymity is stylistically conveyed by their remaining unnamed. The husbands in the latter two stories are led to drastic actions when they cannot live up to their parents' expectations. Not even the love, support, and acceptance of caring wives can overcome their parents' past and present negative influences.

Maraini's approach to the characters and lives of several protagonists in *My Husband* may have been influenced by the literary trends popular in Europe in the 1950s and '60s. Conspicuous among these was the element of the "absurd" that characterizes the works of prominent writers, such as Eugène Ionesco and Samuel Beckett. Maraini reminds us of their concerns and style, as shown by some of her early works, the novel *A memoria* (1967, Memory) and plays such as *La famiglia normale* (1970, The Normal Family) and *La donna perfetta* (1975, The Perfect Woman). In *My Husband*, several principal characters, who remain anonymous, mimic the sense of the absurd in character and actions.[9] Disconnected from social reality as a result of memory loss or regression to the past, Maraini's women escape thought and action through daydreaming and inertia. They are caricatures, victims of time, family, friends, violence, or social circumstances that fetter their daily lives. At times Maraini turns the absurd into a means of ridicule of social patterns, rituals, and values that were no longer viable at a time when Italy was ripe for an economic miracle. In addition, her stories show that the economic miracle — the growth of consumerism, secularization, modernization, standardization — benefited only the lives of the few within reach of a good education and the means to generate income by investing.[10]

But Maraini is also very capable of creating humour, especially in stories where she draws a fine line between the absurd and the comedic. Two stories are certainly imbued with both: "Mother and Son" and "The Other Family." The former is a caricature verging on farce of what Italians call *mammismo* — an adult son's dependence and reliance upon a doting and controlling mother. The young single woman who lives on the other side of the wall dividing the two apartments listens to the daily conversations of mother and son, her expressions of pride at his good looks while she gives him long baths, or helps him to get ready for work in the morning. When the doting mother dies, the narrator, who has developed feelings of curiosity and desire, resolves to break down the wall while the young man is at work. When he returns, the young Adolfo offers no opposition: "Adolfo didn't act surprised, almost as if he'd expected it. He looked at me for a moment without speaking, then went to rummage in the fridge....Then, while heating the water, I helped Adolfo undress. I slipped off his jacket, unbuttoned his shirt and slid off his pants while bending to untie his shoes...." By breaking down barriers, the clever narrator gains a lover, and Adolfo, for his part, gains a lover more appropriate than his mother to offer physical attentions.

Elda, the young mother in the most anthologized and humorous story of *My Husband*, "The Other Family," has made some drastic choices. Written in almost continuous dialogue,[11] this story portrays a thoroughly modern woman about three decades ahead of her time: she leads a secret double life, one in Milan, one in Rome, with two families, two husbands, two careers, and two incomes. She commutes by air between the two cities where she works as a lawyer. Neither family knows of the other, and neither family questions the reason for her extended absences. The absurdity, but also the colour and charm of this story, derive not only from the lively characters of the narrator and her children but also from the uniqueness of her lifestyle and the dramatic differences between her two families, each consisting of a husband and two boys. The Roman family is spontaneous, disorganized, down to earth, and fun; the Milanese family is perfect, efficient, mechanical, and unimaginative. For readers acquainted with life and values in the industrialized Italian North, as opposed to the more easygoing manner displayed in other parts of the country, this story comically and satirically portrays two families representing stereotypes of people from the north and south. With humour and lively dialogue, Maraini brings to life two extreme examples of the modern nuclear family. As in other stories, the husbands-fathers are quite dysfunctional and dependent on the wife's income. The husband in Rome, a schoolteacher, does not earn enough to support the family, and is incapable of adequately disciplining the boys; the husband in Milan works on a never-ending novel and keeps the children in line like robots.[12] Maraini's depiction of the overworked superwoman with two careers and two families, is in part a caricature, in part a thought-provoking allusion to the contemporary urban, suburban, or rural woman who, besides looking after the family, at times holds more than one job.

The first story, which gives its name to this collection, uses black humour to portray episodes of "political correctness" that in reality disguise dishonest human relations. Mario appears perfectly normal and kind to co-workers and family. As personnel manager in a bank, he wins respect and trust, and becomes a confidant of co-workers and friends, who come to him with their problems. But often his tendency to overanalyze and play practical jokes gets the better of him when he offers drastic solutions: a young worker takes his own life after Mario suggests that suicide is the only way out of his predicament. The last episode in the story concerns a kleptomaniac who comes to Mario's house looking for a cure. Mario persuades the man to lop off his hand because that's "what the Romans did to thieves," and that's what the Bible says: "If your hand doesn't know how to obey your will, then lop it off," Mario's wife and narrator plays along with her husband's absurd suggestions, regarding him as a true and devoted helper of people in trouble. At the conclusion Marcella imagines Mario's pleased look when he returns from the sawmill. She plays along with her husband's perverse suggestions and his self-conception of true Samaritanism. She imagines that when he returns with the maimed young man, "The most beautiful sight will be Mario's satisfied face—the happy face of a man who's done his true civic duty." To emphasize Marcella's dependence and doting on her husband at the beginning of the story, Maraini has her invoke, repeatedly, the presence of her spouse: "My husband is a man of class, but he loves practical jokes. Sometimes I find a toad in my bed, or jam in my slippers....My husband is a stamp collector. Sometimes he steals the neighbours' mail and cuts out the stamps for his collection....My husband...." This husband also collects new banknotes fresh from the mint: "So he sneaks them from the cash box, slips them into small transparent light blue envelopes, and affixes them to the pages of the album." Mario is a bank thief leading a respectable and comfortable life. Maraini's biting sarcasm reflects the sadness and the shallow humour of people who live by appearances, unable to assess the consequences of their misconceptions and actions. While Maraini seems to refrain from expressing judgment, her choice of subject matter, nevertheless, draws attention to the empty lives of middle-class and apparently respectable people. The many instances that show men not only as oppressive agents but also as suffering subjects confirm the fact that Maraini's feminism does not exclude sympathy for men and does not pit women against them. Her creative and philosophical discourse is all-encompassing, as it recommends greater wisdom, understanding, and mutual acceptance.[13]

In this early collection Maraini creates a multitude of speaking subjects, men and women who may have given rise to characters in future plays and novels: deadbeat husbands and wives, hypercritical parents, sadistic individuals, or men and women with a sense of humour, doing their creative best to face up to life's challenges. The language in the stories conveys the mood of situations and the temper of characters. There-fore it is often direct and even vulgar: "who gives a shit about his girl"; "The three of us had sex; that is, I sat there looking at the two of them while they fucked in front of me"("Diary of a Telephone Operator"); "Meantime I haven't had a crap in two days"; "Bull!"; and "Who gives a fuck... ("These Hands"). With direct dialogue and stream-of-conscious-ness narration, Maraini employs language as an effective instrument to unlock and lend freedom to the Italian idiom, which for centuries has remained in the grips of a "formal" tradition of structure and vocabulary. In the introductory essay to *La bionda, la bruna e l'asino* (1987, The Blonde, the Brunette and the Donkey), Maraini responds to accusations of "vul-garity" by proposing her own definition of the Italian idea of "vulgar." She considers that the literary constructions Italian male writers have used over the centuries to entertain the reader, masking truths and disguising motives, are more "vulgar" than her use of the living language. Pointing to some of the works of Boccaccio, which because of their "vulgarity" were once banned,[14] she states that women writers ought to take the same freedom as men in the creation and development of Italian, following its everyday usage, and thus giving truth and realism to words, human sit-uations, and language structures. Maraini is the first among Italian women writers of her generation to fully engage language and her art in a broad discourse of issues confronting women and men living in the post-war and Cold War generations. Her focused and inclusive vision has gar-nered for her an international following and a central place in the land-scape of contemporary Italian literature. The current collection, in its first English translation, is an additional testament of Maraini's com-mitment to writing, to art, and to social justice.

VFG, 2004

Notes

1 See list of translations, prizes received, and the Afterword, "The Life and Prose Works of Dacia Maraini."

2 Anna Cento Bull, "Social and Political Cultures in Italy from 1860 to the Present Day," *Modern Italian Culture*, ed. Z.G. Barański and Rebecca J. West (Cambridge: Cambridge UP, 2001) 55-56. See also note 8 in the After-word.

3 Among the best compilations of readings on Italian feminism is *Italian Feminist Thought: A Reader*, ed. Paola Bono and Sandra Kemp (Oxford: Blackwell, 1991).

4 Cento Bull 56.

5 Statistics are derived from *Decennio delle Nazioni Unite per la donna: uguaglianza, sviluppo, e pace* (A Decade of United Nations for the Woman: Equality, Development, and Peace) (Rome: Istituto Poligrafico e Zecca dello Stato, 1985) 24, 25, 31.

6 Data on employment are derived from G. Arangio-Ruiz and Fernanda Guarna, *Le donne italiane e il lavoro.* (Italian Women and Work) Istituto Centrale di Statistica (Milan: Mondadori, 1985) 1, 25-26, 32. For a more detailed discussion of statistics and their implications in the writings of Dacia Maraini, see Vera F. Golini, "Italian Women in Search of Identity in Dacia Maraini's Novels," *International Women's Writing: New Landscapes of Identity*, ed. Anne E. Brown and Marjanne E. Goozé (London: Greenwood P, 1995) 206-20.

7 Translation of the essay by R. Diaconescu-Blumenfeld, *The Pleasure of Writing: Critical Essays on Dacia Marani*, ed. R. Diaconescu-Blumenfeld and A.Testaferri (West Lafayette, IN: Purdue UP, 2000) 21-38. The original essay, "Riflessioni sui corpi logici e illogici delle mie compagne di sesso," is the introduction to *La bionda, la bruna e l'asino* (Milan: Rizzoli, 1987).

8 Maraini's extensive work over the years to assist with reforms of institutions for women has been well documented. (See R. Diaconescu-Blumenfeld and A. Testaferri; Ileana Montini, *Parlare con Dacia Maraini* (Verona: Bertani, 1977); Carol Lazzaro-Weis, "Dacia Maraini," *Italian Women Writers: A Bio-Bibliographical Sourcebook*, ed. Rinaldina Russell (Westport, CT: Greenwood P, 1994) 216-25; Grazia Sumeli Weinberg, *Invito alla lettura di Dacia Maraini* (Pretoria: U of South Africa Press, 1993). In her commitment to social reform and literary activity, Maraini is preceded by two illustrious Italian feminists: Sibilla Aleramo [Rina Faccio] (1876-1960), author of what is considered the first Italian feminist novel, *Una donna* (1906, *A Woman*, 1984), and Veronica Franco (1546-1591), whose life and intellect inspired Maraini's successful play *Veronica, meretrice e scrittora.* (See list of Maraini's works.)

9 For an insightful discussion of the absurd in Beckett and Ionesco, and their significance in post-war Europe, see David I. Grossvogel, *Four Playwrights and a Postscript* (Ithaca: Cornell UP, 1962).

10 Although Cento Bull considers it possible to view Italian development from the 1950s to the 1980s as "a linear process whereby the subnational boundaries increasingly faded and the integration of the lower classes into the nation-state was finally achieved" (55), she acknowledges that the integration was attained in the midst of public unrest in the working-class and student populations who, on one hand, distrusted change, and on the other hand, advocated it: "Admittedly, the student protests of 1967-68, originating from the failures of the education system but soon turning into a frontal attack against the political system, the industrial workers'

struggles for higher wages and rights in the autumn of 1969, as well as 'red terrorism' in the 1970s, were all inspired by revolutionary and anti-capitalist ideologies and do not point to social and cultural integration. Nevertheless they can also be seen as the last remnant of a revolutionary Syndacalist…tradition…or…as representing confused aspirations for greater democracy" (56). The failure of ideals in the student movement is portrayed in Maraini's novel *Il treno per Helsinki* (1984, *The Train*, 1988), which is a flashback to 1968, the year of the International Youth Festival held in Finland (see the Afterword).

11 For an extended discussion of the significance of dialogue in Maraini's works, see Anthony J. Tamburri, "Dacia Maraini's *Donna in guerra*: Victory or Defeat?" *Contemporary Women Writers in Italy: A Modern Renaissance*, ed. Santo L. Aricò (Amherst: U of Massachusetts P, 1990) 138-51. Tamburri concurs with W. Iser, who regards dialogue as a means to a more objective reality: "Direct discourse supposedly represents an objective fact heard by the author who undertakes the role of a reporter faithfully recording verbal exchange. At the same time, the technique forces the reader to act as an impartial and attentive observer and literally requires greater involvement" (140). See also W. Iser, *The Implied Reader: Patterns of Communication in Prose from Bunyan to Beckett* (Baltimore: Johns Hopkins UP, 1974) 235-38.

12 Dysfunctional fathers are found throughout Maraini's writings, including her latest collection of short stories, *Buio* (1999, *Darkness*, 2002). Over the past decades these figures seem to have retained the fascination they held in 1968. A Canadian Broadcasting Corporation program (*The Current*, 22 April 2003), drew attention to the fact that the most popular contemporary TV programs revolve around dysfunctional fathers: *The Sopranos*, *The Osbournes*, and *The Simpsons*, the latter being the longest running sitcom in TV history. The popularity of these programs was in part explained by the conjecture that the roles of the father and the husband do not receive sufficient attention in the media.

13 The question of woman's and man's aesthetics, the place and attitude toward the body, continue to be of great interest to Maraini, who views the body as a site of arrival and of departure. She has stated that a fundamental change or reconsideration of male aesthetics of beauty would go a long way in providing greater freedom for women and men. ("Disinibizione per le donne deve voler dire prima di tutto distruzione dell'estetica maschilista.") This would give both men and women the freedom to view the body with the *joy* of living, which with its own natural energy renders humans attractive. However, in a capitalist society tensions and anxieties stand in the way of this joy because participation in daily life is alienating and contrary to the aesthetics of natural beauty. ("Deve voler dire appropriarsi del diritto di avere un corpo la cui bellezza non risiede nella rispondenza ai cononi creati a uso dei maschi, ma nella *gioia* di vivere. Si è belli

quando si è gioiosi di vivere, si è meno belli quando si prova ansia e tur-
bamento. Nel capitalismo appropriarsi della vita quotidiana vuol dire
appropriarsi l'alienazione, cioè la negazione della bellezza.") In a capitalist society we are all a bit unattractive, and all the more so while we live
through a sense of alienation that no one has ever questioned. ("Nel capitalismo si è brutti un po' tutti e molto di più quando si vive una alienazione mai messa in discussione.") Quotations are from Ileana Montini,
Parlare con Dacia Maraini (Verona: Bertani, 1977) 87. Italics are in the original. Paraphrasing is mine. Maraini has written more explicitly on the
subject of the body in "Reflections on the Logical and Illogical Bodies of
My Sexual Compatriots," in *The Pleasure of Writing: Critical Essays on Dacia
Marani*, 21-38.

14　This essay clarifies in detail Maraini's ideas on writing as a creative act.
Just as Maraini has participated actively in social reform, she has also been
vocal in literary debates since the beginning of her career, having been
since then part of significant groups of the neo-avant-garde, including
artists and writers such as Pier Paolo Pasolini, and Alberto Moravia who was
her companion for over eighteen years. Maraini makes the important point
that what is considered vulgar today will be easily accepted tomorrow,
and this has long been the working dynamic of writing by men: "Almost
always, the idea of vulgarity refers to the use of certain words, considered
obscene. But the border of this obscenity changes from moment to
moment, from place to place. It's hard to keep up with it. Books, even
yesterday rigorously banned, are suddenly read as innocuous....Crudity
makes people suspicious, even if it also attracts. There has always been,
toward authors considered pornographic, an attitude of attraction and
repulsion, morbid curiosity and condemnation. Think of Henry Miller,
Bataille, and, going back in time, Lawrence, and further back, Belli and Boccaccio" (25) (see note 7 for quotation reference).

◠‿

My Husband

My husband is blond, has a receding hairline, white teeth and light skin, with big brown freckles. My husband is elegant, dresses with care, and always scents his hair with cologne. He oversees the work of tellers in a bank and earns a good monthly salary.

Whenever my husband speaks I listen carefully. His voice is soft, velvety, and a bit tense. The things he says are always very precise and correct. I've never heard him say anything out of place or foolish.

My husband is loved by his friends and respected by superiors; whenever he wishes he can also be a man of the world. He can sit right in the centre of a circle of people and just talk or discuss things. He defends the truth and checks his friends' enthusiasm, driven as he always is by perfectly good sense.

My husband is a man of class, but he loves practical jokes. Sometimes I find a toad in my bed, or jam in my slippers. Once he even served me a dessert he'd made with a dead mouse inside.

My husband is a stamp collector. Sometimes he steals the neighbours' mail and cuts out the stamps for his collection. He has two albums, thick as phone books, stuffed with valuable stamps. He says some day he'll sell his stamps and with the money he'll build us a house in the country.

In those albums, besides the stamps, my husband keeps new banknotes fresh from the mint. He says that the first of a new issue brings good luck. So he sneaks them from the cash box, slips them into small transparent light blue envelopes, and affixes them to the pages of the album with Scotch tape.

His colleagues think he's very wise and intelligent, so they come to the house to confide in him, ask his advice. They come on Sundays for the most part, and I'm usually the one who answers the door. When I find myself staring at a stuffed and dumb face, eyes rolling nervously around, I know it's one of Mario's colleagues and immediately show him to the living room.

The man follows me down the hall, then hesitates before entering the room, looking around, unsure. If he has been at our house before, he heads with nervous relief toward the reclining chair at the far end of the room, away from the window. If it's his first visit, he waits, standing, hands in pockets till I ask him to take a seat.

Our living room is very dark. The blinds are always down because Mario says light fades the furniture. So, our guests seem a little intimidated or even afraid whenever I open the door that leads from the hallway to the living room.

One man came every Sunday until a while ago. He was small with curly red hairs poking out from under his shirt cuffs. He used to come to talk about his wife, who was sleeping with the bank manager. At first when this red-haired man began to talk about his wife, he got all worked up, punched the furniture, and shouted. He was in a real bind. If he wanted to keep his job at the bank, he had to pretend not to notice what was going on between his wife and the manager. This bothered him to the point that he couldn't eat or sleep.

On one occasion Mario found a way to console him by talking for hours in a soft, persuading voice. Deciding not to go out so as not to interrupt the session, Mario asked the man to stay for dinner three times in a row. During the sessions this friend became peaceful and even regained a rosy complexion where before he'd been pale and prone to fits of anger.

"He still has some traces of sadness in his eyes, but I'll get rid of them," said Mario. "Make us some good coffee, Marcella. I want him to feel like a new man when he leaves here."

Mario convinced him (his theories were so beautiful that I myself was mesmerized) that the bank manager is a superior being, something of an angel.

"Can an angel be accused of meddling in human affairs?"

"No. But what if he isn't really an angel?"

"Come now, after all our discussions, after all the time we've spent analyzing him and his qualities that are anything but human…I thought you were convinced."

"I am. But sometimes I have doubts…."

"Weak men have doubts, a strong man doesn't. He acts in harmony with himself; his heart, his head, his liver. Even his intestines must follow his actions. Are you convinced?"

"I guess so."

"Good. I'll ask you again: can an angel upset human affairs?"

"No, of course not."

"In fact an angel is an angel. He can only do good. Wherever he descends only happiness and good can result for us."

"He may be an angel, but my wife is no angel."

"Your wife is not an angel, all right, but her relations with an angel can certainly help make her better, more pure and pleasant."

"My wife isn't pleasant."

"She isn't now, but she could become pleasant. Being close to a pleasant man her character will lose its moral and intellectual impurities. Little by little she'll grow out of her weaknesses and you yourself will hardly recognize her. She'll be like a new woman."

"But I married her. As a matter of fact, it's enough for me if she's the way she was when I married her."

"You disappoint me, Carlo. You don't love the good as much as I thought you did. Instead you're attracted to evil, chaos, and darkness."

"That's not true, I swear."

"Well then, listen to me. Tomorrow you'll start keeping an eye on our manager. Try to stay as close to him as possible, pay attention to the sound of his voice, notice how he walks, and moves, how he bends over the desks stacked with papers. If you can strip this veil of indifference and passivity from your eyes, if you can see with your heart, you'll discover his angelic nature."

"I've watched him lots of times, but I've never noticed anything special about him."

"That's because like your other colleagues you are stained with evil; you know how stupid and vulgar they are. To them a manager is just a manager, a cashier just a cashier, and a mailman nothing more than a mailman. For them only appearances matter. Nothing exists beyond appearances."

"It's true they're stupid. All they do with their time is tell dirty jokes and criticize clients."

"See, you notice it too. That means you're different from them, you're better. You're already seeing their behaviour for what it is. And soon it'll be quite clear to you that just as our colleagues are animals, our manager is a noble and pure spirit. Then it will seem perfectly natural to you that he and your wife should look for and love each other just as good and beautiful people search out and love each other."

"This is all well and good. The only problem is that if I complain he'll fire me."

"This is an evil thought on your part. The manager never fires anybody unless it's for a good reason. And then, why should you complain if you're convinced that this union is all for the best? Can an angel do wrong? No. Then, let it be, give in to it, be better than the others; be different from those animal-like colleagues of yours who can't see an inch farther than their noses. In fact you should take your wife to him yourself so she'll come back to you purer and more pleasant."

My husband usually speaks with such ease that everybody listens to him as if under a spell. Not only did he manage to persuade his colleague to give his wife up to the manager but he induced many others to do even more incredible things. A friend of ours with a reckless son used to come weep in our living room. My husband finally convinced him that the boy was not truly his son. So he no longer despaired and kicked his son out of the house. Two days later the boy killed himself. The father came wringing his hands. Mario convinced him that what had happened proved that the boy was really someone else's son and that evil can only lead to another evil, death.

Another man used to come in the early mornings. He'd sit in the living room and stay there till evening, lighting one cigarette after another. At times Mario came and went from the house, forgetting he was there. The man just waited quietly, chainsmoking in the dark, smoky living room. He seemed perfectly fine, not sick or poor; no family problems like other men. He was simply tired of living and wanted to die, but didn't know how. Now and then he'd find out about some new poison and become fascinated with its chemistry. He consulted books, tested it on mice and other animals. He'd discuss his experiments for long stretches with Mario, making drawings on a piece of paper. By drawing human shapes, he'd show the effects of the poison on the body in all its progressive phases from intoxication to eventual death. Beneath the sketches he'd show with tiny numbers the time needed for the poison to take effect. However, just when everything seemed ready, he'd usually lose interest and would not mention it anymore till he came across some new, more powerful potion.

Mario often said that his was a difficult case. Words had no effect on him. He didn't know how to listen. He was invariably passive, coming to life only when they talked about poisons.

So Mario let him smoke, slouched on the reclining chair in our living room, and rarely stopped to talk to him.

"Marcella, bring him a strong coffee, he needs it."

I'd make coffee and take it to him. He thanked me, but whenever I came back for the cup it was still full. The man had stirred only to light his cigarettes.

"Do you think he'll stay with us for good?" I asked Mario.

What upset me most was that stench of smoke throughout the house, settling on the furniture and the curtains. Aside from that, it was as if he wasn't there at all.

"He's a strange man, more dead than alive. I can understand why he wants to kill himself; death is his natural condition. We should help him, but how?"

"Today he told me about a poison taken from the blood of a parasite," I said.

"There's something eerie about him, something that keeps him stubbornly alive despite his will to die. I'd like to understand what it is."

"Maybe he just wants to talk about it but doesn't really want to die," I replied.

"I'd say he's already a dead man, but whatever lives in him is superfluous and abnormal, something perverse and useless that needs to be destroyed."

"Why don't you talk to him with your beautiful words?"

"Because he doesn't listen; his hearing is dead," Mario said.

My husband began to suffer because his friend was not able to kill himself. He became nervous, maybe because he doubted his own abilities. At night he tossed and turned, unable to sleep.

One night he and his friend went out. I expected both of them back for dinner, but at ten they were still out. Dinner got cold. I had some bread and a glass of wine and fell asleep. Around midnight the sound of the key in the lock startled me.

"Is that you, Mario?"

He didn't answer. A minute later I saw him come in with messy hair and red cheeks; his eyes were bright with satisfaction.

"And your friend?"

"He's dead."

"Did he kill himself?"

"Yes. Now he can be himself and won't have to pretend anymore."

"How did it happen?"

"We went for a walk around town. As usual, he was talking about his poisons. Then we went up to the top floor of an apartment building under construction. It was on top of a little hill by an embankment that runs into the river. We sat down on a low, fresh cement wall and started to smoke. We smoked for two or three hours. My fingers were frozen, and my back was so cold I thought I'd pass out, but he wasn't cold or uncomfortable. He just looked down the embankment in a daze. 'Wouldn't you like to throw yourself down?' I asked him. 'I'd like to but I can't.' 'Why not?' I asked. 'Because I can't harm myself. It's not natural.' 'Well then, what do you want?' 'How about if you give me a push?' he asked."

"Did he say that?"

"Yes, just like that. 'If you're a true friend please give me a push and I'll finally be happy' 'You don't have to beg me,' I said. 'I came here just for this, to bring you to the edge and then push you over.' 'Then you really love me,' he said 'because you understand me better than I do myself.' 'It's my job to understand others and help them be honestly consistent with their true selves.' 'Thanks,' he said to me. 'Let me smoke one last cigarette.' 'Take your time. We've got lots of it,' I said. He lit a cigarette, took a few drags, and then with it still between his lips he stood up on the little wall. I gave him a push with two fingers. A very light push was enough and he just went down, had a very beautiful and elegant flight down. He rolled smoothly along the side of the embankment and ended up in the river. He couldn't have met a better end."

My husband is so wrapped up in his mission that at times he even forgets to take his holidays. For instance, this year we haven't left Rome. I would have liked to get away from this quiet, dark house as we do every year to spend a couple of weeks with my in-laws in Riccione by the Adriatic. But I didn't want to bother him; he's got some difficult cases and he can't just pack up and leave.

These days a young man often comes over. He's a skinny, dark type with a scarred face and two deep grooves around his mouth. He says he's a compulsive thief. His face is very tense because of his constant effort to control his urge to steal, his strongest urge; whenever he's tempted he'd rather die than deny himself.

Mario loves order, rules, and things done properly. He has a very strict and precise idea about civic duties, so he's become committed to curing this young man. Up to this point he hadn't succeeded. After several days of therapy, the young man stole again.

"Last night I had a bright idea," Mario said.

"What?"

"Do you know what the Romans did to thieves?"

"No."

"They would cut off the hand that stole."

"No! Why?"

"To punish them. If your hand doesn't know how to obey your will, then lop it off. That's what the Bible says, and I think that's the only solution."

More and more I'm convinced Mario possesses the attributes of a magician. Just as if he were the high priest of some terrible, archaic religion, he feels neither pity nor doubt. And his self-assurance is so contagious that in the end everybody does what he orders.

Mario convinced the young man that in order to get rid of his obsession for good, he'd have to cut off his hand.

This morning they both left very early to go to a friend's sawmill. There, while Mario looks on, the dark young man will instantly cut his own hand off with one spin of the saw. Afterwards, they'll come back here for coffee.

That's what they told me, but I think the young man will need bandages and sedatives rather than coffee. I've made up a bed on the couch in the living room where he usually sits. On the glass table I've placed some pain killers, bandages, and a glass of cognac.

The most beautiful sight will be Mario's satisfied face—the happy face of a man who's done his true civic duty.

$\mathcal{D}$azed

$\mathcal{U}$*ntil a few months ago I saw myself as a slug,* sliding along, brushing against things, hurting myself with each movement, unable to rise above things. I felt as if I were going about life following the slow, level trail of a slug with my long, meaningless, and awkward body.

It felt as if all my skin had peeled off. What scraped and bumped into things and was penetrated by them was not a well-polished and silky body but a skinless one whose aching, raw flesh lay exposed. So I suffered, moving blind and dumb, longing for the human security I never found.

For a while I asked my parents for some financial assistance; though I'd always lived with them they never helped me out. Later on, when both of them died only a few days apart, I was left completely alone.

Now I can say that the moment I began to learn to live came at the moment of their death. One morning, sitting beside my mother's bed as she lay in agony, I kept looking at her, my eyes open wide with pain and revulsion. Suddenly I was overcome by extreme tension, the fear and horror of what was happening. My eyes drooped while staring at a corner of the bedsheet. Yet my body was not at all asleep and neither was my mind because it continued to work slowly, in circular motion, like a funnel sucking away heavy, fatty foods. But my eyes and senses were asleep.

I must have remained inert for over two hours. When I came to I felt rested and lighter, almost stronger. Meanwhile my mother had died.

That day I decided to do this exercise deliberately. At first it was difficult for me to reach the saturation of tension and nausea that allowed me to sleep with open eyes. But after several attempts to keep to my decision, I almost succeeded in gaining total control over my body.

When my father died, I still hadn't fully succeeded. I remember one very long night when short moments of dazed sleep were followed by endless, painful periods waiting for sleep to return. Finally, toward morning, I began to cry. With tears streaming down my cheeks into my mouth, I discovered that all the strength I needed was right there, around my lashes and beneath my moist pupils, between the arch of my eyebrows and my nasal passages. I had simply to focus that strength at the centre of my iris, projecting it outward in order to free myself from all my pain.

A few days later my new life began. I cleaned house and got rid of some old furniture that was just taking up space. I took down my dusty curtains and washed them, burned all the newspapers and periodicals piled up in my father's law office, and got rid of all my mother's old dresses, necklaces, useless things stuffed in drawers and closets.

The money I inherited vanished in a few weeks, so I went out to look for work. I found a good newspaper ad and went for the interview. About twenty other girls showed up. But as soon as I saw them, I knew I'd be the one to get the job. While the others tried to appear beautiful, different, made-up, with shoes in the latest style, I made no effort to hide who I really was: a girl neither too young nor too old, neither beautiful nor ugly, hard-working, honest, careful, meticulous, and serious — all ideal traits for someone wanting to work for an employment agency.

Just as I had imagined, after they interviewed all of us, they ended up hiring me and they put me to work right away behind a desk full of papers.

My female colleagues were not as pleased with me as my superiors were. My silence and mechanical ways upset them. But finally they got used to me and learned to ignore me. Sometimes they joked about my dazed eyes, how I'm always on time and careful about my work.

The truth is that I'm training myself to sleep while I work, and I must say that I've almost succeeded. At times my waking is sudden and painful, especially if a colleague touches me on the shoulder, bumps accidentally against me, or laughs in my ear to spite me. Then I'm startled, seized by a fever that luckily lasts only seconds but leaves me exhausted and lifeless.

When I don't work I stay home asleep on a kitchen chair. My eyes stay open; I can even talk and move about, do simple chores while my pupils draw on all my body's strength, keeping it suspended as if in a sleepy, motionless daze.

I even forget to eat at times. A few days ago I fainted in the street. Luckily I didn't bump my head. Feeling weak, I leaned against the bumper of a Fiat and seconds later I was flat on the ground. When I regained consciousness I found myself on a bed at Rome's First Aid Clinic on Via Arenula; a doctor was taking my blood pressure.

I knew right away I'd fainted from hunger. I remembered that I hadn't eaten for three days. The doctor gave me a little lecture and told me to go home, gently tapping my cheek.

Once in the kitchen I headed straight for the refrigerator. There were two dry yellow pieces of mozzarella, a plate of shriveled spinach, and four chicken soup cubes. I boiled some water with the cubes and dropped in the spinach. I ate two dishes of that hot stuff and could have eaten more, but didn't feel like going to the store for groceries. I promised myself the next day I'd eat a good meal. But then I was too busy with my self-hypnosis to remember to eat. When I got home from work that evening the refrigerator was still empty. So, I set a pan with some oil on the stove and fried the two pieces of mozzarella. They were spoiled and tasted awful, but I ate them just the same, with some biscuits I found in the kitchen drawer. They must have been quite old, because when I bit into one a chip broke off my front side tooth.

After fainting, my waking time is much shorter. I spend most of it sleeping restlessly, always tossing, but now that has become second nature.

At night when the house is quiet and dark I wake up at times. As I try to reactivate my consciousness my pain is so great that I can scarcely breathe. Then I get up, turn on the lights and get some music going. But more than anything else, it's human voices that have the hypnotic power to set me back into my sleepy, lucid trance. I go back to bed leaving the lights on, holding the radio close to my ear, resting on the pillow and keeping my eyes shut.

At seven the alarm goes off. The yielding and mechanical part of me begins to walk around lightly like a machine, going about all the typical morning motions: getting up and going to the bathroom, washing and dressing, going out, taking the bus, getting off the bus and going to the café on the ground floor of the office building. I have a cappuccino, get into the elevator, sit at my desk, type some letters, make calls, lay out the newspaper ads, and so on.

During the holidays I need more sleep, so I fall into deep trances. Since I don't have to go to the office, I stay in bed all day with the window wide open and eyes staring at the house opposite. At times I see some children playing with a cat. Other times I see a woman in a slip arguing with a man in an undershirt. But I can't make out whether I see the woman and the man when I sit in the kitchen, and the children with the cat as I lie on the bed, or the other way around.

In order to remind myself to eat, I've hung up signs throughout the house: white pages with "Eat!" written in red. But I realized that after the first two or three days, I no longer noticed the pages. So I decided to change the colour of the writing and the shape of the signs every day, but this didn't work either because I forgot to do it.

Finally I had a bright idea. I bought some small cans of meat, which I scattered on the floor throughout the house. Whenever I bumped into one, I'd bend down and pick it up so I'd remember to eat.

The other day, when I thought I was finally in complete control, something happened to take away all my self-confidence.

I was sitting at my desk focused on solving a problem. Just by chance I lifted my eyes and for the first time I saw the face of my colleague sitting right across from me. The bright, sad beauty of that young man (I noticed at that very instant that he was quite young) transmitted such a joy over to me as I had not experienced since I was a child. I stared at him for some time, till my eyes were tired and empty—that is, until I fell again into a stupor.

That same evening, once I was home seated and facing my kitchen window, the memory of the young man's fresh, clear face came back and kept me awake. I tried to recall something more about him, the shape of his shoulders, his teeth, the colour of his eyes. But try as I might, I couldn't remember a single feature.

My vain attempts at recalling details kept me awake and troubled. That night I couldn't sleep, so I turned on all the lights and danced around the house to the music, hoping I'd get tired. I had two small cans of meat, three eggs, and some wine. Finally I went to bed with the radio on my pillow. But the lights, the food, the voices, my tossing and turning, didn't bring on sleep as before.

So I took a pad of white paper and tried sketching the face of the young man just as I remembered it. But each time I came up with different unlikely faces.

The entire night passed, with me sketching sheet after sheet. In the morning I got dressed earlier than usual and reached the office when the door was still locked. I waited on the landing, stomping to warm my cold feet.

Just before nine a short, balding young man arrived, wrapped in a bulky raincoat of a strange mix of green and purple. He drew close to the door, looked at me for a moment, and smiled. I returned his greeting by bowing my head. And as I observed his wide, calm eyes, I realized this young man was none other than the young man who the day before had created such a stir in me. This bald man who reminded me of a monkey smiled as if we two had a quiet understanding.

I fixed my eyes on his big, oily head. A few seconds were enough to bring on the trance. The sight of him had suddenly become meaningless to me. He was nothing but an object among all the other objects around me.

After this incident my life went back to being mechanical, even humdrum. But I was convinced of one more thing: whatever seems beautiful to me is in reality a figment of my imagination. So I must take care never to wake up again.

Mother and Son

I rented this apartment because it's cheap and because it's got a beautiful view over the square. I furnished it carefully, partly with furniture from my family's old house, partly with new furniture. I found the bed, for instance, in a large department store. It's a cool, pleasant, modern Swedish bed. I could not go on sleeping in my old, dark wooden bed, a metre and a half off the floor, or in the large gold one where my parents slept and died at almost the same time. I also bought lamps of coloured glass, wicker chairs, and even a large wooden monkey with movable limbs that hangs in my bedroom and is company to me.

At first I was lonely. After living at home for thirty years I felt lost in this strange place, but soon I discovered that while living alone I could participate in my neighbours' lives. The wall dividing my apartment from theirs was very thin, almost transparent, and this made me feel less alone.

Adolfo and his mother woke early, around six-thirty. As soon as they were awake, they went to the kitchen and talked to each other, so I could hear them while still in bed in the dark. Actually, Adolfo spoke only a little. What I heard most often was his mother's hoarse voice. In my drowsiness, I couldn't make out her words because I could hear noises of cups moving, a spoon scooping inside the coffee tin, the sparker for the gas stove, water running in the sink, the fridge door opening with a click and closing with a thud and hiss.

The mother's words were overcome and hidden by these noises coming into my still drowsy awareness with sharp clarity. Then, as I gradually awoke, the objects grew more quiet and the voice of Adolfo's mother grew clearer, serious and very loud.

As soon as their breakfast was over, mother and son went back to the bedroom, and because the door between the kitchen and their room stayed ajar I could still hear their voices, or rather the mother's thick, heavy voice, now louder, now more quiet, like the rhythm of strained breathing interrupted once in a while by her son's grunts and monosyllables.

"Now your Mom'll put your shorts on you."

"You're tickling me."

"What tickling? Lift up your arms, like a good boy. Now Mom'll slip on your undershirt. Lift your foot, like a good boy. Now your Mom'll pull up your pants. Stand up straight, can't you see you're slouching all over? If you don't learn to stand up straight you'll twist your spine and you'll have to walk around with a steel brace."

"A steel brace?"

"That's right, a steel brace. And you won't even be able to sit down because the spine ends at the buttocks and you'll be all wrapped up in steel. You'll need to have a plastic tube up your ass so you can make caca."

"What?"

"Yes, a plastic tube a metre long. And you won't even be able to bend over to pee so you'll do it all over your legs."

"Ugh!"

"What do you mean, ugh! I can see you don't know about war. When you go to war you'll know what it means not to have your Mom with you."

"Oh, no!"

"In war, you sleep alone on a wood pallet and you'll be eaten alive by bedbugs and lice. You'll get scabies. Nothing's more likely in war than getting scabies."

"What's that?"

"Your body'll get red and swollen with blisters. And when you scratch them, they'll fill your fingernails with pus, and then you'll get covered with scabs. Nothing's more likely in war than that you'll get dysentery. Your ass will burn; it'll burn like hell and you'll shit blood. You'll feel your bowels churning and I won't be there."

At ten to nine I leave for the tailor shop. Sometimes I meet Adolfo in the elevator and am astonished to see him so strong, tall and handsome. Each time he raises a hand to push the elevator button, I watch his giant hand, fascinated: a broad, light-skinned hand, criss-crossed by veins and raised tendons. I was taken by his big stubby fingers that moved stiffly with a solemn calm.

When I got home at one, the neighbours were already at the table in the kitchen. As soon as I turned the knob I was overcome by the proud, loud voice of Adolfo's mother. From the clinking of the spoons against the bowls I could tell whether they were having pasta rather than soup, and from the continual thudding of the glass on the tablecloth, I understood that Adolfo was drinking a lot, as usual. So, each thud was followed by her reproach.

"You drink too much, my precious. You'll become impotent. Wine makes you impotent. You'll become epileptic. Wine makes you epileptic."

"Ummmmm."

"Do you believe it or not? I must have told you a hundred times. Now get the clean dishes. They're behind you, on the sink. And take the meat off the burner. But where's the salt? the salt? I could swear it was on the table. Reach into the drawer, dear. Now tell me, what happened this morning at the bank? No news? Eat more slowly, or you'll choke. If you don't chew your meat properly, it'll sit on your stomach. Each bite should be chewed thirty times. If you don't do it, you'll get an ulcer, spit blood, and then you'll die consumed by unbearable suffering."

Soon I was living completely through their lives. As soon as I finished work, I locked myself in and, lying on the bed with my eyes closed, I participated in their private lives.

I listened carefully. My long observations enabled me to guess all their movements on the other side of the wall. I recognized the hurried, heavy steps of the mother and the son's slow, timid ones; I knew when and how she undressed him, beginning with the jacket, the shirt, undershirt, down to the pants and socks. I could tell when she knelt down to undo his shoelaces and when she stood up, snorting and grunting.

On Saturday nights, with my eyes closed and ears cocked, I took part in the preparations for the bath. The woman roamed the house in slippers, searching for the soap, which she could never find because at times she used it in the kitchen, other times in the bathroom, or for the laundry. Meanwhile I could hear the boiling water thundering into the bathtub. She would return to the kitchen and cut two lemons in half. Then she'd squeeze the juice into the bathwater. Finally, when the tub was almost full, she'd turn off the tap and start to call out to her son.

"Your bath, my precious."

"Not too hot. You know I can't stand it."

"Don't worry, it's just lukewarm. Come here. There, see, your Mom'll take off your shirt. Mom'll take off your pants. Mom'll take off your socks. Mom'll take off your shorts. You're so handsome! You're really well put together. Not like your Dad, thin and shrivelled up. You're filled out, bursting with health. You've got a flower between your legs."

"It's too hot, I can't get in."

"Always tantrums, nothing but tantrums for thirty years. Here. I'll turn on the cold tap. Try it, try it with your foot. It's lukewarm. Get in. Now bend over so I can soap your back. Your back's so beautiful! What are you doing? Keep still or the soap will get in your mouth."

"You're hurting me."

"Quiet, amore. Let me give you a good scrub. Now turn around so I can soap your chest and hips."

"Mom, you're tickling me!"

"What do you have at this end, a little bird? A little worm? A baby snake? Your Mommy's made you really handsome, you look like a Christ."

"I'm cold."

"Sure you are, with all this cold water. Now get back down and rinse yourself off very nice, and then I'll come dry you off."

While Adolfo rinsed himself, his mother returned to the kitchen to get dinner ready. Happily knowing her son was busy getting washed, she'd sing a lullaby in a slow, serious voice.

But a few days ago, instead of being awakened by the usual harsh voice and the noise of crockery next door, I opened my eyes to silence; no sound from my neighbours' apartment. I thought they might have gone on a trip. Yet on reviewing their conversations of the previous night I couldn't remember a single mention of a trip. So I thought either Adolfo or his mother might be ill. But if that were true I should have heard the footsteps of one of them, a moan or a call. Instead the silence was total, deafening.

I got up slowly, nervously, and put my ear to the wall. But the silence continued, broken only by the faucet dripping in the sink.

I got dressed quickly and put on my coat and shoes, but couldn't bring myself to leave the house. I sat on the bed motionless, studying the wall in front of me as if I could go through it with my eyes and look into my neighbours' mystery.

Finally, around ten, I left to go to the tailor's, but I worked badly because I was nervous and anxious. At ten to one I came home. The moment the elevator door opened I saw the neighbours' apartment door ajar and people in dark clothes standing at the entrance. I drew closer. Through the bedroom doorway I saw the large body of Adolfo's mother laid out on a violet spread, a rosary between her fingers and a big bunch of gladioli resting on her chest.

After that morning, life became very boring. When I finished work, I didn't know what to do. I'd lie on the bed like before, but no longer felt peaceful or happy. Often, my only company was Adolfo's long, weak cry as he paced up and down unceasingly all night. So, yesterday I made a major decision. I called a carpenter and ordered him to tear down the wall separating my apartment from Adolfo's. I had him do the work while Adolfo was at the office, so when he came back, he'd find everything finished.

That's exactly what happened. While the carpenter tore the wall down, I picked up the pieces and swept the room, so when the work was finished there would be no debris left.

Adolfo didn't act very surprised, almost as if he'd expected it. He looked at me for a moment without speaking, then went to rummage in the fridge.

I didn't say anything either. I went to the cupboard where the dishes are stashed and began to set the table. I lit the stove with the sparker, filled the pot with water, and adjusted the gas flame.

Then, while heating the water, I helped Adolfo undress. I slipped off his jacket, unbuttoned his shirt and slid off his pants while bending to untie his shoes....Then I ran to the kitchen when I realized the water was boiling.

~

The Wolf and the Lamb

My husband is a rather handsome man. I can't imagine why he married an ugly face like me. "To get at your money," says my mother, who's got no brains and can't see farther than her nose. She's never understood anything about men; the fact that she married my foolish father proves it.

"He's wasted everything you had," she lamented. "Too bad you wanted a handsome and superficial husband. Now you're stuck with him. But don't say I didn't warn you."

My mother's way of thinking is simple and rough. She can't see that Emilio is a clever man and that some day he'll do something that will surprise her.

First of all, he's a thoroughly good and generous man, able to rise above any kind of pettiness. For instance, some months ago a childhood friend of ours, Fiorenza, came to stay with us following the death of her parents, who'd left her poor and homeless. Without saying a word, my husband moved out of his study to make room for her. And although now Fiorenza lives with us like a relative, and seems to have no intention of leaving, Emilio never complains. In fact he treats her with increasing affection and consideration. Fiorenza is discreet, kind, and a bit shy. She doesn't want to worry us.

"We do worry about you. You don't have anybody."

"I've got relatives in Florence."

"Relatives are like snakes, you can't count on them."

When Fiorenza laughs she bends over as if she had a stomach ache. Strands of blond hair scatter over her forehead while her body shakes and quivers. Emilio stares at her, charmed. He likes beautiful, delicate things like Fiorenza, who's as pretty as a flower in spring.

"We'll never let you go," he says.

"You're like family to us now."

"You're really too good to me, both of you. I'm embarrassed."

"You'll stay with us."

I like to see Emilio cheerful, happy, and busy as a bee around the house. Before, he was out all morning or till dinnertime, but now he hardly sets foot outside and I'm sure I owe it all to Fiorenza, who charms him with her laughter and unpredictable fits of wistfulness.

"You're a naive fool," says my mother. "They're carrying on right under your nose while you're stupidly happy and satisfied."

"Fiorenza's a friend, mother."

"A friend doesn't make herself at home so you can wait on her hand and foot."

"She's all alone."

"But she doesn't lift a finger. Why doesn't she look for a job? Anyway, it's not wise to keep a beautiful woman like her in your house next to a superficial and unscrupulous man like Emilio."

"I know Fiorenza and I know Emilio. They'd never do anything to hurt me."

"He's wasted all your money and now he's destroying your life. That scoundrel will send you to your grave."

My mother has a small mind. Though she's very kind and warm, she's also completely blind and confused about family matters.

Fiorenza's looking younger than ever since she's been with us. She's put on some weight and regained her healthy complexion. Now she really is an attractive woman. The other day she asked me for money for a pair of shoes. I immediately gave it to her and apologized for not having noticed that her shoes had holes.

Emilio too seems more youthful than ever. He shaves twice a day and uses some of my cologne on the sly. I don't let on that I know. It's just his superficiality, as my mother calls it, coming through. But in my opinion, these actions show a kind and loving personality.

In the evening after supper we play cards on our red Formica table. Emilio's hands move with self-confidence and excitement, while Fiorenza's hands are more careful, graceful, small and transparent. At times I'm fascinated by the four hands mingling rhythmically over the table as if in a ballet. At times I even forget to play.

"It's your turn, Elisa."

"My turn? Oh, yes."

"What were you thinking about?"

"Nothing. I was looking at your hands," I reply.

"What's there to see?"

"It's as if they can talk."

"And what do they say?"

"I don't know, I don't understand. But they can speak very well."

"Not if you can't understand them," he insists.

"Perhaps they don't say anything; they just dance."

"Come on, play. It's your turn."

"Yes, all right. I wasn't paying attention."

Fiorenza puts out a hand, lifts a card and smiles. Her flowered blouse opens slightly. She sighs, staring at us, resting both her elbows on the table.

"Have you two been married long?"

"Ten years."

"Are you happy?"

"I am. How about you, Emilio?"

"I'm very happy. Now, shall we move on, please?"

"Are you really happy with me?"

"Yes, of course. When we make love, we're happy."

"And do you love me?" I ask.

"Do you doubt it?"

"No. But I'd like to hear you say it."

Fiorenza bursts out laughing. She bends over the table and her hair falls over her hand of cards she keeps spread out.

"Why are you laughing?"

"Because."

"What are you thinking about?"

"I think maybe I'll never get married," Fiorenza replies.

"Why?"

"Because I can't do a thing. I'm not good at anything."

"You don't need to know how to do anything. You're so pretty."

"I'd like to work and earn some money. But I don't know how. I just don't know how to do anything."

"You don't have to know how to do anything when you're a wife. You're just a wife and that's all," Emilio replies.

"Nobody wants a woman who's just a wife. She's got to have money, at least."

"A lot of men do; you can have children."

"I don't feel like having children."

"Why get married then?"

"I don't know. I'd like to find a wealthy man who adores me and doesn't ask for anything. A man who simply worships me."

"You'll find him," I say.

"But he must adore me to the point of doing anything I ask."

"What, for instance?"

"Everything, even kill somebody for my sake. Will I ever find him?"

"Perhaps you will—you're so beautiful," says Emilio.

"I don't think I'll ever find him, I'm so unlucky."

At midnight we say goodnight. Fiorenza goes to sleep in Emilio's study and the two of us head for our bedroom.

"Fiorenza doesn't have any luck," Emilio says.

"Why?"

"She had a house and lost it, parents, and lost them, a boyfriend and they broke up."

"Yes, she's unlucky, but she's found us and we take care of her like family."

"It's not enough."

"What more could we possibly do?"

"You must trust her completely and love her like a sister."

"But I already trust her."

We fell asleep hugging each other. The following morning, Fiorenza came to me in tears.

"What's the matter?" I asked.

"I'm so unlucky; everything I do goes wrong. I really do have bad ·luck. Life's against me."

"Tell me what happened."

"I'm pregnant."

"Pregnant? And who's the father?"

"A man I met a while back. We had sex once, then he left for America with another woman."

"So what will you do now, will you keep it?"

"What?"

"The baby."

"I don't know, I'm really unlucky, so much bad luck."

"If you want to get rid of it I'll help you. I'll give you the money for the doctor."

"You're so good, Elisa. I don't deserve all your kindness. You're too good to me."

"And if you want to keep the baby I'll help you raise it."

"Do you mean it?"

"Of course."

"Well, if you give me the money to get rid of this baby, I'll be forever grateful to you."

I gave her some money and drove her to the doctor. That evening Emilio looked pale and thoughtful. I asked him what was wrong.

"Nothing. I'm sorry Fiorenza lost the baby."

"Fiorenza's unlucky."

"That man shouldn't have done what he did."

"What man?"

"The man who loved her and then left her in a mess. He's a pig."

"But maybe he left before he found out about the baby. If he knew he might have stayed."

"He knew it, all right. He's a dirty, selfish pig."

"How can you know? You don't know him."

"I'm sure that's how he is."

My mother keeps saying I'm an idiot. She comes to the house, sits in the kitchen, and gabs on and on, and I can hardly keep up with her.

"You're an idiot."

"Mother."

"It's an understatement to say you're naive. At a certain point naivete becomes idiocy. It's incredible how little you know about life and men."

"Well, what do you think I should know?"

"That men are like wolves devouring each other."

"And who are the wolves in this case?"

"That rascal husband of yours is a wolf in sheep's clothing. You'll be sorry, you'll be sorry the day you realize what a fool he's made of you!"

"Well then, mother, we're the real wolves because we're the ones with the money. Whoever has money is a wolf and comes from a family of wolves."

"You're the most ridiculous little lamb I've ever come across. You don't even know what sort of creature a wolf is."

"Wolves are the people who 'have'; people who 'don't have' are lambs. Emilio is a lamb and I love him for it."

"And you think you're a wolf? Don't make me laugh."

"We are, you and I, because we're wealthy."

"You haven't got a penny left. That man has ruined you."

"I'll always be rich enough. I belong to a class of wolves."

"I've got such a stupid daughter. What can I do? Please tell me."

"Please don't talk to me about Emilio."

"But can't you see he's cheating you right under your nose?"

"What do you mean cheating me?"

"He and that deadbeat Fiorenza, can't you see they're making fun of you? The baby you all got rid of, whose baby do you think that was, whose?"

"Enough, mother. I won't hear another word about it."

Fiorenza's feeling better today; she's still pale, but seems stronger. After lunch the three of us went to Rome's Borghese Gardens for fresh air and a walk in the park. Emilio walked in front of us deep in thought. Now and then he stopped to stare at a tree with a pained, faraway look on his face. Fiorenza followed slowly, gazing around with a wistful smile.

"Is something wrong?" I asked.

"No. I'm just a bit tired."

At that point the heel of my shoe broke. I took it off and hopped for a while on one foot. Fiorenza and Emilio burst out laughing. I laughed too, waving the broken shoe in the air.

"Wait here. I'll go get the car."

"I'll go with you."

"No, don't leave Elisa alone."

"Nonsense, go ahead, Fiorenza. I'll wait here."

I sat on a tree trunk watching them move away holding hands. They certainly were a nice couple. From a distance they even seemed related, like brother and sister.

A few minutes later they came back with the car. Fiorenza was quiet and thoughtful, her lips tense. Emilio seemed happier and more relaxed.

"I've made a decision."

He glanced at me with a sly, affectionate look as if to say that his decision was mainly about me.

"What have you decided?"

"I've made a serious but clear-cut decision."

"Well, what is it?"

"When a person has a goal, but obstacles get in the way, what should he do?" he asked me.

"Get rid of the obstacles, I imagine."

"That's what I intend to do."

"What are you talking about?"

"It's a secret. Some day you'll know. I can't tell you right now."

"Does it involve me?"

"Yes and no."

"Why won't you tell me?"

"Because you wouldn't understand."

"I could try."

"No."

"Does Fiorenza know about it."

"Fiorenza has nothing to do with it. It's only my business."

"Will you tell me?"

"No, not now."

"When, then?"

"You'll know. But when you realize it, you won't mind!"

"You're so mysterious!"

Since we had this strange conversation in the car, they've both been unusually kind to me. Now and then I smile to myself, noticing Emilio acting more and more like a rascal.

A few minutes ago they brought me coffee in bed where sometimes I linger with my diary. I thanked them both. Now they're the ones who do everything around the house.

"Sugar?"

"Yes, two teaspoons. Why do you both feel you have to do everything? Aren't you tired, Fiorenza?"

"No, not a bit. By tomorrow I'll be just fine again."

I brought the cup to my lips. Suddenly I had a feeling of revulsion. I wanted the coffee, but my lips remained stubbornly closed.

"Aren't you going to drink it?" she asked.

"I had just a moment of nausea. I'll drink it now."

"Drink it all down while it's hot."

"Yes, you're right. I'll try."

I made the effort of opening my lips to drink from the little espresso cup. I felt the bitter liquid slide along my tongue. A strange, metallic taste. But I didn't say anything so as not to offend Emilio, who'd spent time in the kitchen getting it ready for me. I drank every last drop.

As I put the cup down and looked at them, their eyes filled with curiosity. I smiled and they responded with a grin. They both looked as if they would never smile again.

~

The Two Angelas

As a child I couldn't understand why I suffered and was miserable. I couldn't ask myself why I had so many unpleasant feelings in the morning, dizziness, and migraines that left me so breathless I'd have to press down on my chest to stop myself from vomiting.

I thought I must be sick because there was no other reason for my suffering. My parents were just like other parents, no better or worse, no richer or poorer. My school, my teachers, and friends were as one would expect, normal and ordinary. And yet, I suffered for no apparent reason.

On those rare occasions when everyone was out of the house, I'd stand naked in front of the mirror trying to see, to understand where the pain might be located. But my body seemed as healthy as the bodies of all other children. I thought that the source of my trouble might be inside my body; I'd get closer to the mirror hoping to see inside. I'd search under my skin—a child's transparent skin—trying to spot something to help me with this mystery.

I'd spot small blue veins along the inside of my arm, by my crotch, under my neck, but nothing else. Standing motionless and worried in front of the mirror, my eyes wide open with curiosity and amazement, I wondered what those snake-like little veins could mean.

But when I looked closer, I detected many other mysterious clues. My moles, for example. I was sure they meant something; for sure they were symbols of some complex and obscure message I had to decode. I noticed I had four moles on my back that almost formed a square, with one side longer. There were two others closer together, like very dark twins, at the base of my spine. When I walked they moved like two little crossed eyes. Even my nipples, though they were just like all other nipples, intimated something very special about me though I didn't understand what.

Falling asleep in the dark, I imagined various solutions to my problem, but none satisfied me completely.

I was convinced that every person was like a box containing a complicated machine, with screws and wheels moving much like a clock. So I thought my machine must have broken down somewhere: maybe I had migraines and nausea because my machine was malfunctioning.

But really, in reality, everything was much more complicated than that. There was something vague, uncertain, uncontrollable in me that had nothing whatever to do with the workings of a machine. Perhaps some unknown activity was the cause of my unhappiness.

My mother's voice always rang in my ears, giving me practical advice. Whenever I was at school, in the playground with friends, in the cafeteria eating soup, or on the bus on my way home I'd push her voice away for as long as I could. But as soon as I'd relax and think about something else, there came her voice again, suddenly, as if out of my lungs and on its way to my ears and nose.

I think I was ten when I first realized how very happy I could be. Till then I didn't know what happiness was. The sensation surprised me, leaving me dumbfounded, almost tipsy, for a few days.

I had discovered that my bitterness, my nausea, and disgust were caused by my living very much in the present, regardless of where I was or what I did, whereas my joy and happiness derived from my remembering the past, regardless of whether I'd been happy or sad. I was delighted by the sweet familiarity of the enchanted, remote past. The more the recollections were distorted, incoherent, almost erased from my memory, the greater the pleasure.

I could have lived for several years with pleasure rather than pain if only I'd been able to systematically recall my past or my recollections of the past.

Everything had been horrible and painful for me because I'd been unable to escape the humdrum of everyday life: my mother's voice, school and friends, waking up, relatives and teachers.

Only later on did I begin to understand myself better. This enabled me to develop my memory, to stimulate it so that I could recall happy moments.

At fifteen I fell in love with a girl at my school. I stole some of mother's money to buy presents for her. I'd walk with Angela to and from school, lend her pens and coloured pencils. I even did her homework. I did everything to please and win her over, but she was never happy, nor was I. Then, one night, while we were alone in her bedroom, I hugged and kissed her. She broke a hairbrush over my head. But when she saw me on the floor, holding my head with bloodied fingers, she began to caress and kiss me, weeping sweetly.

I never saw her again after that night. I was in bed for six days without eating or sleeping, my arms and legs tense as if in a trance. As she talked to herself, my mother's voice pained me like a distant, remembered, hated, and endless nightmare.

On the eighth day I woke up as usual with nausea and chest pains. Hardly able to breathe, I kept my eyes shut. Whenever I opened them I'd feel the ceiling bearing down on me. I could even taste the plaster chalk in my mouth. The slightest opening of my eyes caused a painful burning sensation around the sockets.

While lying in bed in a rare moment of peace, instead of pushing Angela's image away, as I'd done before, I allowed myself to welcome her into my aching head and look at her in my mind's eye as if she were a picture in front of me. I immediately felt better. Through the thick, hard, and ugly present, I tried to carve a tunnel into a world of distant, pleasant, marvelous recollections that I could recognize.

That evening I got up and started to eat and study again. My mother's voice, as usual, dragged me down like a heavy load. But now the deadening impact didn't last.

Once in a while I still suffered, thinking of Angela as a part of the present. Yet, I'd learned how to react. In my memory I'd recreate the scene of our first meeting at school, especially the details of her dress, hair, puffy little lips, and her shoes, and I'd soon feel better. In this way, my past began to exist as a framework for heartwarming images: gestures and objects were unreal yet tender, desirable but distant. They would slide in and out of me, along the pathways of my memory, as when warm wine pleases and does not weaken us.

From that day on my suffering stopped. I dedicated myself entirely to the work of organizing my memories. Mere sensations of past flavours, smells, colours were now enough to trigger a flood of events and people loved and lost.

The problem is that, in order to go on living, I need to gather present memories for the future, although I find living in the present almost unbearable. But I know this process is irreversible. So, in the present, I am now obliged to search for new experiences, even if painful. Once these experiences are over, I neutralize their sensations as soon as I can in

order to reorganize and keep my desensitized experiences in the odour-
less, tasteless yet very clear fluidity of my memory, which alone can preserve the vitality of life's details.

In my effort to collect new memories, I'd fallen in love several times
with different men who had similar characters. They'd be whimsical,
self-centred, hypocritical, stingy, and lazy—exactly like my school friend
Angela, my first love. I even married one of these lovers. With him, I
had a baby boy who died, so we went on our separate ways, living alone.

At one point I thought my supply of memories was saturated. I had
so many that I assumed I'd be able to live the rest of my life with a complete disregard for the present. But after a while even the most beautiful
and sweet memories wear out, fade, and die. Constant recollection blunts
their freshness and vitality.

Now I am twenty-eight and I feel like seven. My past no longer gives
me pleasure. I am in love with a fifteen-year-old girl. Her name is Angela,
just like the other Angela, my adolescent friend. She has Angela's empty
eyes, full lips and wispy hair, her thin, light body and thick, strong legs.

For me it was love at first sight, and from that very moment I turned
her into the stuff great memories are made of. I took note of all her
words and movements, rearranging these later into scenic canvases I'd
contemplate when I was alone, as if they were already in the dead past.
Yet the image of Angela herself refused to become a thing of the past
because it kept reappearing in front of me with the dynamic vitality of the
present.

Angela comes to my house every day for history tutorials. Even
before the doorbell rings, I am aware of her presence on the stairway, like
a cat waiting for its mistress. I dash for the door to see her come up the
last few steps out of breath, her big bag hanging across her chest and
down her side, her deerskin jacket open at the neck, her messy hair scattered over her shoulders, her small but full and curled lips pouting.

I step to one side and she comes in without a sound, throws her
bag on a chair in the hallway, heads for the study, and sits down. When
she asks for a glass of water I run to the kitchen and in my haste I spill
it, refill it, and bring her a full glass. She takes it sadly and doesn't even
thank me. She drinks it all in one gulp, with one hand pressed flat against
her chest.

I ask if she has studied. She shakes her head and I'd like to scold her
but can't. I open the book, leafing through the pages. As I bend down to
see better I can feel her breath, smelling like dry figs, in my nostrils. I
begin talking to her about Tiberius, but she doesn't listen so I have to beg

her to pay attention. She looks up at me amused, saying she's paying plenty of attention. I go on with my lesson on Tiberius.

Is it really true that he was corrupt and depraved, she asks. What does it mean to be depraved, I ask her. Well, it's somebody who goes to bed with young boys and likes orgies. I say it's all gossip. Tiberius was a talented astronomer, a clever and just ruler.

She laughs in my face. Well, then, what was he doing on the island of Capri from morning to night? I tell her he was studying the heavens. She says she'll lend me a book about him, a book that says Tiberius was a ruthless and fierce emperor. I say that though Tacitus agrees with her, he was not right. And why not? Because, I answer, Tacitus belonged to the party of the senators. It was a matter of the republic pitted against the empire.

At home I have a print showing Tiberius wearing a laurel wreath, she replies. He has a red nose from too much boozing. In one hand he holds a naked boy by the neck, in the other, a whip. Nonsense, I say; Tiberius was a benevolent emperor and a good administrator. Anyway, she insists, I like to think of him as reckless. Why, I ask. Because that way I find him more interesting.

So I go on with my lecture on the Roman Empire, Tiberius, Octavian, the army, the slaves, and serfs. Angela cuts me off to ask whether she can make a phone call.

Certainly: the phone is right there. I watch her get up, stretch her arms, yawn, then lift the receiver with two tiny, pale fingers.

I relax for a moment, recalling a very distant memory: Angela, my young friend, in a pale blue dress, turning around running toward me, surprised at hearing my voice.

But the image is worn and weak. Just one outburst from the present Angela is enough to make it crumble like a cracker.

I can hear her laughing, holding the receiver against her cheek. I bend down over the books, pretending to read. I can't now, says the soft voice behind my shoulders. I can hear her still, laughing with pleasure, satisfaction, and amusement.

The call lasts nearly fifteen minutes. I haven't the courage to complain. I look at her tiny feet in her red leather boots. Realizing that I'm looking at them, she begins to move about as if dancing.

Finally, she comes back to my side, smiling, and sits down, gazing vacuously at her nails. I can hardly catch my breath or speak. One hour later, she leaves. I remain listless near the door, sniffing my hand that shook hers for a moment.

I am unable to eat or keep calm. I pace up and down the apartment, fussing with objects that sit on the furniture. The light and the noises bother me. All the memories that formerly made me so happy, now lie like dead rags on the shelves of my lifeless recollection.

My only consolation is in knowing that sooner or later this, too, will be part of the past. I hope time will go by quickly, very quickly.

But it never passes quickly enough. A day has twenty-four hours. I spend one hour with Angela. For the other twenty-three I'm alone, prey to my childhood nausea.

I try hard but in vain to recall the past, to reassemble the old images and stimulate my listless imagination. My quiet love for Angela is inhibited by the brutal reality of the present.

I have never in my life contemplated the future, which always seemed empty and uninteresting. Now I'm surprised to catch myself fearing and hoping for the time when these tutoring sessions will be over and I will again be free.

Eight months have gone by.

I haven't seen Angela since the morning when, faint with passion, I kissed and gently nibbled her ear. Angela, contrary to what I had imagined, burst out laughing. She said she knew I was in love with her and would return my love out of curiosity and fun. Let's try to love each other, she said at one point, taking her clothes off in a hurry and throwing them all over the room. A minute later, she stood naked in front of me, wearing only her red booties and a mocking, provocative smirk on her small, fat lips.

At that precise moment all my love vanished, disappeared, evaporated like water on fire. I preferred to close my eyes and think about the Angela she was before, the one I loved secretly, fearfully. I could not bear the sight of this small, bare, pale, indecent body offering itself to me.

Angela got dressed quietly but in good spirits. She left laughing, but I was furious with myself because I felt like a stupid coward.

Once again circumstances made me realize that I have a shameful sickness: a fear of the present forces me to go on as if dead to life, helped along by floods of memories, the only things that can awaken in me a living joy.

The Other Family

*Peter and Paul wake me up in the morning jump-*ing on my chest. I open my eyes feeling as if I'm suffocating. Peter sits astride my stomach, rearing up and down as if riding a horse. Paul kneels over my thighs and laughs.

"Mommy, time to get up."

"What time is it?"

"Six."

"Can I sleep a bit more?"

"No, you've got to help us get dressed and get our breakfast. Get up."

"What time is it?"

"Seven."

"You liar! You're giving me the wrong time just to make me get up, you liar. Let me sleep some more."

"Peter, Mommy wants to sleep. Get off her."

I turn over and try to get back to sleep. But the silence of my two boys makes me suspicious. I turn my head and there they are, busy lighting a fire in the middle of the room with two scraps of paper and some matches.

I jump out of bed, smack them, and go back to bed. But I can't go back to sleep: I lie there for a few more minutes, my arms crossed behind my head, my eyes half shut, trying to get accustomed to the light coming through the wide open window. Then I get up and start the day.

I go into the kitchen to get breakfast ready for George and the boys. At eight we're all sitting at the table. Peter tries to get his older brother to play a game by filling his mouth with milk and spraying it all over him.

"Tell your son to cut it out," says George.

"Stop it, Peter."

"Paul did it too."

"Stop it, both of you."

"Tell your son to cut it out."

"I did."

"Slap him then."

Peter runs off before I manage to grab him. I run after him and when I get close to him he sprays a mouthful of warm milk in my face.

"Give him a smack!"

"Smack him yourself," I reply.

"You know I'm against violence. But your son is a pest."

"He's your son, too."

"He's my son, but he takes after you. Paul is more like me. In fact, if it weren't for Peter, he'd be different, he'd be great."

"Now run along, boys, because it's late. Where are your school satchels?"

"My satchel is broken," says Paul.

"How did it break? Where did you put it?"

"I threw it out. It was all busted."

"But how could you break a wooden satchel?"

"Peter played ball with it."

"Tell your son he's an ass and a pest, too," shouts my husband.

"It wasn't me, it was Paul, I swear."

"No, it was you."

"And tell him he's also a liar besides being an ass. Give him a slap, why don't you?"

"I already slapped him."

"Slap him again."

"I can't spend the day slapping Peter."

"I'm against violence, but that stupid kid deserves what's coming to him."

I chase Peter through the house while Paul and his father simply look on, holding their milk bowls, their hair neatly combed, their eyes serious and dazed.

Finally I take the children to the elevator, send them off to school, shut the elevator door, and go back to the apartment. George is getting ready for work.

"When are you going to Milan?" he asks.

"Tomorrow."

"Your working part-time here and part-time in Milan is getting on my nerves."

"Why?"

"Because I can't get used to it. Sometimes I think: today we'll be alone because Elda is off to Milan. Then I come home and there you are, playing with the children. Other times I think: when I get home I'll tell Elda the joke Strapparelli whispered in my ear at school. But when I open the door there's a smell of burning and suddenly I remember you've left and at the same time I realize Peter has set fire to something, as usual."

"But that's my job. What can I do if it forces me to commute between Rome and Milan?"

"You could find some other sort of work."

"I don't think so. I make good money this way. You know your salary isn't enough for all of us."

"But at least you should decide on which days you spend here so I won't always get confused."

"I can't. It depends on the work, not me."

"Sometimes I think you must have somebody there, in Milan, waiting for you."

"Who could I possibly have?"

"Another man."

"Don't be silly!"

George smiles complacently. He bends to kiss me on the cheek, straightens his tie with two fingers, and goes out.

I tell the housekeeper what to prepare for lunch and then shut myself in the study to work. I get my reports ready, study the new cases, and write them up. My head is completely empty. I work mechanically, almost mindlessly.

At one, the door is suddenly thrown wide open. Peter rushes in, hugs and kisses me, gluing his ice-cream-covered lips to my cheek.

"How did things go at school?"

"Great. I didn't go."

"What do you mean you didn't go? And Paul?"

"Paul came with me. We went to play soccer."

"What should I do with you, can you please tell me?"

"I know, I'm a pest. But where's Dad? Don't tell him, please."

"I won't tell him, but I'm going to slap you just the same."

"When are you leaving for Milan, Mom?"

"Tomorrow."

"Will you take me with you?"

"No."

"Why not?"

"Because I've got work to do, you know that."

"But I'll behave and I'll just wait for you in our hotel."

"I said no and that's final."

Peter and Paul eat lunch quietly and with great pleasure. Then they run to play on the terrace. George reads the paper. Shortly after we both go and lie down to rest.

At four George goes out again. Peter and Paul go to the nearby park to play with friends. At about seven-thirty they come back to do their homework, but it's too late and they're tired. They sit at the table but after ten minutes fall asleep on their books. I spend the evening doing their homework.

"Peter is a bad example for Paul. They'll be a couple of bums, or two gangsters. It'll be your fault."

"Why my fault?" I reply.

"Because you're not bringing them up right."

"And what about you?"

"I've already got enough on my hands teaching forty students at school. When I get home I'm tired. You know what? I think we did wrong; we shouldn't have had children. The two of us just aren't suited to having a family."

"Maybe you're right. We should have stayed just the two of us. But then, maybe we would have been separated by now."

"Why?"

"Because two people alone can get very bored with each other. After a while they run out of things to say."

"You always come out with unpleasant ideas. Why don't we go to see a movie tonight?"

"I don't feel like it. I'm dead tired. You go."

"No, I'm not going without you."

"Well, then let's go to bed."

The next morning I am awakened at the usual time by Peter riding astride my chest as if I were a horse.

"What time is it?"

"Five-thirty."

"Peter, be a good boy and hand me down the suitcase from the closet, please."

"Paul will do it. I'm busy now."

"Get down, Peter. You're hurting me."

"No. A horse can't tell the rider to get down. Shut your eyes and trot, Mommy. I want to go to Milan."

"Peter, get off me, otherwise I'll throw you off."

I pack my suitcase and get my briefcase ready with the papers for the legal case I have to defend. Then I take my purse, my coat and dash off. Peter walks me down to the taxi. Paul stays behind with his father and they both lean out the window to wave goodbye.

On the plane I doze off. It's the only time I feel completely relaxed. The noise deafens me and the slight movement of the plane rocks me to sleep. I wake up shortly before landing, opening my eyes just as the plane descends from the clean, clear blue altitude of 12,000 feet down the bank of dull fog and whitish, bright clouds hanging over the Northern Italian region of Lombardy.

By now everybody at the airport knows my routine. As soon as I land I go to the bar, set down my suitcase, buy a coffee and a token to call home.

"Is that you, Charles?"

"When did you get in?" he asks.

"Just now."

"Did you have a good trip?"

"Yes, very good, I slept well."

"I'll come get you."

"You don't have to. I've got a taxi waiting."

When I open the door to the apartment, I find Gaspare and Melchiorre already up and waiting for me. As usual, they're smartly dressed, well-groomed, polite, and helpful.

"How are you both?"

"Gaspare has gotten some great marks at school."

"Melchiorre had some good ones, too."

"And Daddy?"

"He's fine; he went out to church just now."

"What a pious and neat family I've got."

"Would you like something, Mommy?"

"No. I have to run off to the office. I'll see you at lunch."

The work I find piled up in my Milan office is always more than I can foresee and I end up going home late. When I get in I find the table set, my two sons and my husband sitting waiting for me.

"You shouldn't have waited. You should have started."

"We wanted to eat with you."

"Did you have a lot to do?"

"Yes, a lot. I felt very tired."

"Flying is tiring," he says.

"Yes, flying is tiring."

"Even the change of air is tiring."

"Yes, even the change of air is tiring."

"Even getting up early is tiring," he jokes.

"Yes, even getting up early is tiring."

"How did things go in Rome?"

"Okay."

"Rome is very boring."

"Yes, mighty boring."

"There are so many unnecessary stop lights."

"The people are so lazy there. It's us Milanese who support the peninsula."

"What peninsula?" I ask.

"Italy, of course!"

"Ah yes, Italy."

"Gaspare, Melchiorre, go do your homework," Charles shouts.

"Yes, Daddy. See you later, Mom."

"They're becoming two hypocrites," I complain.

"Who?"

"Your two kids."

"They're yours, too," he insists.

"They're mine, too, but they take after you. They're quiet and hypocritical. They pretend they're great, but they're up to all sorts of tricks. They've already learned to play their parts perfectly. They don't give a hoot about me."

"What's so bad about them?" he asks.

"They're fakes, I tell you. They're fakes and liars. Well, have you finished your book?"

"No, sweetheart. But I'm near the end. Only eight more chapters."

"What's the story about? I don't remember."

"It's the story of a man who's living a double life," he replies.

"Interesting. But I wish you'd hurry up and finish it. It's been dragging on for years now."

"That's because I've got to work it out. And yet, the more I think about it, the more complicated it becomes. Do you think a man can have not just two women, but two families at the same time?"

"I suppose it's possible."

"Do you think it's moral?"

"No."

"Well, that's the problem that interests me: how to reconcile what is moral with what is most vital and rooted in us, like sex, the need for independence, our fascination with whatever is unusual and uncommon."

"Will you finish it this year?"

"Oh, sure. Even if I work on it only a little at a time, I do work sometimes, you know."

"And who'll publish it?"

"I don't know. I'll find a publisher, I imagine. But it's difficult, very difficult."

In the afternoon I take the boys to the movies while Charles stays home to work. When we get back we find him sitting in the hallway playing with the cat. We ask him if he's been working. He says yes, of course. Gaspare and Melchiorre smile, not quite believing him.

At eight-thirty we have supper, but I feel so tired that I'm no longer hungry. The boys chatter away, boring me with their stories. Then we all settle down in front of the TV and don't move again before eleven. I can't concentrate on the programs because I'm already asleep with my eyes wide open. My eyelids are burning, and my pupils stare blindly in front of me. Gaspare and Melchiorre startle me from time to time with their laughter.

"When are you leaving for Rome, Mom?"

"Thursday."

"So this time you're staying with us for four days."

"Yes, four days."

"When are you taking me to Rome, Mom?"

"Never."

"I'd like to go to Rome and see if it's really as ugly and dirty as Daddy says."

At eleven the two boys go off to bed. Charles and I are left alone together in the dark room illuminated only with the TV's bluish screen.

"Listen, tell me what you think of this opening," he says.

"What are you talking about?"

"My novel, sweetheart."

"Oh, yes, how does it start?"

"This is the beginning of chapter ten: 'On a warm, windy summer evening while the leaves of the holm-oak quivered lightly sending a green shiver through the air...' do you like it?"

"Isn't the sentence rather long?"

"Not at all. Listen again: 'On a warm, windy summer evening while the leaves of the holm-oak that I could see from the window at the back of my room, quivered lightly sending a burning shiver through the air…' which do you think is better 'burning' or 'green'?"

"I don't know."

"'On a warm, windy summer evening while…' Listen how good it sounds; it's like a wave advancing slowly and powerfully. You feel it coming, and hold your breath, waiting for it to break. Is that right?"

"Go on, what's next?"

"'On a warm, windy summer evening…' maybe instead of 'warm' I'll write 'hot,' what do you think? It creates more of a sensation of stifling heat. The intense heat is important here. Meanwhile the wave advances. You can feel it coming. Here it is… 'While the leaves of the holm-oak quivered lightly sending through the air around me…' at this point I want to add 'around me,' it's better that way, don't you think? Well, 'a shiver around me,' what did I say next?"

"Shall we go to bed?"

"You go ahead, I'll go on working."

"What do you have to do?"

"I must find the right sentence. It's very important to find the exact sentence."

"I don't think you'll ever get this book published."

"Why not?"

"Because you're not inspired. Where did you get the idea of the double life?"

"Once when I was young I loved two women at the same time. But I felt so bad, so guilty about it."

"And in the end, how did it go?"

"Bad. We can't live divided within ourselves for too long. We get sick."

The next day I return to my usual life in Milan. Gaspare and Melchiorre go to school; I go to the office. Charles shuts himself up in his study to work on his novel. At one we all have lunch together. In the afternoon I go back to work, Charles plays with the cat and the two boys do their homework. Some times we go to the movies around seven, otherwise we spend the evening at home with the TV.

A few days later, I pack my suitcases, fill my briefcase with letters and accounts as well as papers and the lawsuits I have to prepare. Then I head back to Rome. Charles comes with me to the airport.

"Goodbye. Try to get that novel finished."

"I work on it a lot, you know that. I'm counting on finishing it this year. Then I'll be able to support you. I'll make a comfortable life for you."

As soon as I'm in Rome I buy a token, go to the nearest telephone, and call home.

"Is that you, Mommy?"

"Yes, I've just landed now."

"Guess what? Peter set fire to Daddy's study!"

"Goodness! And what did Daddy do to him?"

"Nothing. He's waiting for you to get home to punish him. He says you should spank Peter with the belt of your dress."

~

Diary of a Telephone Operator

Fifteenth, May

It's nice and sunny today. Tomorrow I'll start my new job at Spen. I left Crispino because he drove me crazy with his thing about marriage. I'll never get married.

22th May

I like working at Spen. The girls are nice. Our boss is all right and the supervisor's kind. I'm not yet used to the loud voices continually buzzing in my ears. I've learned to eat lunch in ten minutes and digesting is really difficult. Maybe I'll have to eat less.

30th May

It's beginning to get hot. Yesterday I found Crispino waiting outside Spen. Again he brought up his plans for our marriage. But I don't waste my thoughts on him. I walk on and he tags along. Just can't shake him off.

3rd June

No holidays for me today because I haven't worked a year yet. That settles that. But I don't mind working at Spen. Like the boss says, for me the place is like a big family.

7th June

Since we split up, Crispino seems more handsome. I'm tempted to get back with him, but he won't settle for sex without marriage. He wants to get married and I don't.

20th June

At night I wake up talking to myself. In life I'm still a telephone operator. In my dream I say: "Hello, who's speaking? Can I help you? Just a moment, sir. Just a moment, madam. Hello, this is Spen. How can I help you?" Nanda says she can't sleep because of me. But it's not my fault.

27th June

I haven't seen Crispino for a while. He must have found another girl. Or better, a wife, because he's looking to get married. He's only twenty-three. He earns a small mechanic's wage. He's out of his mind.

3rd July

It's hot. The trees along Mille Avenue have come to life. It's a pity the neon lights at Spen have to be on all day. At night my eyes sting as if they're full of soap.

8th July

I saw Crispino again. He's really handsome. It's a pity he's fixated on marriage. I asked him if he had found another girl. He says no, that it's me he wants.

16th July

This month Nanda hasn't earned a cent. I have to pay all the rent. She quit her manicurist job because she had an argument with the owner.

19th July

Yesterday I made love by phone with a stranger with a very sweet voice. If the boss hadn't come by we would have gone on till one. He wanted to go out on a date. But I already knew I'd be disappointed. If his face were as nice as his voice, he'd be the sweetest man in the world.

24th July

I met Steve, the man I made love to by phone. He's thin and nervous. I don't like small men. He's Nanda's type. I'll arrange for them to meet. He offered me an ice cream. While I licked the cone he stared at my mouth. I stared back. I asked myself whether I liked him. I decided I didn't.

26th July

Steve's come over for a visit and met Nanda, who's small like him. She likes the nervous types that look older than they really are. She offered him coffee, some special cookies somebody or other gave her, and American cigarettes she bought on the black market.

1st August

It's unbearably hot at Spen. Some of the girls are on holidays. But there's as much work as ever. I'm required to do overtime each evening for half pay because I'm training. I don't have a contract yet.

3rd August

It's damned hot! The girls want to strike, hoping to get air condition-ing installed. The boss came over to give us a pep talk. He's actually very kind, a family man. He said tomorrow he'll buy us twenty fans.

6th August

No sight of the fans. Our supervisor smells like a piece of cheese gone bad. I notice right away when she goes by because of her body odour. Yesterday Steve came to get me when I got off work. His car is a new model, lime green. I asked what work he does. He said he's in sales; he must make good money. His gold ring must weigh a couple of grams. His key chain's gold too, like his tie clip and his two teeth that shine like stars whenever he smiles. I suspect Nanda's taken him to bed. I don't like him. Today he came again and gave me a box of little chocolates. I took him home to see Nanda. Then I went out and left them alone.

8th August

Tomorrow's Sunday. We're going dancing with Steve, Nanda, and two girls from Spen with their boyfriends. I phoned Crispino but he doesn't feel like going.

10th August

I met Carmelo at the party. He's quite dark, but cute like a lap dog. We had sex in the bathroom standing up.

14th August

No fans yet. To make us feel better the boss made another rousing speech. He's really a very nice guy who understands everything. He said we'd get the fans by Saturday. I don't know why we sweat so much in this type of work; we just sit all day answering calls but we drip like faucets.

18th August

I saw Carmelo again, but secretly, because he's dating one of the Spen girls, a blond who works only a couple of metres away from me.

22nd August

The fans arrived, three of them for four big rooms measuring at least six by ten metres. Nanda and Steve are always together now. In the evening I often have to leave so they can have the apartment while I go for walks with Carmelo, who's always afraid to be found out by Giulietta, his girl.

27th August

Saturday. This evening we're going dancing at Steve's. He has a huge house and a record player with lots of records. Carmelo will also be there with his date.

29th August

Nanda found out that Steve is married. His wife lives in Brazil, and nobody knows why. He also has three children; the eldest is fifteen. Nanda kicked the hell out of him and called him a bum. Steve was pale as a sheet, and was afraid she'd bust his car. He stood there trying to protect the front end. He cares more about his car than his eyes. Nanda knew it and so tried to kick in the glass of the side window. Suddenly Steve got in without saying a word and drove away. That night Nanda couldn't sleep. I had to go down and buy some mild sleeping pills for her. Luckily the night drugstore is not far away. When I came back Nanda was crying, banging her head against the wall. She took two pills and calmed down. Toward morning she woke me up to tell me she didn't give a damn about his being married, that she'd call him up to start their affair all over again because she's in love, period.

4th September

Steve has disappeared, nowhere to be found, at home or work. Nanda's beside herself. She asked me to ring him up every half hour to see if he's back. If my supervisor finds out I'm phoning for personal reasons she'll fire me. Today one of the fans is blowing air right on my back. I get some wonderful icy gusts. Yet I'm always wet, and feel I'm catching a cold. Who knows why telephone operators sweat so much. Our supervisor says it's our fault because we use our nerves instead of our brains.

8th September

Nanda lost four kilos, all because of that fool Steve. Fortunately she found another job at a car dealership and earns a good monthly wage. She's got to repay me part of a month's pay. She said she'll give it back a little at a time.

15th September

Carmelo comes over every evening. We have sex, eat, and then he leaves. The room is too small for three people, but we get by. When we have sex Nanda goes out for a walk, then she comes back and eats with us. When it's time to sleep, we kick Carmelo out and turn off the gas stove. Nanda says I should give him an ultimatum, me or his girl. But who gives a shit about his girl? She's a bore and wears too much makeup. Carmelo says he can't leave her because he loves her and will marry her. But he says she's not very good in bed. For me it's okay like this.

18th September

I'd forgotten about Crispino. He came yesterday to pick me up at

Spen. He's grown even more handsome. I asked him whether he'd like to have sex. He said yes, and wants to marry me. He's really hung up. I told him I'll never marry. Never!

19th September

Crispino knows I'm friends with Carmelo. But he doesn't complain. He says that where it counts I really do long for him, but won't admit it to myself because I'm afraid. He says I love him and I'll end up marrying him. He's crazy.

24th September

Nanda's fallen in love with Carmelo. I knew it would end up like that. They had sex Thursday afternoon while I was at Spen. She was in bed with a temperature. I sensed it all right away as soon as I walked in. I told her she could keep him if he wants. I'll find somebody else. She said it shouldn't have happened and wouldn't happen again. But I know her well enough; whenever she falls for somebody she doesn't give him up easily.

20th October

For a month we shared Carmelo. First he made love with her, next time he came over, with me. But Nanda's not happy, nor Carmelo. I decided to give him up. I'm tired of this threesome, actually foursome, because he's still got his girl, Giulietta. Carmelo's always exhausted.

29th October

I haven't had sex for nine days. I've got a headache. I don't like to work. I'm beginning to hate the telephone and those shrill, impatient voices in my earphones, calling me every minute of the day. Sometimes I say: "Just a moment, madam," and let them wait for fifteen minutes, especially the women. With men I'm more patient if they've got a nice voice. Even our supervisor noticed my lack of interest. She says she expected it; at first a worker is eager, then gets nervous, begins to hate the job, and gets depressed; finally, people get used to their routine, and then they're okay. She says I'm at the hate stage.

5th November

I met Pietro. He's dating a girl from Spen, just like Carmelo. But he told me right away he's about to ditch her.

10th November

Nanda complains. She says she's unlucky because she always falls for the wrong guys. Steve was married, and Carmelo's engaged. Why are you looking for a husband? I asked. If you stop looking, you'll find as many men as you want.

27th November

It's cold. At Spen the radiators don't give much heat. Fortunately there are lots of us, but in the morning when we all get in we die from the cold. Then, at about eleven, the room warms up. We've got a ten-minute break; I bring buns and an omelette from home. But I can never get them down in ten minutes and digest them right. Our supervisor says we shouldn't eat a lot; the less we eat the better we work. But I'm hungry; I feel hollow in the pit of my stomach when noon comes around.

13th December

Now I take turns with Nanda: on Mondays, Wednesdays, and Fridays she stays home with Carmelo. On Tuesdays, Thursdays, and Saturdays I stay home with Pietro. No sex on Sundays. When we don't have outings or parties all four of us stay home and listen to records, then we eat some spaghetti and go to bed. Carmelo usually arrives late because he spends the afternoon with his girl.

18th December

Christmas is almost here. Yesterday I saw Crispino. He grows more and more handsome. I'd like to have sex with him, but it's too bothersome and he doesn't want to. Pietro doesn't want us to, and Carmelo hates him for liking me.

20th December

Pietro has a very balanced figure; he's tall, just as I like a man to be; he's blond, just what I like, with two big dark eyes, teeth wide and well spaced. His lips are thin, his shoulders wide, hips narrow, and his legs are long. But he's a bit bent, so at times it seems he's got a hump. I like him because he doesn't talk as much as Carmelo. He's not vain like Steve, or hard-headed like Crispino.

24th December

Nanda's still sad. I can't figure out what's wrong. Maybe she thinks about Steve, and yet she seems to be in love with Carmelo. Sometimes he spends the night with her and I hear them gabbing for hours. Then they have sex, trying not to wake me up. But I can hear them just the same, and I have to bury my head under my pillow so I can sleep.

25th December

This evening we're cooking at our place, Nanda, Carmelo, his girl, Pietro, and me. The girl seems not to have noticed anything yet. She's really dense.

27th December

We decided to get married. Nanda's excited, as if she were getting married herself. She wants to come along when we choose my gown; I told her she's crazy. That's the last thing I'm thinking about. We don't have any money. We'll marry just as we are, and that's it. Nanda doesn't agree. Carmelo said he'd buy me a refrigerator with the help of his girlfriend.

29th December

I wrote my family to tell them I'm getting married. After a couple of days my mother and father arrived with a suitcase full of fresh meat and cheese. They wanted to meet the groom and find out whether he's got money, his job, and stuff like that. When they saw that Pietro's poor, they went to his place to tell him I'm a fool and I'll make a lousy wife. Pietro told them to get lost.

8th January

Fortunately those two assholes—my parents—left. They took their stuff because they were mad at me. Too bad for them. New Year's Day was a disaster. We were supposed to visit a friend of Carmelo's girl in Ostia, just outside Rome. But this friend got sick at the last minute. On the way back we ran out of gas. Carmelo had a fight with his girl. Nanda was furious. Pietro was bored. I was the only happy one, but I was so cold I almost froze to death. I wore a sleeveless knit dress and there was a fierce wind blowing off the sea.

22nd January

For the past four days I've been in bed with the flu. Pietro comes to visit as often as he can. Crispino comes by, too. He's convinced as usual that I'm in love with him. I told him I'm marrying Pietro. He said I'll be sorry.

23rd January

When I'm in bed with nothing to do I have a great urge for sex. Carmelo came to visit; Nanda was out. So I had my revenge.

26th January

It's not cold, but it's been raining for five days, nothing but rain. Suddenly Pietro has become jealous of Carmelo. I told him I don't think about Carmelo anymore, and it's true. I had sex with him more for revenge over Nanda than for pleasure. But Pietro doesn't believe me, so he's still jealous and makes a fuss about Carmelo always being around. Nanda went to buy the rings. I found out that Pietro has no father, no mother. He's nobody's child. We're looking to rent an apartment at low monthly rates.

2nd February

Still no apartment; can't find fuck all for what we can afford. At Spen they promised me two days off when I get married.

7th February

We got married. No money, no honeymoon. Where could we go with two days off? We haven't found a place yet. For some nights I'll go on sleeping at Nanda's.

28th February

We found an apartment: two rooms, kitchen, and bath for next to nothing. Naturally, heating and phone are not included. The bath smells like a sewer; a pipe must be broken. I take two buses to get to Spen, and have to get up an hour earlier. In the evening I drop off into a dead sleep.

7th March

Pietro's a good husband. He doesn't complain. He helps me with the house chores and he certainly is great in bed.

16th March

I've been working at Spen for almost a year now. I've asked for a contract. Without a contract there are no sick benefits, no overtime remuneration, no paid holidays. But I haven't received anything yet.

21st March

. I saw Nanda again. She's getting fat. I asked her about Carmelo. Seems he's still with his girl, undecided whether to marry or ditch her. I suggested she ditch him. She said she's in love. Always the same story.

3rd April

I'm already sorry I married. I've no desire to clean house or iron Pietro's shirts. I don't want to do anything; even sex gets boring when you're married.

8th April

Carmelo ditched Nanda. Seems he decided to marry Giulietta. Nanda came to my place crying. I gave her a mild sedative and she fell asleep in the kitchen with her head on the table. I didn't have the heart to wake her up. When Pietro came back, I went out with him. We went to the movies, but half way through we left because we were dozing off. When we came back Nanda was still at the table, sleeping.

22nd April

Yesterday Pietro invited a certain friend of his to dinner, a guy called Harry from Massachusetts. He lives here, in Rome. He's an actor, good-looking, with squinting blue eyes and yellow teeth.

30th April

Nanda killed herself. She slit her wrists. When Carmelo called I was already sleeping. I don't know how he found out. He came on his motorbike to get me. I didn't even get dressed, just put my coat on over my nightgown. As soon as I got in the door, I slipped and almost fell. Nanda's blood was everywhere. When Carmelo saw her, he fainted and got blood all over his overcoat. I had to stop myself from vomiting.

7th May

At Spen no news about a contract. The other day our boss made a nice speech to say unemployment is high, that a lot of young women come in asking for work, so we should consider ourselves lucky, and all that. He sure knows how to talk. Everybody just looks at him and nods.

16th May

At night I wake up with the sensation that Nanda is in bed right beside me, her arms and legs dripping with blood. I start to kick and Pietro moans.

23rd May

Harry usually stays at our place now. He eats a lot. He brings presents for me and Pietro. I don't quite understand him and can't figure out what he wants. Always seems resentful, sad and quiet. He just sits there, looks at us without a word. I wonder what's on his mind.

27th May

Carmelo and Giulietta got married. We went to the wedding Sunday morning. They had a traditional church service, white dress, music, witnesses, then lunch at a hotel restaurant near the train station. Harry came with us. He hoarded three whole helpings of baked pasta, two helpings of pork, and a slice of cream cake so big it didn't fit on his plate. Giulietta wore heavy makeup as usual, and a small bunch of fake flowers that made her look gauche. Carmelo was half asleep from the champagne. It was sweltering hot.

30th May

Coming home earlier than usual, I found Pietro and Harry on the bed hugging each other. When they saw me, Pietro went to sit on a chair and started to cry. Harry started to speak English. I took off and just walked around, then went back. Harry was still there, sleeping. Both of them were sleeping. I carried two blankets off to the bathtub and crawled inside to sleep.

4th June

Harry lives with us now. Pietro is happy and at times even has sex with me, but he's changed. Sometimes he fakes his pleasure. I said if he wants, I can go back to living on my own. He says I mustn't leave because we're husband and wife and we must stay together.

7th June

Everything's wrong at Spen. It's hot. This work is harder than ever. I haven't got a contract yet. Our supervisor is nervous and stinks even worse. The girls fight. Yesterday two girls were at each other's throats with jealousy. I have an abscess. Voices pierce my ears like steel rods. Tomorrow I'll have to go get my gums slit open.

15th June

The three of us had sex; that is, I sat there looking at the two of them while they fucked in front of me. Harry looks like a newborn when he's naked. He's pale, a bit on the heavy side, all covered with freckles and beauty marks. He smells like sour milk.

19th June

Crispino came to get me at the Spen exit. See, he said, everything went wrong. How can you possibly know? I asked. He didn't answer. He was cheerful and happy, and took me home, all along trying to convince me I'm in love with him.

22nd June

Harry stays home all day, sleeping. When he goes to the bathroom he takes stuff to read and sits on the john for hours. Whenever Pietro comes home he brings something for him: an American paper, a pair of new socks, some roast chestnuts, bananas. I finally concluded I have lost him as a husband. He says he really loves me and can't live without me. But I'm beginning to get fed up.

27th June

Harry does nothing but drink beer; he leaves empty beer bottles all over the kitchen. He's always got money, not much, but enough. I asked him where he gets it. Says his mother sends it to him from Massachusetts. Pietro got a raise. Me, still no contract.

4th July

It's hot. Again this year all the phone operators at Spen have threatened to strike unless we get reduced hours and air conditioning. Our boss made a great speech. He said the phone industry's going through hard times. Profits have decreased to half what they used to be, and there's a lot of competition. He also said he's very happy with our work, that we're excellent employees, and he loves us like daughters.

18th July

Now and then Crispino comes to pick me up at Spen. He's handsome, clean, and quiet. I feel again the urge to have sex, but it's too complicated. With him it's marriage or nothing.

24th July

Harry has disappeared. When I got home I found Pietro, beside himself, waiting for Harry, who hadn't appeared at dinner or at bedtime. Around one I kept dozing off, so I went to bed while Pietro waited. He went out, then came back, but not to bed.

27th July

No news of Harry. Pietro doesn't eat or sleep. If I say something he tells me to keep quiet. He paces around the house like an idiot and every two minutes rushes to the john. He's got the nervous runs.

6th August

We got a card from Harry; he's in Spain and sends greetings. That's all, just greetings. Pietro's beside himself and refuses to go to work.

15th August

The heat's killing us. At Spen still no sight of a contract, and no holidays. If I complain they tell me there are lots of young women who'd like nothing better than to take my place. And it's true. Pietro has calmed down. He's gone back to work but he's lost a lot of weight. He's become ugly because of his fasting. We don't even bother to talk about sex. Sometimes he hugs me and tightly holds on to me out of fear, as if I were his mother and he's my child.

28th August

Giulietta's expecting. She's still working at Spen, but often has to go to the john to throw up. She wears no makeup now. She used to be blond, but has turned grey. Marriage hasn't been good for her. I learned from my neighbour at work that Carmelo cheats on her with a French girl, a babysitter for a countess from Naples who's loaded and always gives her expensive outfits. That's what they told me. Carmelo's too handsome to stay faithful to a rundown wife like Giulietta.

4th September

Another guy has come into our lives, Peter, a German mechanic. Here he doesn't work. He's kept by a wealthy guy, an antique dealer named Pupilla. Peter has a white Jaguar, and wears suede shoes with silver buckles, silk shirts, and black leather bands ten centimetres wide around his wrists. He's handsome like an actor, but has false teeth you can see from close up. From a distance, he's perfect. He's twenty-six.

13th September
Peter comes looking for Pietro and they leave together in the Jaguar. I eat alone and then go to bed because I'm always sleepy. Once in a while Peter gives Pietro some money. We have some new things at home now: an electric stove like a balloon, but we never use it because it wastes too much electricity, a bird cage with two fake parrots that sing only when the air is damp. We have a cigarette lighter that must weigh half a kilo, an Indian carpet with gold dragons, and a set of flower-shaped water glasses.

20th September
My entire back is sore. The supervisor says I sit the wrong way. But I can't sit down any other way. The metal headset presses against my temples. I can't get used to the voices. She says they'll give me a contract next week.

22th September
Peter gave Pietro a gold bracelet inscribed with his name and the date they met. It's been too long since I had sex. I feel I'm getting sick.

25th September
No contract. Instead, it seems they'll let some employees go because a lot of phone lines have become automated and they'll no longer need all those female operators.

10th October
Pupilla is dead. He was found drowned in the sea in front of his villa. He's left Peter a big inheritance, two valuable apartments, the Jaguar, and a box full of jewels. Pupilla's wife has contested the will. Peter's very happy, and Sunday we went for dinner to old Ostia to celebrate. It was sunny and there was a beautiful scent of jasmine in the air. I ate a fish as big as a house, but it tasted like cardboard.

16th October
Peter's sad. Says he can't forget his patron and lover, a very kind and lovable man. He takes flowers to the cemetery every day. Pietro's jealous. I said it's stupid to be jealous of a dead man. He said a jealous person is jealous of everything.

24th October
I met Aldo, a young man with curly hair. He's got a wide mouth and small eyes, a type of black beauty. Sex with him is great, but we never know where to go for some privacy. Pietro's always home and I don't want him to know. The public parks are always wet. One day we had

sex at the movies, made some crazy moves, and we were scared silly somebody would spot us.

30th October

I left Aldo. He was too stuck on me.

4th November

Pietro will go to live with Peter in an apartment in the hills of Rome, Monte Mario. They go around buying furniture, holding hands like sweethearts. Pietro will leave the print shop and stop working. They'll travel around the world. That's what Peter said.

19th November

I saw Crispino again, says he knows everything about me. I don't know how he finds out because I never said a thing. He says he saw it all coming and that now I'll marry him just as I should have done from the start. He says I won't have problems getting an annulment because of Pietro; so we'll live together and have kids. But I don't want to marry him or even have sex with him.

24th November

I saw Pietro's new house. It's small with two big yellow and red tile terraces. Peter bought several pots of flower, geraniums, azaleas, oleanders. They even have a cat named Hans. Pietro offered me French cognac and almond pastry. Then he put on some records of German songs. Peter was sleeping under a fur blanket stretched out on the carpet in front of the unlit fireplace.

28th November

I met Nino. He's tall and stout and works in a bar. Whenever we have sex he talks and cries out. It's like an earthquake. He's twenty-two and as beautiful as a Madonna.

4th December

I lost my job. Without a contract, I can't even apply for severance pay. Maybe I'll end up with Crispino, but maybe not. He's so dull. I've got to find myself a new job.

Beloved Death

It happened a month ago. We were headed for Ostia. Gigi was driving and I sat beside him, legs crossed, and my arm round his shoulder. Gigi was in a bad mood.

"What's the matter?" I asked as soon as we passed city traffic.

"Nothing."

"You look sad."

"No. I'm just a bit discouraged."

"What happened?" I insisted.

"Nothing. I don't know. I feel stressed, that's all."

"But why? Don't you want to tell me?"

"If I knew why, I'd tell you. I'm just depressed and don't know why, that's all." I didn't insist because I know Gigi well enough, and whenever he decides to keep quiet there's no way to get a word out of him. I stroked his hair and made him feel my closeness and my love.

We entered the freeway. Gigi began to drive at full speed. The glaring sunlight reflecting off the hood hit his eyes. Now and then I turned to look at him sideways: a bit puffy and pale, the fleshy cheekbone, the tense eyelid, the transparent half cornea of the eye struck by the sunlight, the cracked skin on his large, lifeless lips, his chin with a light afternoon shadow, his neck red from the heat, his shirt collar open.

When we stopped for gas, I couldn't help asking again what was up. Gigi took off his gloves, laid them across his knee, and turned to me with a mischievous look.

He paid for the gas, took the change with casual indifference, turned on the ignition and took off. After ten minutes he stopped again to put on his gloves, then roared off. The sun now warmed his shoulder while his profile seemed less pale and tense.

We were headed for the sea. To my left, the hedges of the median went by so rapidly that the natural green of the plants seemed black. Unable to distinguish leaves or branches, I could see instead a heavy, dark and shiny serpent, turning and twisting, no beginning, no end. But as I lifted my eyes, the view suddenly cleared and stretched ahead so I could see green fields of grain, row after row of chestnut trees, and far away in the north, an immense belt of pines so green they were almost blue. Beyond, there it was: the white, white sea.

Once in a while I left the landscape to look at Gigi. His determined, pale profile, framed by a thick head of curls, was enough to move me.

"Well, I feel mighty good today," I said, stretching out my legs, lifting my arms and flattening my palms against the car ceiling, pressing my feet against the rubber mat and pushing my chest forward like an arch.

"I feel great, and almost happy," I said.

Gigi turned for a moment, resting his chin on his shoulder with a frown.

"Why almost?"

"Because you're in a bad mood."

He didn't answer. He looked at the road in a thoughtful, fixed stare. The corner of his shirt collar flapped against his neck from the gusts coming through the car window.

I opened my purse, pulled out a compact and snapped it open. In the small, square mirror I saw my face. I like it a lot. Each time I see myself I'm surprised by the perfection of my features, and often I run to the mirror to assure myself that the perfection is still there, intact. If my face has a defect, it is precisely the fact that it has an almost inhuman perfection. I gazed at length at my shapely nose, my glowing cheeks, shimmering eyes, faultless forehead, and well-defined chin. Then with a click I snapped the compact shut.

That's when it happened, while I was still so self-absorbed. Or perhaps not; it may have happened later. I don't remember clearly. I was looking at my firm, sunlit hands spread open over my breast like a cross. I thought they had the pure and absolute beauty of statuary. They seemed chiselled from marble or priceless porcelain. They are tiny, motionless, snow white as if bleached by salt, sparkling and smooth without stains, dark patches, or traces of blue veins.

I lifted my back gently to study my bare feet lying close together flat on the floor. I wanted to sit up to see them better: they were so pearly, creamy. However, a new sensation, a weariness, closer to drowsiness than to pain, caused me to shift back to my former position.

I was bent over, intently staring at my hands when it happened. Or perhaps it happened before, while I was studying Gigi's somewhat grim profile. I don't remember. I heard the screeching of brakes. The car went out of control.

I wish I could talk to him now, ask him what he was thinking at that precise moment. I wish I knew why he was so stressed that day. More than once I have wondered whether he might have been bothered by a premonition. Perhaps he felt that something was going to happen that morning, and in his attempt to understand his own feelings, he became more quiet and sad. I don't know. Then at times I also ask myself whether he may have been hiding secrets. I'll never know now because I've lost him. And besides, after what happened that evening, I'm afraid to go near him or talk to him.

I've been wanting to do this for a while. Sometimes I've gone as far as his door, but I never dared go inside. The other evening, after waiting for him by the road, I saw him arrive with some of his friends in a big American car. All five got out. Gigi's face suggested he was out of sorts, just as he had been on that day. His friends joked and laughed aloud. One of them drew closer, twisted the cap of a small bottle of liquor and handed it to him. Gigi pushed his friend's arm away. The other insisted. Finally Gigi put the bottle to his lips, taking several sips. But he choked on the liquor and started coughing nervously. His friend slapped him gently on the back. Meanwhile the others were fooling around, chasing each other up and down the sidewalk and around the parked cars. Two of them ran into each other, then hugged, and, leaning on each other's shoulders, laughed till tears ran down their cheeks. A third took off his coat and threw it over the top of the car, while the one with the bottle started drinking again.

Gigi began walking up toward the house. The other four blocked his way by joining hands. Gigi was annoyed, and so they jumped on him with smirks and sounds of fake kisses, giving him friendly blows and pats.

At that moment the bottle slipped, fell to the ground and smashed to pieces. The glass hit the legs of the young men. Suddenly everyone was quiet, as if following a signal; the friends went their separate ways, saying their goodbyes in low tones. Gigi went in the door, the corners of his wide, white raincoat flapping round his legs.

I decided to go visit him. The scene had filled me with an eager curiosity, and I felt I could say some words to console him. So, why not?

Perhaps I could beat him at some card game, laughing and joking, just like his male friends.

I waited till he was in bed. But perhaps I waited too long, because when I went in the light was out and he was asleep. I walked around the room, studying the furniture and other things by the feeble light that came through the window overlooking the road.

Everything was like before. The doors of the wall closet were ajar. Inside I could see Gigi's light suits, his only grey-and-blue plaid coat, and his white raincoat. Near the window was the table standing on three legs with a pile of books serving as a fourth. The wood surface had spots and stains; I could see pens and cigarette butts scattered everywhere, books and headless ceramic figurines recalling Etruscan times. Leaning against the lamp's steel stand was the framed portrait of me with one corner blackened. I picked it up. It really was me. Looking at that fresh, bright face with its soft features I felt a strange sensation. Almost automatically, I brought the portrait to my lips and kissed it.

Without thinking, I walked away from the table, and moved toward the window. I looked down on the road, almost deserted by now, cars parked in a row by the sidewalk with two familiar swinging lamps, one chipped and opaque from the dust, the other new and sparkling. I looked up at the house across the street. One of the windows was lit. A man stood facing me with his head leaning against the pane. He looked like Gigi. For an instant I thought I was in the wrong house and was about to go out. But when I looked to my right into the darker corner of the room I was reassured I was in the right house. I gazed at Gigi all curled up in his bed.

Drawing away from the window I glided toward the bed. Seeing his curly head pressing on the pillow and his full lips almost open in a restful self-abandonment, I felt a rush of joy. I brought my hands to my chest. At that precise moment as if responding to my surge of emotion, Gigi woke up. Tense and motionless under the covers, his eyelashes blinked several times as if he were trying to make sure he was not dreaming. His face muscles tensed up in a fearful grin. Then he suddenly sat up and started to shout, his sweet eyes wide open with horror.

I ran out. Since then I haven't dared to show my face again. I'm afraid to frighten him. So, now I take pleasure in looking at him from a distance.

~

The Red Notebook

My husband keeps a diary. I came across it a few days ago while I was tidying up the wardrobe in our bedroom. The flowered paper in the drawer had come unglued in one corner and under it I found a small notebook covered with red plastic.

I picked it up, opened it, and read: "January 13th. Nothing happened today. Elena always stays home, in her room. I can hear the rustle as she turns the pages of her magazines. I can't concentrate on my work. When will she make up her mind? This waiting is almost unbearable."

I shut the notebook quickly, put it back and sat on the bed to think. I couldn't understand my husband's words. What does he want from me? I wondered. What is he so anxiously expecting from me?

That evening when Lattanzio came home I looked at him with different eyes. I realized he had changed a great deal. His face had grown old and his eyes behind his glasses were painfully small.

We had supper as usual, served by old Amalia in the large, dark dining room. Each time the telephone rang I watched Lattanzio lift his eyes, straining to listen. He'd stop eating—waiting for Amalia to reach the phone, come toward me, bend down and whisper the name of the caller in my ear.

"Who is it?"

"My mother."

"Aren't you going to talk to her?"

"No, I told Amalia to ask her to call me back."

"Did anyone else call today?"

"No."

I thought I should ask him about the diary. But his lifeless, grey face, slightly twisted by a secret smile, made me change my mind. I knew that if I asked him he'd lie to me.

"Do you realize how long we've been married?" I asked.

"Ten years. Why?"

"Do you think we're happy?"

"Well, what about you, what do you think?"

"Maybe we're bored with each other."

"Don't say silly things. We get on just fine together. Everything's all right."

"Maybe you're right."

We didn't talk about our marriage again. But now that I shared one of his secrets I couldn't look at him again in a normal, casual way.

I wait for him to leave the house so I can read his diary. But Lattanzio works at home and rarely goes out. Even when he's shut away in his study, I know that he's aware of every little movement in the house. I know that when the telephone rings he tries to listen: whenever I move he follows the sound of my steps through the rooms. Every moment of the day he knows where I am, what I do.

While he works at his math, surrounded by books on calculus and countless papers piled up on his desk, I stretch out on the living room couch, my feet resting on the arm, smoking, leafing through some magazines.

Sometimes I go out to visit Aldo, or my mother in the hospital, or do some shopping. Before leaving, I go by Lattazio's study to say goodbye.

"I'm going out."

"Where?"

"To see my mother."

He looks me up and down for a minute while his glasses slip down his shiny nose. Then he gives me his peculiar grin filled with exasperation and longing.

"Well, bye."

"Wait! What time will you be back?" he asks.

"I don't know. About seven."

"And you've made yourself look so elegant just to go see your mother?"

"This dress isn't elegant, it's the one I always wear."

"You look nice just the same. You've even put on perfume."

"I always do. What's wrong with that."

"Nothing. I like you when you go out all dressed up."

"Can I go now?"

"Yes, of course. See you soon."

So, I shut the door and go out. I walk to the taxi stand, and tell the driver the name of the clinic. I sit upright, my back straight, and fix my gaze on the nape of the driver's neck.

By now they know me at the clinic, no need to ask me which floor I want. I find my mother sitting on the balcony outside her room, wrapped in her flowered robe. I sit beside her and listen to her chatter. I know that after gossiping for an hour she feels better. I let her criticize and scold me in her tense, monotonous tone. Meanwhile I smoke and watch the patients strolling in the garden below, the cypress trees swaying in the wind, the small clematis vines on the wall of the house across the road growing thicker and bigger by the day.

But now and then when I feel like it, I go see Aldo instead of my mother. Even though he doesn't like me to be seen by the head mechanic, who happens to be his father-in-law, I go to his garage anyway. I like to watch him work, dirty with grease in his blue overalls, a blond lock of hair hanging over his blackened, oily forehead.

I wait till he cleans up and changes. Then we climb into his Fiat 500 and drive to his house.

"You know you shouldn't come to the shop."

"I know."

"My father-in-law can't stand the sight of you."

"But if you and your wife are separated, why should he care what you do?"

"Sure he cares, because he's determined to bring us back together. And your being around spoils his plans."

"And where's your wife?"

"How should I know? She ran away. Even he doesn't know, and he's her father."

"Well then, how's he going to bring you together?"

"He's stuck on the idea. What can I do? He's convinced she'll come back soon and he'll have us back together."

"But would you go back to her?"

"Maybe, who knows."

"Do you love your wife?" I ask.

"Some times I do, other times I hate her."

"All right. Next time I'll wait for you at the street corner. Now, give me a kiss."

"I'm still dirty. I'll take a bath first. Will you scrub my back? My wife never liked doing that."

When I get home I find Lattanzio waiting for me, bent over his books, his eyes shining and his forehead covered with perspiration.

"How did it go?"

"As usual."

"Is she feeling any better?"

"Who?"

"Your mother."

"No. I don't think she'll ever get better, but today she was more cheerful than usual."

"You're looking pale. Are you tired?"

"No."

"You have dark circles under your eyes. Every time you go to see your mother you come back exhausted."

"I'm not at all tired. It's the bad lighting in this study. It's so stuffy in here, isn't it? May I open the windows?"

"No, leave them. It's time to go and eat."

And so, we take our usual places at the table. While Amalia serves us, I study my husband's face across from me. It's dull and lifeless as always. But now and then I detect a suppressed flash of satisfaction.

Finally, a couple of days ago, Lattanzio went out for the afternoon. I rushed to the bedroom, took out the little red plastic diary, and opened it. I read: "Thursday, the 22nd. Elena has given in. After resisting for some time, she finally went to see him yesterday. My afternoon was wonderful. I really felt great."

I put the little book back in its place. Opening the shutters, I leaned on my folded arms and looked out over the balcony. This is what my husband wanted from me. He wanted me to be unfaithful to him.

Then I suddenly remembered that Lattanzio had been the one who took me to Aldo's garage. He had drawn my attention to Aldo's youth, his slimness and fairness, as he bent over a car to look at the motor.

I realized that while believing I was affirming my independence and freedom by having an affair, I was instead being more than ever submissive to my husband because my unfaithfulness was nothing less than what he really wanted.

When he came back at supper time I decided to confront him.

"I read your diary today."

"What diary, sweetheart?"

"You know very well what I mean. The one where you write about me and...."

"You're imagining things. There's no diary. I don't know what you're talking about, my dear."

I ran to the bedroom and opened the doors of the wardrobe. I bent down. The diary was not there. And yet, after the moment I had held it in my hands no one else had been in the bedroom. I looked at him dumbfounded.

"See? You must have dreamed about that diary. It doesn't exist."

"Of course it exists. I saw it."

"Pass me the salad, dear."

"Here."

"Aren't you going to see your mother after supper?"

"No."

"And tomorrow?"

"No."

"How naughty of you."

I looked at him for a moment while his round, grey face lit up with a fleeting expression of mawkish pleasure.

~

Suffering

Suffering wears us down. I realized it too late. When I was a girl, I didn't take care of myself. I really suffered. My father, my mother, school. Now these seem remote and incredible.

My parents, with their endless pretence, turned our family into a model of happiness—at least that's how we looked to others, relatives and friends.

Everything about our family was perfect. My father was a business-man, honest and hard-working, able and rich, my mother a kind, affec-tionate, and traditional housewife. They never had fights or argued, but always agreed. And they always put on the appearance of being happy and in love.

I was their only daughter, spoiled and loved, but also raised fairly strictly. I always wore embroidered smocks, bows in my hair, white shoes, and as a grown young woman I wore angora outfits and coral necklaces. I attended school, was punctual, and got good grades. My parents came to get me at the end of my classes and the three of us walked slowly home, aware that others looked on us as an image of domestic bliss.

I lived with them till I turned thirty, and I never avoided the role my father made me play. Our life was orderly and serene, no interruptions, moments of doubt, or discomfort.

But I continued to suffer and didn't know why, nor perhaps did I ever wonder why. With all my strength, I carried on with my duties as daugh-ter and student.

When my father died, my mother and I found ourselves alone, not knowing what to do. My face had become old—almost comic with my pitiful wish to seem satisfied at any cost. Even my mother aged, looking like a little monkey, her face all wrinkled and withered.

But in a few months a lot of things happened. I can hardly remember them. First my mother dyed her hair red, and then she found a lover on whom she wasted all the money my father had left us. When she ran out, the young man left her, and she killed herself.

I was penniless and homeless then because our apartment was sold. So I started to look for work and for a little while, I was a secretary in a retail office. But I didn't get along with the owner, maybe because he reminded me of my father. Well, actually, I was a poor worker with no enthusiasm, unable to keep organized schedules or type letters without errors. Finally I resigned, or maybe they fired me, I don't remember anymore. For a while I went to stay with a girlfriend, Giulia, a manicurist at Parioli's.

It was while talking with Giulia that I realized what was wrong with my life. I accepted suffering as a necessary or inevitable part of life. Giulia had very different ideas.

"Suffering spoils your skin, have you noticed?"

"I never thought about it."

"To keep healthy, you mustn't suffer."

"I've never given it a thought."

"It's not easy, you know, because everybody out there tries to make you suffer. It's worse if you're poor. So many things go wrong, and you have to put up with so much just because you're poor and powerless. And there are so many idiots out there you can't call idiots just because they give you a job."

"It's really true."

"But you have to free yourself from suffering."

"How?"

"I told you many times. Think of life as a room full of old, filthy rags, dirty windows, dusty floors, closets packed with stuff, curtains reeking with awful smells. Would you live in a room like that?"

"No, I wouldn't."

"What would you do if you were forced to live there? You'd clean it up, right?"

"Right."

"Well, just imagine that room being your heart."

"I never thought of anything like that."

"I can see that. You look ten years older than you are."

"In what way?"

"Your face, for instance, it's twisted, stiff. I'm your age, see, but I look way younger."

"Yes, you do."

"See? You know how I did that? I did away with suffering, wiped it out."

"But how?"

"Just like I said, throw away all the litter and useless stuff; clean up and sweep away all the dust till you feel like a nice fresh box, empty and roomy."

Giulia's words made a lasting impression on me. I had never imagined I might be able to get rid of my emotions, or eliminate suffering.

"Look at your face in the mirror. These lines, these blemishes are nothing but the result of suffering. How stupid to suffer like this when you don't have to."

"I tried to change, but I couldn't."

"You don't happen to be in love, do you?"

"Well, yes, I am."

"There, that's why you're not succeeding. First you've got to stop being in love."

"But how can I?"

"You've simply got to convince yourself that the emotion of love is just like one of those cluttering, useless pieces of furniture that fill up old rooms. You've got to get free, just as you get free from bothersome, useless objects."

That same evening I phoned Giorgio and told him to stop calling me. Afterwards, though encouraged by Giulia's words, I felt so sick I didn't think I'd make it. But Giulia helped me.

"That boy could only cause you unhappiness," she said. "He took up too much space inside of you. Now you've kicked him out. Maybe for a few days you'll miss the weight you were used to. But after, you'll see how much better you feel. You need to become convinced that freedom is being empty, totally empty and free of emotions."

Suffering wears us down. I didn't need Giulia to understand that. The skin on my face was tight and dry, it tended to peel, my eyes were feverish and wide, sticking out like two moist, red balls.

Giulia looked after me for a few months. I became quite changed. Looking at myself in the mirror, I took on a new expression of self-control; my eyes became normal, rested and calm under my still lids, without expression.

One day Giulia came into my room while I was sleeping and told me I had to leave because she was getting married.

"But how can you? You said one must never fall in love and now you're getting married?"

"Sure, I'm getting married but it doesn't mean I'm in love."

"Then why get married?"

"Because I found a rich husband; with him, I won't need to work."

"Don't you think you'll suffer without your independence?"

"I don't think so. I don't love this man so I'm still free. Freedom doesn't depend so much on being autonomous as on avoiding having an inner life."

I looked at her with admiration. Giulia has succeeded, but I've only come halfway.

"And now what will I do? Where will I stay? I've no work, no money."

"You'll manage. I need the apartment and you have to be out by tomorrow."

The next morning I packed and Giulia took me to the elevator, hugging and kissing me. While she pressed me against her, I looked at her closely and had the sensation she was really empty and happy. Her face was clear, white and perfect like a painted wall, no wrinkles or spots, but also lifeless.

For a while I was a nanny, then a secretary for a printer. Now I've taken Giulia's job at Parioli's, where I give manicures for a small monthly wage.

Suffering wears us down. I repeat it to myself in the evenings before I go to sleep, when I'm eating alone in the landlady's small kitchen. I think I'm tired of being alone, tired of working and just existing, tired of not having friends, a husband, or a home of my own. But, following Giulia's instructions, I try to convince myself that all these emotions are unnecessary baggage I carry with me and I must get rid of them.

I saw Giulia again a few days ago. She came to the shop. She parked her beautiful car in front of the sidewalk and came in, shouting good morning to everyone.

"How are you, Giulia?"

"Great. Do you know I'm pregnant?"

"Well, have you given up on emptying yourself?"

"No, I haven't given it up at all. Do you think all it takes is a baby to fill me up again with clutter? Don't you know that my inside is so empty there isn't even room for a pin?"

"If it's empty, there's room."

"Empty space, when it's really empty, feels like filled-up space, don't you know?"

"But I can't do it, I don't know how."

"I can see you don't; you look miserable."

"I'd like to get married."

"You say it as if you'd like to be filled-up with honey. You long for all the old pieces of furniture and the dust that kept you company before your big housecleaning. Go ahead, do it. But you'll find that you'll always feel awful."

At that instant I remembered my father. I hadn't thought of him for some time. I realized that he and Giulia had something in common. Only, he had used an old method to gain happiness: by always pretending, he had managed to turn his life into a game that he secretly hated, whereas Giulia, more modern and courageous, had the strength to truly free herself of suffering by ridding herself of her emotions. There she stood, pale and beautiful like a statue, her large blue eyes staring at nothing, her cold, elegant hands resting lifeless in mine while she smiled, hardly moving her lips.

~

The Linen Sheets

This morning I found a hole this big in my sheet.
I'm sure Helen made it with her damned cigarettes. She knows I'm very
fussy about the linen. She knows these sheets are part of my dowry, that
I'm proud and jealous of them. That's precisely why she spites me.

As usual, this morning, as soon as George woke up he asked for his
coffee. I was already in the kitchen getting it ready. "I'm coming," I cried
out, and hurried to get the little cups out of the china cabinet.

I boiled the milk, cut the bread slices into four, placed everything on
the tray and went to the bedroom, pushing the door open with my knee.
George and Helen were in bed, watching me as I came forward holding
the tray. George was sitting up with his hair ruffled, his head leaning
against the headboard, his pyjama jacket unbuttoned, showing his hairy
chest. Helen was still under the covers, her big round head sticking out
from under the sheets. She was still sleepy, but her big blue eyes lazily followed my movements.

"Where should I put it?"

"Here, sweetheart."

"Where's here?"

"On my knees."

"Helen's still sleeping," I said, just to say something, though I'd seen
her eyes open.

"I'm not sleeping. Did you bring me the milk?"

"Yes, it's there on the tray. Oh, I forgot the sugar."

"Run and get it, you little mouse."

I've told him many times not to call me little mouse. But he doesn't
pay attention to anything I say. I went back to the kitchen, grabbed the
sugar bowl, and placed it on the tray near the milk.

"What will you make for lunch today, little mouse?"

"Please don't call me little mouse."

"I'm your husband, aren't I?"

"So what?"

"Well, a husband has the right to call his wife whatever he likes."

Laughing, Helen pulled herself up lazily. She stretched a hand towards the tray, and it wobbled on George's knees. Then she grabbed a slice of bread and dunked it in the milk cup.

"Sit down here, mousy."

"I ate already."

"Well, sit down just the same and tell me what you dreamed about last night."

"You know I never dream."

"That's impossible."

"I never, never, dream."

"It's a bad sign."

"Why?"

"It means you've got nothing inside of you."

Helen started to laugh. I couldn't understand why she found what George said so funny. She laughs a lot, often for no reason at all. When she shakes her head, her hair falls over her eyes and cheeks. George likes to see her laugh. He smiles with satisfaction as he watches her shaking her head and hair.

So much has changed since we married, especially in these last few months since Helen has been staying with us. I've never known George to be so awkward and sly. On the surface our life together seems much like before, but in reality nothing's the same.

I still remember the day he brought her home. He appeared at the door, very cheerful and excited, holding her hand. "Ada," he said, "I brought you a friend."

"A friend for you or me?"

"For you and me. Starting today, she'll live with us."

"But I don't know her," I said.

"You'll have time to get to know her."

"Where will she sleep?"

"In the double bed, with me. Do you mind?"

"In the double bed? Between my linen sheets?"

"If you want, I'll buy us some cotton sheets."

"No, no, you can keep them."

"You can pull out the couch and sleep in the living room," he said to me.

"That's a very hard bed," I complained.

"Helen can help you cook and clean house. You'll see, she'll be a big help to you."

"Can she cook?"

"I don't know. Look, Helen is a bit spoiled. But I'm sure she'll get used to the new house, and she can help you with the housework."

"How do you mean, spoiled?"

"Well, you know, in her house she never does anything and sleeps all day. But she's so good and willing to help. I'm sure you'll like her."

Up to that moment I had not looked at her. I was annoyed at the idea that she'd be using my linens. I hoped I could make her vanish simply by not looking at her. But, there she was, tall, fair and nodding with approval at George's every word. So I lifted my head to take a good look at her. The first thing I saw were her big, peaceful blue eyes staring at me with curiosity. Except for those almost exceptionally large eyes, her face was nothing special, round, pale, regular. Her body, like her face, was plump, regular, normal.

That evening George stayed home to help us bake a big apple pie. He put on an apron and peeled the apples while talking to Helen. Then I realized Helen didn't know how to do anything. Whenever she tried to help, she'd get in the way. From that evening on, I never asked her to help in the kitchen. I prefer to do everything myself to save time.

That evening, to celebrate her coming to stay with us, we even opened a bottle of champagne. Helen had two glasses and got tipsy. George picked her up and put her on the bed. Then he called me to help him undress her. I saw her naked. Dressed, she looked like twenty-eight. Naked, she seemed more like thirty-eight. I don't know why it pleased me to realize she was older than I am. Giving a last glance at my delicately hand-embroidered linens I went out, leaving the two of them alone.

What George says is true: Helen is nice and very affectionate; the only problem is she often gets bored, and to pass the time plays practical jokes on me. Usually she spends the day reading comic books, putting on nail polish, or brushing her hair. At times she falls asleep and I don't see or hear her till seven when George comes home. Just before he arrives Helen dresses quickly, puts on her makeup, heels, combs her hair, and as soon as he opens the door she runs to greet him with cries of joy.

At times the three of us go out together. We go to the movies or for a walk downtown. I must admit that on those occasions George is very nice to me. He treats me like a real wife: we walk arm in arm, he whispers funny and sweet words in my ear, and holds the door for me. And Helen follows us slowly, somewhat jealous. Whenever we meet a friend of his, he introduces her as his wife's cousin, mine, that is, saying, "She's lost her husband. So she lives with us now because she doesn't have anybody, poor thing."

Helen never breathes a word. She smiles, and asks for ice cream, her great passion. At times George buys it for her. Other times he scolds, saying ice cream is bad for you in winter, and keeps walking.

As soon as we're home, things change. George doesn't look or talk to me unless it is to make Helen laugh; that's when he calls me his little mouse. This reassures Helen and she starts talking about boring things. Other times she lies on the bed with her comic books and expects me to run to her with a cold glass of milk whenever she's thirsty.

My problem with Helen is not that she wants me to leave the house — in fact she's asked me not to leave — how could she ever get along without me anyway? Who else could put up with her pouting, her tantrums and practical jokes? My real problem is that she doesn't realize I just cannot put up with the way she mistreats my bed linens.

"If you go on making holes in my sheets, I'll leave this house," I told her one day when I got really angry.

"Don't say that. George would get very upset."

"That's his problem."

"But he's your husband."

"So what?"

"He could take you to court for walking away from the marriage."

"Do you think my leaving would hurt George?" I asked.

"I don't know. But if you leave I can't live with him anymore."

"Why not?"

"You know we're not married."

"Well, what does that matter?"

"Pretty soon everybody will know we're lovers."

"So what?"

"I don't like it. What will the neighbours think?" she asked.

"Who cares about the neighbours?"

"I do. I don't want to make other people think I've no morals."

Actually, I have no intention of leaving the house. I would get bored on my own, and furthermore, George is my husband, and I believe my place is beside him. When I threaten to leave, I do it just to frighten

Helen. Now and then I like to see her being thoughtful and listening when I speak.

Soon George will be back. I've made a big decision this evening. I'll tell George to buy himself some cotton sheets for our bed where he sleeps with Helen. I won't stand by and watch them turn my linens to shreds.

~

Marco

When I married him he was still attending uni-
versity, two years short of his engineering degree. He never studied. He
used to say he'd rather look at my feet.

My feet, for him, are very "attractive," long, hard like two corpses pre-
served in ice with the stillness and heaviness of dead weights. You could
say I walk with my legs, not my feet; in fact, my feet move heavily, like two
marble slabs anchored to my ankles.

Marco used to take pleasure studying my feet, lying on the bed for
hours motionless, holding my bare feet on his chest, examining them
closely. I got somewhat bored, but I'd let him be. I never had a special liking for my stupid and meaningless feet.

Whenever Marco was not staring at my feet, he'd sleep or whisper his
childhood memories to me, keeping his eyes half shut. Actually, Marco
lived for his memories. His head was always full of them, recollections
of people and events from his past. He never thought about the future
and saw the present as something bewildering, painful and absurd.
Whenever he could, he completely forgot the present and escaped into
the past. So his grades were nothing to be proud of, and his father, an
engineer, supported him and always badgered him.

Marco used to say my feet reminded him of a statue standing in a garden in the region of Lombardy, where he spent his youth.

"What was the statue like?"

"A bit like you, small and white, plump, with two strands of hair
falling over the ears, small breasts, heavy legs, white, beautiful feet like
yours with a little bump of flesh on top, just like yours."

"Why did you like them?"

"I liked to look at them. Sometimes, when I was sure nobody was
watching, I'd bend down to kiss them and even lick them a little."

Often he talked to me about his mother, the real and mature person, symbolized in his imagination by the statue. Whenever he talked to me about her, his eyes smiled.

"Do you know what my mother looked like?"

"I can imagine; she was extremely beautiful."

"No. She was weightless. When the war came, she flew away."

"Did she die?"

"No. She disappeared. I don't know whether she died, she just disappeared. In those days she still looked like the statue, young and beautiful even though she wore ugly dresses, black flower prints."

"What did your mother do?"

"Nothing. She usually lay down on some chaise, reading the paper or staring at the empty air with a disappointed look on her face. I'd play nearby, never straying away. At times I'd bother her and she'd send me away with a gentle push. I liked my mother a lot: the most beautiful woman in the world."

After Marco and I had a few months of this quiet life, his father threatened to cut off our allowance if Marco didn't resume his studies. To please him, Marco started studying again, but without commitment; he'd stop continually to talk to me about himself, his childhood, his mother, the marble statue, and the garden.

Every day around four I went out to get groceries for supper, leaving him at his desk bent over his books. When I came back I always found him as I left him, in the same position, motionless, staring at the empty darkness. I'd stretch a hand toward the wall to turn on the light. Marco didn't move.

"Did you study?"

"Yes, sure."

"Why don't you turn on the light when it gets dark?"

"You know what I was thinking about a minute ago?"

"What?"

"My mother when she was seventeen. My father was a farmer....She was from Milan, with a city air about her that scared people off. My mother was a beauty in her teens; every week she showed up with a different man. Her skirts were so wide that whenever she moved they'd sway, showing her ankles."

"But how can you know anything about your mother when she was seventeen?"

"I can imagine it."

"Why don't you get down to studying?"

"She put her hair up in a soft style and decorated it with little fabric roses. I can see my father falling in love more with her fancy hairdo and her Parisian skirts than with her, always the sucker. Do you know what he used to call her when they were engaged? 'Kitten.' What can be more disgusting? And he thought she married him for love. What an idiot!"

"Why did she marry him then?"

"Because she was bored. He'd been after her for ten years, while he was a young boy and she was still an unattractive girl with a low forehead. She used to love handsome men, dance, laugh, make love, whereas he always worried about papers and documents. But he wanted her at any cost, and in the end he got her. She was tired of avoiding him and married him to spite another man who wanted to marry her but couldn't bring himself to ask. So, after ten years of saying no, she said yes, let's get married and go live in the country."

"And then?"

"Then, nothing. She got bored stiff, and when war broke out, she vanished."

"Did she run away with a man?"

"When I was little she used to put her fingers in my mouth."

"Who?"

"My mother, to see if I was getting my new teeth. I was a bit shy, especially when dad was there. But I used to like the feel of her fat fingers in my mouth. First she'd stick one finger inside, sliding it along my gums, feeling and pressing down; then she'd stick in another and another. When she pulled out her hand, dripping with my saliva, I blushed and ran away. She laughed and patted me on the head."

"Why don't you study instead of thinking about your mother?"

"I studied, now I'm tired. You know how mother ended up?"

"How?"

"Burned alive under the bombardment."

"Didn't you tell me she vanished?"

"Yes, vanished, burned, it's all the same."

"Now study for an hour and then we'll eat. After, if you want, we'll go to a movie."

"I don't feel like going. You know I don't like to go. We'll stay home and I can tell you about my mother when she was a girl."

"You already told me."

"I could tell you endless things about her. You know, she used to suck the egg out of the shell after making two tiny holes with her nails. She was so good at it, a tap with the index finger and a bit of shell fell off. Then she tapped on the other end and started sucking. Or I could tell you about the times she took a steam bath and I squatted down behind the door to listen to the stove humming. I cried and I wanted in, but she laughed, refusing to open the door. Then she came out wrapped with a towel, looking all red. She slipped on her nylons and I'd say, let me see, and she pushed me away with her foot. She gave me a gentle kick to get rid of me, but I wouldn't leave because I was so glad to be near her."

"I'm going to get your supper ready."

"No, wait. Did I ever tell you about the time when she caught me hugging the feet of the statue?"

"If I don't get supper ready, we're not eating tonight. It's late."

"Okay. I'll come and help you."

After two years of courses Marco had taken four exams and failed two. His father cut our monthly allowance in half. Marco and I ate poached eggs and salad as if we lived in wartime, but he wasn't sad or annoyed. Living like poor folks didn't bother him because, he said, it reminded him of his childhood.

"Maybe I'll go out and look for a job," I said.

"Do as you like. I've got a lot to study, but what am I going to do the whole day without you?"

We stretched out on the bed and Marco held my bare feet, petting and kissing them, keeping his eyes shut and still as if he were asleep, but he wasn't.

"What are you thinking?"

"The time when I was a boy."

"Why don't you think about now, about me? You're a man now."

"On Mondays I used to get up at five with the butcher's son to watch the farmers kill the sheep. I walked into this big, dark room with the cement floor all spattered with blood. On one side there was a heap of hay, and a table with pails, knives, and razors scattered all around. It was pretty cold in there, even in summer. My friend's father came in wearing a big plastic apron, grabbed a sheep between his legs, leaned it against a stump, and slit its throat with a knife. The blood didn't splash, but I always expected it to. Instead it dripped bright and black, creeping along the floor, ending up in a deep hole, clotted and smelling with a sweet, heavy scent. That hole was always covered with flies. The sheep looked straight at me as if to say: What are you doing there, you fool, you pig? I'd feel a stab in my stomach that was mixed with a sense of pleasure or excitement. I just couldn't take my eyes off the butcher's hands or the dripping blood."

"Why don't you think about me? I'm here. Your childhood is dead now."

"Some things never die."

"I don't remember anything about my childhood."

"That's because you live in the present, and you're not happy because only the past can give us happiness."

"What's so beautiful about remembering the past?"

"It's the most beautiful thing in the world. Whenever I remember things I'm alive, but when I don't remember, I don't feel well, I'm already dead."

"Why's that?"

"Because the present is only what it is, whereas memories are always something more."

"What are they?"

"A wonderful distortion that makes my head spin."

One day Marco's father came to visit in the late morning while we were talking on the bed, naked. I listened as Marco talked with his eyes closed about his childhood in a low, delirious monotone, all the while holding my feet pressed against his chest.

I can't imagine how the door to the house could have been unlocked. We noticed Marco's father only after he appeared at the bedroom door and saw us naked.

I shrieked and pulled the blanket over my chest. Marco opened his eyes, saw his father, and just lay motionless.

"What does that idiot want?" he said in a mocking and sad tone, still lying naked.

The old man started to shout so loud we couldn't understand his words. Marco didn't even try to cover himself. After a few minutes his father began to kick the furniture, upsetting everything in his way, breaking the mirror on the wall into a million pieces with a single blow. It took only one violent kick to topple Marco's desk and all the books on it. His head was bloody from the slivers but he wouldn't calm down. After a while he grabbed the back of a chair and brought it crashing down over his son's back.

Marco said, "You're an old idiot."

Marco's calm, angry tone made him stop, so he let the back of the chair fall to the ground and threw himself on the bed sobbing.

"My son died," he said between sobs. "My Marco's dead; I won't ever see him again. Everything's finished."

"Go and cry somewhere else, you crocodile," Marco shouted in his ear.

The old man got up, dried his tears with the corner of a sheet, and left mumbling that his son was dead and everything was over.

From that day we received not another cent from him, so for a while we earned our living by selling furniture. Then I found work in a travel agency and Marco came to meet me at the end of the day. As soon as he appeared I asked if he had studied.

"Of course," he answered. But I knew it wasn't true.

My small monthly salary allowed us to live very modestly in a one-room studio apartment. Marco was always home, whereas I was out working. Now and then he'd phone me from the café below to ask how I was.

"I'm okay. Are you studying?"

"Yes."

"What point are you at?"

"I'm at a good point. I think I'll take an exam in October, but I'd like to tell you about something that happened to me this afternoon while I was studying."

"What?"

"I was figuring something out when I felt a blow to my head. I turned around, but nobody was there. I couldn't understand what it was. I wasn't feeling well and I kept hearing a buzzing noise in my head. My eyes were burning and I ran to the bathroom to put my head under the shower. I stayed there for a while, under the jet of water, somewhat startled. Then, with my face wet and my eyes puffy, I looked out the window. You won't believe it .... I realized that what I was seeing was not the usual parking lot with rows of cars but a garden with hedges and trees. I couldn't quite understand what was going on. Meantime I was feeling really very good. The pain had gone and I had started breathing normally again and then I finally realized what I was seeing in front of me was my garden."

"Marco, you had an hallucination."

"No. It was really my garden. And guess what was at the end of it, behind the hedges and the oleanders. The statue, my mother's statue! Even from far off I could make out her bare feet shining in the sunlight. I stood there mesmerized, staring at everything, afraid it might disappear any minute. But can you imagine who I saw at one point toward the back, squatting, playing with the pebbles? It was me. It was really me! I was wearing shorts and a yellow cap, busy playing so I didn't even notice somebody was watching me. Then I heard my mother's voice coming from the house and soon I heard her steps on the gravel. My heart raced. I thought in a minute I'd see her. And I prayed she'd be wearing the dress with black tulips. Sure enough, there she was. She walked slowly, lazy and playful, and her flowered black dress danced around her legs. Then a car horn startled me and everything disappeared. It all vanished just like that. I sat on the edge of the bathtub, so disappointed."

That night when he came to meet me after work, I realized he was ill. His face was somewhat contorted, his eyes bloodshot and swollen and his jaw tense.

"Why don't we go to the movies, just for fun?"

"No."

"What do you want to do?"

"Let's go home."

"It's so uncomfortable in that small room with all this heat."

"Come on, I'll show you something."

When we were home he asked me to sit on the bed and put a book in my hands. I opened it. Above the title on the first page, a child's hand had written his own name and the date: Marco Annoni, 1 June 1942. Glued beneath was a faded photo of a thin, sad, frowning face with two bright but sad eyes.

"Is this you?"

"I'll never be like that again," he said.

"Why would you want to be like that? You're better now, a handsome man."

"My father's right; Marco's dead."

"And you, who are you?" I asked.

"I'm an abnormal growth, a wart, something I don't care about, a ridiculous appendage."

"And what about me, don't I exist?"

"Neither one of us exists. Our lives are dark, sad, meaningless, and ordinary, like the lives of all the others. When I was a boy I was different, I was special. Now I'm repulsive."

"Don't you love me?"

Instead of answering, Marco sat on the floor, bared my feet, took them in his hands and started to lick them.

Two days later he again phoned me at work, and I could tell his voice was nervous and elated at the same time.

"What's the matter?"

"It's happened again."

"What?"

"The knock on my head, the pain, the vision of the garden from the bathroom window."

"I'll call a doctor, maybe you're sick."

"I'm just fine. It was very beautiful."

"What?"

"The vision. My mother was coming forward along the path of dahlias, walking lightly, deep in thought, wearing the black tulip dress. Her face was very pale, with dark rings around her eyes. But when she saw me, instead of smiling, she tried to give me a little nudge with her foot like when I was little. Her voice got harsh and stern when she said to me: 'If you hadn't grown up I wouldn't have changed at all. If you didn't have such long arms, I'd still be alive. If you hadn't had such long legs, I'd still be young. If you didn't have that beard, I'd still be a girl. If you didn't have that hard, bristly beard, I wouldn't have aged and died. But you spoiled everything. You wanted to grow up and become a man.' When she drew closer I saw her face was pale and hard, as if made of stone. Her voice became sharp, painful: 'If you hadn't grown up, you selfish child, all these awful and horrible things wouldn't have happened. Now I'm ugly and decomposed. If you hadn't grown up, everything would have stayed as before.' That's what she said, and I didn't want to cry, but I cried all the same; I wanted to cry out that it was not my fault, that I would have given up my life to go back to the past and give her youth back to her. But I couldn't open my mouth. So she went away, angry, turning her back on me without saying goodbye."

I thought I should go and have a talk with my father-in-law. I was afraid Marco was really ill. But two days later, in the office, I was told to run home because Marco had thrown himself out of the window. I ran to the house. They found Marco's body, already cold, down in the courtyard, on top of a long, light blue car. He had hit his head and died instantly.

I've come to stay with my sister, where I lived before marrying Marco. Of all the things we had in the house, I've kept only the book with the picture of him as a child. But I never look at it because it's a bad memory, and so I never look back at the past.

～

The Blonde Wig

I've never liked trends and fads. As far as I'm
concerned, it's stupid to worry about what's in and what's not. My girl-
friends make fun of me because I always wear the same styles, male-cut
suits, coloured blouses, and a worn-out purse with a shoulder strap.

For instance, for a while wigs have been the rage here, in Rome. Several women with whom I work in the firm wear them. Some own dark
or red ones, others blond or brown ones. Some wear them straight and
long, others curly and short. The girls pass them around and have fun
wearing each other's wigs.

Naturally, I laugh at their superficial taste and say I'll never buy
myself a wig. First of all I find it revolting wearing some dead woman's
hair, and moreover, I think it's senseless to change the appearance of my
hair as easily as I change my clothes. One of the girls laughingly said that
it isn't true wigs are made out of dead women's hair.

"Where do they get the hair, then?" I asked.

"They buy it from the vendors from the East."

"What East?"

"Don't you know who the Orientals are?"

"Of course I do, but I still don't get what you mean."

"For example, the women from Vietnam. There's a war going on
there, don't you know? Aren't they poor there? Well, a salesman goes
around saying: I buy hair for ten dollars a pound. The women go for it.
They need money, so they cut their hair off and sell it."

"So all the hair is from Vietnam?"

"Of course not. It comes from Persian, Arab, Chinese women, from
Indian women too, from poor women all over the world. Get it?"

"But Orientals are dark. What about the blond wigs?"

"They're dyed, that's easy to do!"

"Well then, are wigs all black at first?"

"Sure. I've got three of them, red, blond, and black."

"How much is a wig?"

"A good one can come to over a hundred dollars. But some sell for sixty, fifty, even thirty. A synthetic wig can cost as little as twenty dollars."

"And where do you find the money to buy so many wigs?"

"I buy them in bulk with my friends."

"That's immoral."

"It's fun."

"It's immoral, I tell you."

"If wearing a wig is immoral, so is wearing makeup, or a dress, or even getting an education. All things that are artificial or added on or not natural would be immoral, then. But civilization is like that, artificial and masked, made up and manipulated. A wig is only a little added padding, what's wrong with that?"

More than Gina's reasoning, what made me change my mind about wigs was my hairdresser's mistake. One day I went to get my hair done. While I was busy looking through a magazine, the hairdresser, by mistake, slipped a wig me instead of the lady next to me. I looked up at the mirror and for a second saw a face I didn't recognize. The hairdresser quickly took the wig off and apologized for his mistake.

But the image of my face, unfamiliar and completely transformed by a mass of thick blond curls, stuck in my mind. In my dark eyes and my usually cold demeanour I had suddenly detected a flash of unfamiliar tenderness: my usual severe and distant look had vanished in favour of a childlike, helpless insecurity.

Naturally, I didn't even think of buying a wig, nor did I tell Gina about my experience. I went about life as usual, working full time without time off for fun or love.

But in the morning, whenever I combed my short, straight hair, I'd search in the mirror for that expression I'd noticed on my face when I first had the wig on.

Try as I might, I couldn't find that excitement or joy in my eyes again. No matter how hard I looked at myself or pretended to put on airs, I was nothing but a middle-aged young woman who wore on her face the signs of duty and boredom.

I gradually tried to convince myself that buying a wig wasn't a crime, and that I could wear it just around the house now and then. But something in me wouldn't give in; I felt I'd be disloyal to myself if I changed my hair colour or style. Only vain and silly women do that, I thought. It's an inexcusable silliness. But I began to feel I'd soon go along with the idea.

One day I finally made the decision. Somewhat embarrassed, I went to the hairdresser's and asked for a wig like the one I'd tried on once by mistake. The hairdresser looked at me amazed, since he has always known me to be strict, conservative, and unyielding to whims of vanity.

"You'd look nice in something like this. Look at this beautiful brown hair and these waves with red highlights."

"No. I'd like the blond one."

"We've got so many. What about this one?"

"No, the short curly one."

"But that's a doll's wig. I assure you that's not for you. It would look terrible on you."

"Please get it for me."

"Each person can wear only a certain type of wig. In your case, you'd suit this one, this, or that one there. But the blond, curly wig is definitely not for you."

"Why not?"

"You'd look like a puppet with the wrong head stuck on your neck, that's why."

"How much is it?"

"Sixty dollars. But listen to me, it's completely out of place on such a conservative and sensible person like yourself. That wig was made for a flirt, not for you."

"Here's the sixty dollars."

I didn't ask him to put it on me, but had him wrap it up in a piece of paper. I quickly took it home. I didn't touch it until the evening. Meanwhile, I devoted myself more than ever to my work of business manager.

At eight I went home, prepared supper, and ate while reading the evening paper. Later I got ready for bed, the wig lying there on the dresser, soft and blond like the frame of a painting waiting to be filled. I couldn't go to bed without first trying it on.

I combed my black hair back to keep it all under the wig, which fit me perfectly. Then I tightened the elastic on my nape.

Lifting my eyes to the mirror I suddenly faced a stranger: a young woman just beginning to show her age, with large, round eyes, light cheeks, thin lips, and a playful mouth. I thought all this was quite indecent and tried to frown and tighten my lips. But instead of revealing a frown, the face in the mirror smiled and put on such a sly, calculating expression that I quickly pulled the wig off to regain my composure.

That night I hardly slept, and the next day I worked hard but without interest since I was troubled by my very new, unfamiliar image and feelings.

I didn't touch the wig for three whole days. As if in a trance, I heard but didn't pay attention to the silly conversations of my female employees. Now and then I'd tell them to work more and talk less.

"I saw a platinum blond wig."

"Platinum hair is for older women."

"Sure, for women with lines on their faces. But if you have smooth skin, the effect is really extraordinary."

"Does it have blue highlights?"

"No, silver."

"Silver is in now."

"So is gold."

"Platinum blond with silvery highlights."

"Is the hair long?"

"Short."

"Curly?"

"Wavy."

"Shall the four of us buy it together and then share it?"

"I want it for next Saturday."

"A party?"

"Looking from the back, there's always some doubt about platinum hair: a man wonders how old the woman might be. But when she turns her head he's completely taken by the freshness of her face. When you're young, platinum blond makes you look even younger."

"Shall we buy it?"

"How much is it?"

"Platinum blond on a summer's night."

"Platinum blond close to his lips."

"Platinum blond against a black velvet jacket."

"Platinum blond and green eyes."

"And silver nail polish."

"Are you sure it's got silver highlights?"

Drawing closer I noticed their voices turning to softer, quick, low whispers. I bent to look at the coloured, padded head of one of them.

"You're all overdoing this wig thing. You'd better get down to work," I said.

That evening, even before dinner, I went straight to the bedroom and slipped the wig on. My employees' chattering must have brainwashed me, because wearing the wig and stepping out of the house for a breath of fresh air suddenly became very important to me.

But this time what also happened was that as I lifted my eyes to the mirror I was shocked. The woman facing me wasn't me but somebody else. My bashful but severe face had vanished, replaced by a youthful, restless face with a gently sly and deceiving smile.

I knew this type of face needed makeup because its paleness made it look almost coarse. I started looking for some old cosmetics I never use. I put on red lipstick, black eyeliner, and a very light blush, combed my hair to let the blond curls hang loose over my cheeks and forehead.

But once I was made-up, my head felt detached from my body. My old-fashioned clothes, like the long, male-cut jacket, looked ludicrous. I searched in the chest where I kept my old clothes and found a red dress from my teens. Tried it on. It was tight and short, but I thought if I ironed it and let out a couple of seams, it might fit fine.

Doing just that, my fingers moved with unusual agility and excitement. Then I slipped the dress on with a pair of high-heeled shoes, and without looking in the mirror I went out.

On reaching the street I remembered I had not eaten. I started out toward a trattoria and as I was about to enter, I remembered I had no money. So I walked along the street, just looking at store windows.

I stopped in front of a supermarket that was all lit up. A printed sign read: Open till midnight. I started to wander among the stalls, staring greedily at all the produce that was openly laid out.

I tried stealing a banana and made it. Nobody saw me; then I sneaked into the phone booth and ate it quickly, slipping the skin between the pages of the phone book.

Moments later I stole a piece of Swiss cheese, letting it fall inside my purse. But I soon got bored just stealing food and made my way toward the costume jewellery department because at a distance I'd spotted the glitter of a beautiful ring shaped like a snake with a ruby set in the head. I looked around; the crowd wandered about slowly and aimlessly. The salesgirls seemed tired, tense, uncaring. I soon realized that the best way to put my plan into action was to pretend I was studying the object closely. Then, with very smooth, precise gestures, I could slip the ring into my purse and still linger around, not hurrying away to avoid attracting attention.

By the time I decided to leave, my purse was bulging and heavy. On my way out, I grabbed a small bottle of cognac. As soon as I was outside I tore the plastic wrapping off with my nails and downed it all standing up, with my head turned toward the darkening sky.

As I threw away the empty bottle, I met my own reflection in the store window. I felt as if all my usual inner seriousness and pride were about to break through in a scream of outrage against my new self. Instead, in the reflection my head was slightly bent over my shoulder and my face smiled gently. It was so beautiful and fresh, so delicate and fragile, that I didn't have the courage to scold myself. What does it mean to be a thief, anyway? It's just something silly. My reflection in the glass, with its clever and joyful expression, seemed to say that although the stores were closing now, the next day I would no doubt go downtown to steal something significant and valuable. Promise? I dared myself. I swear it, I replied to myself aloud, placing my right hand flat over my heart.

On reaching home, I went to bed immediately, as I was very tired and sleepy. But before falling asleep I placed my beautiful blond wig on the cardboard head on top of the dresser and washed off my makeup with soap.

The next day I went about life as usual. At the office I was strict as usual, watching that nothing got stolen. I devoted myself to my tasks with determination, in order to dispel the memory of that disgraceful evening.

I promised myself I'd never wear that wig again, and I think I kept my promise.

But two days ago I found a diamond bracelet at the bottom of one of my purses. I took it immediately to the lost and found, saying that I'd found it on the ground. I don't want to keep any stolen property in my house.

~

Diary of a Married Couple

February 12th

We got married. Giulio's father sent his curses in a letter from Sicily. I don't give a shit! Anyway, I'm the one who works and he lives in my apartment. What can that old fart do about it? Giulio's skin is beautifully smooth, like silk.

February 18th

So his father won't cut off his allowance, Giulio goes on writing to say he's studying and taking exams. His father answers with long letters that Giulio throws in the basket, since the only important thing is the cheque.

March 8th

We've been married for almost a month. Giulio doesn't look happy and he's become nervous and lazy. He doesn't say a word and our sex life is almost zero.

April 10th

Another month. Things are terrible at the office: work increases but not the pay. I realized Giulio's a man of habit, always doing the same things. Our lifestyle is regular and boring: he studies, I work. In the evening we have supper in the kitchen and then we sit in front of the TV. No friends, no movies, no evening walks.

May 16th

Now that the weather's hot, we go sit in the Galleria Umberto or in a café in the evening. Giulio likes to have ice cream, sitting there surrounded by miniature trees, listening to the little orchestra playing. I get bored to death, but I keep quiet for his sake.

June 3rd

Giulio is sad. I don't know what's the matter with him. He studies all the time, but so far he hasn't taken any exams. He wrote to his father to say he's graduating next year.

June 20th

If I tell him he's a cold and irritable husband, he doesn't answer. If I tell him I want to have sex, he gives the excuse that he can't study after. If I tell him that going to the Galleria for ice cream is something old people do, he gives me an angry look.

July 7th

Another month gone and Giulio doesn't change. We sleep in the same bed without touching. I told him that he was different before we married; he liked sex then. He answered that animals have sex. I pointed out he didn't think so before we got married. He said before marriage it's all right to be passionate. Love is like the trees blooming, there's a proper time when trees become beautiful, smell great, and are full of flowers. That's the time for love. After that, *basta*, enough. We put things to rest for another year. But we aren't trees, I said to him. We're like trees more than you know, he answered.

July 16th

It seemed as if he would write exams this time because he'd studied so much. And then, at the last minute, he didn't show. He's got a bony, stubborn face and hard eyes. He says he loves me, but I can't understand how he can possibly love me because all he does is study.

August 30th

It's sweltering hot. I asked him if he wishes to go to the beach for awhile on my holidays in a week. He didn't even bother to answer, but started to write furiously in a notebook. When I come back from the office I undress and get into a bathtub full of cool water and I go around the house naked to arouse him; but to him I don't exist.

September 7th

My holidays have started but we don't leave Rome at all because Giulio says he has to study and I hate and curse him while I sleep off my frustrations.

September 15th

The holidays are over. We're still in this awful, dark, hot apartment. Giulio studies and says he'll take four exams in October. Every five minutes he asks me for some iced coffee.

October 6th

Exams begin in a few days, so Giulio hardly sleeps. It's impossible to get along with him. He drinks too much coffee and his hair is so dirty. I told him to wash it but he threw a slipper hitting me on the head. He doesn't eat either. The ham rolls I take him while he studies end up in the waste basket.

November 10th

It's November. The exam period is over. Giulio never left the house. He studied till he got a fever and when the time came he said he wasn't ready. All along he sat in his room at his desk.

November 22nd

Yesterday was my birthday. I'm twenty-three. My sister Agostina invited us to dinner at her house, but Giulio didn't want to go, saying he had to study. I met Candido at Agostina's. He talks a lot, smokes like a chimney, and has blue eyes.

December 6th

Giulio's hair is getting grey. When I married him he was blond and handsome. Now he's a different man. He wrote to his father to say he has taken four exams. His father's happy, sends money and writes long letters Giulio doesn't read but throws in the basket.

December 15th

Candido would like me to stay with him, but I've got to work and look after Giulio. Without me he doesn't eat, drink, or sleep. But whenever I can slip away I go visit Candido in his basement. There's no heat, no bath. We have sex on the floor, on a mattress under a blanket full of holes. Bursting with life, he tells me about his paintings; weeping and laughing he covers me with kisses. It's such fun to be with him.

December 25th

It's Christmas. We've been without running water since yesterday on account of the frozen pipes. When it's this cold, Giulio doesn't even get dressed. He goes from bed to desk, and studies in his pyjamas with a blanket on his shoulders. He says he'll take five exams in June.

January 3rd

A new year. Giulio refused to go out for Christmas and New Year's. He says he must study and can't waste even a minute. I said I was going to Agostina's. I know he won't phone. I spent the night with Candido, and to celebrate I gave him a little gas heater and a bottle of French cognac. When I went home I found Giulio sleeping on his books. He studied till 3 a.m.

February 2nd

It's freezing. The office where I work is badly heated so I got the flu. I want to buy myself a pair of boots tomorrow. Giulio doesn't bother to dress anymore. He's become plumper and sallow and never leaves the house because he's always studying.

February 20th

I bought my boots and told Giulio about Candido. He told me not to bother him because he has to study, and that's that.

March 6th

March already! Giulio's beginning to get nervous about exams. He's become filthy. When I married him he was clean. Now he never showers and if I tell him he smells, he gives me an angry look.

March 8th

Candido sold a painting for four hundred dollars. He had a basket full of tropical fruit for me and little cans of crabmeat in oil. We ate till we got a stomach ache. He also bought a new gas unit for the heater, so we had sex in a warm room.

March 20th

Giulio never asks me what I do or where I go. Sometimes I get home late after visiting Candido. He doesn't care at all, and feels satisfied if at some point in the evening I bring a dish of soup right to his desk. Sometimes he eats it, other times he doesn't. Eventually I go to bed while he stays up till two. I don't even notice when he comes to bed. Once, when I was half-asleep and turned around to give him a hug, he pushed me away with a kick. I think he's sick. It's not normal for a twenty-seven-year-old man to abstain like that.

April 16th

I have to play tricks when I want to change his pyjamas because he doesn't want to change or wash. He drinks about thirty cups of coffee a day. The other month I added up our grocery bills and we spent the most on coffee. It's crazy.

May 8th

It's impossible for me to sleep anymore beside a man who stinks like sweat and dry urine. One of these nights I'll take him and push him into a tub full of water. He becomes increasingly obnoxious as exams draw closer. Now he's begun to fast again. Strange thing is that instead of losing he puts on weight and he's got a stomach bulge.

May 18th

Last night I waited for him to fall asleep. Then I slowly took off his pyjamas and washed him with a wet, soapy sponge. I think he woke up at one point but didn't open his eyes. He lay there without moving, as if surrendering with his legs stretched wide open. I washed and dried him without wetting the bed. I don't know how I possibly did all that. The dirt had formed patches of crusts all along his legs and his pubic hair was tangled and matted with sweat and body oils.

June 3rd

Every five or six days I wake up at night to bathe my husband. He pretends to be asleep while I slide a towel under his body and, keeping a wash basin full of warm water handy, I sponge him clean. By the way he breathes I think he loves all the attention. Once he even got an erection. I thought he wanted to have sex, but nothing happened. He went on pretending to be asleep. During the day he treats me as he usually does and has never referred to the nighttime baths or given any indication that he wants to have sex.

June 8th

It's almost exam time. Giulio doesn't sleep or eat anymore, nor can I wash him because he spends the days and nights at the table studying.

June 6th

Candido sold another painting for six hundred dollars. The buyer is a restaurant owner. The painting is a dish of onions set against a quartered cow.

June 20th

That's it. Exams have started. Giulio has a fever. I can tell from his shiny eyes and his face full of red blotches. He says he'll go to the university in a couple of days.

June 25th

He put on his best suit, even washed his hair, leaving the bathroom like a pigsty. He took his books and notebooks, and left. At two he came back, pale as a sheet. I asked if he'd written the exam and he nodded. But I knew it wasn't true. He wants to fool me like his father. He sat at the table, but didn't eat. When I came back from work at six-thirty I found him sleeping with his head on the kitchen table.

July 3rd

We got a letter from his father, saying he's coming to celebrate the happy outcome of the exams with us. Giulio started kicking the furniture, the chairs, the bed, turning the entire apartment upside down. Then he fell asleep on the john with angry tears streaming down his face.

July 7th

Giulio sent a telegram to his father, asking him not to come because he's not well. Result: the next day the doorbell rang. It was his father.

July 15th

Giulio's father is staying at a hotel on Via Veneto. Every morning he phones and talks in his cheerful, bossy tone. At one he comes to visit with cream-filled pastry and strawberry-flavoured wine. Giulio goes on with his act, saying he'll graduate in October since he has by now taken all his exams. I don't breathe a word, but his father believes, or pretends to believe him, and cannot decide to leave.

July 25th

Last night I woke up feeling cold because the covers had fallen off. Giulio lay beside me, sleeping, naked as if surrendering, quietly implying that he wanted a sponge bath. I got up, poured water in the wash basin, and began to wash him. Now and then I looked at his face; he kept his eyes shut but seemed pleased, his sallow skin perspiring lightly and his grey lips tense and shiny. I was sleepy, but I continued till I felt my arms heavy like lead.

August 13th

Candido continues to produce paintings, but nobody buys them. I lent him ten dollars because he hadn't eaten for three days. The damp air gives him a backache. He moans, whines, and complains, but soon his mood improves and he's his old playful self again. The other day he painted his buns green to make me laugh. He sat on the bed, leaving a big heart-shaped image on the sheet. Now he's obsessed with painting onions. They're everywhere, on the floor, hanging on walls, on his easel, on the windowsill, the mattress, the stove.

August 16th

Giulio's father's still in Rome, making great plans for the future. He's trying to find a job for Giulio for next year when he graduates. He hasn't found anything yet, or he's just pretending. I don't know. They're such hypocrites, father and son, and I never know what's on their minds.

August 22nd

We ate at home yesterday with Giulio's father. After coffee, Giulio said he was going out to buy a book, but he never came back. Later, toward evening, my father-in-law went to the police. Then we both did some hospital rounds, but we didn't find him.

August 28th

No news of Giulio anywhere. My father-in-law never stops phoning. He's such a nuisance, sweating as he talks, talking as he sweats, dressed in white, with a raffia hat. I had to tell him that the news about Giulio's exams was all a lie. He said he knew it already; so why did the fool make all that fuss?

September 2nd

Giulio's body was found in Rome's Tiber River by the Magliana. I didn't go to identify his corpse because I didn't want to see him in such an awful state. I asked his father with his white linen suit and raffia hat to go identify him.

September 8th

Nobody but myself and my father-in-law went to the funeral, the church, and the cemetery. Nobody brought flowers. Where were his friends? his father asked. What friends? Giulio didn't have friends, I replied. He continues to wear his white outfit. It gets on my nerves, that raffia hat with the black silk band. I hope now at least he'll leave. I feel sick just looking at him.

October 30th

Candido has come to live with me and keeps me in good spirits. He goes around the house naked, scandalizing our women neighbours, who can see from across the way. All the furniture is repainted yellow or red. His Arabic and Chinese cooking fills my apartment with smoke. When he's tired of painting, he squats down in the hallway beating on a drum, in fact a metal pan, and keeps on drumming till night.

November 8th

We got married. He dressed in black and I wore bright yellow. After the ceremony, Candido's friends came over. There were about thirty guests, all penniless artists, together with some unemployed actors. We ate cheese sandwiches and drank beer till 3 a.m. Then they all left together, leaving my apartment in a total mess. One of them even pissed in a dish.

December 3rd

We spend all our time in bed. If Candido could paint as well as he makes love he'd be a great artist. He has the best cock I've ever seen, surrounded by curly red hair. Luckily he's given up painting onions, but now he paints all kinds of corpses, hanging bodies, cut-up or frozen corpses, poisoned, stabbed, or strangled.

December 25th

It's Christmas. Last year at this time I was shut up in the house with Giulio. This year I'm always out. This evening we're going to Nando's. He's a short, thin actor whose special talent is impersonating gays. Tomorrow night we'll be at Telemachus's, a painter who produces huge gold canvases. On New Year's Eve we'll pay a visit to Esther, an actress who poses for photo-romance magazines. She always wears blond wigs with hair down to her waist and never smiles, hiding her rotting teeth.

January 2nd

Another year gone, scampered away like a mouse. Candido is always on a high, saying this year he'll make a lot of money from his corpse paintings. I hope he does. All the guests got drunk at Esther's New Year's party. Then they threw up all over the house; somebody barfed on my foot. Candido waited to vomit till we got outside. Around two it started to snow.

January 18th

When I got home I found Candido stretched out on the kitchen table having sex with Esther. I got so mad I insulted him. He said it's stupid to be jealous, but I don't give a damn whether it's stupid or not: I'm jealous. He grabbed the girl by the arm and took off with her.

January 22nd

Candido hasn't come back for two days. I'm beginning to think it was crazy to marry him. I don't even know whether or not I love him or if it's just because he's so good in bed. I'm such an idiot!

January 28th

Candido's back, claiming Esther's an idiot. I knew it all along. He said he wants nothing to do with her. We had sex right there with our clothes on.

February 4th

Candido's taken up painting again and has locked his friends out of the house. He paints all day, bent over the canvas. In the evening we have sex and then go to bed.

March 6th

Candido's given up painting. He's sick of corpses and spends the day squatting on the floor, beating on a pan. I already know something bad is going to happen.

March 17th

Esther's back. I found them together in bed sleeping, holding each other. I kicked them out of bed and threw them out. Candido kept shouting I was a fool to be jealous since our marriage was a true marriage based on freedom and love. I don't give a damn about his kind of freedom, because whenever I'm nice to somebody else he blows me away with his jealous fits. He's a hopeless egotist.

April 7th

Candido's back. We had sex. But it's all over. I don't love him and don't want to be with him. Now I like Amadeus, a young actor I once met at Esther's. He's young and slim, like a sardine. He's got yellow eyes, light blue cheeks from the fuzz, black hair, green lips, and a great sex drive.

~

$\mathcal{P}$lato's Tree

$\mathcal{I}$ *have a very bad memory, but on the other hand* I'm fussy and picky. Attempting to organize my life better—orderliness escapes me like water evaporating in sunshine—I've always kept a diary with a detailed list of all my daily commitments.

A few nights ago when I opened my notebook, as I usually do, to record what I had done that day, to my surprise I found two blank pages.

I was astonished because I'd never missed recording a day since I was fifteen, except for one time, just once, when I had an ulcer operation and couldn't write for a week.

September 4th and 5th were missing completely, only blank pages. I quickly tried to prod my memory into action, but as I just said, it's so weak there's nothing there. Question it as I might, it never talks to me.

That's why on the first page of my diary I've written this: "Following Milena's advice, I've read some strange stories, Plato's dialogues—they made me yawn. I would have put the book down if at a certain point I hadn't come across an observation that seemed to apply directly to me. Socrates says that the nature of memory is one of two possible kinds: like a stone that always keeps the information carved on it, or like a tree full of birds that at the first gust of wind fly off, leaving the tree empty. No doubt my memory is of this second kind."

I reread slowly what I'd written the two days before September 4th, trying to find clues to the puzzle, but I didn't find any.

The page for September 3rd is full of small writing and stains. I copy it here, hoping to restore my memory: "September 3rd, 8:00 a.m. Discussion with Carmelo about a piece of soap which, he says, I left in water all night to dissolve. Our argument was cut short by the insistent ringing of the doorbell at the building's main entrance below. I ran down without saying goodbye. Giacinta was impatiently waiting for me in the car, her foot on the accelerator. She was in a terrible mood. We reached the office without saying a word. She drove in fits and starts. At one point I was afraid we'd go crashing against some truck. Ten o'clock. It's unbearably hot in the office. The air conditioner is out of order. Mr. Martelli gave me a new ballpoint pen. I thanked him and thought to myself: 'He's so kind; maybe he's in love with me.' Then I discovered he gave me the pen because the ink had almost dried up; almost each time I put it in my pocket it releases a few drops of ink.

One o'clock: I'm home. Started fighting with Carmelo about the soap again. He says I did it deliberately to provoke him. Of course it's not true. I hadn't even noticed that the soap had dropped in the water.

We sat at the table. He ate a portion of yesterday's boiled meat and then threw the dish on the floor. He said the meat was hard and stringy. Of course fresh meat is expensive, and we can't afford it. He said he can't chew it and it sticks to his teeth. I told him to go see a dentist. He said we haven't any money for a dentist. I said it's all his fault if we have no money. He wanted two families, so now he's got to support all his children. He said I'm a silly fool.

I hadn't finished my helping of boiled meat when Giacinta started leaning on her car horn in the street below, so I was forced to rush out, gulping down my food, skipping the fruit. Carmelo looked out the window; I saw him looking down at us. I'm sure he wanted to ensure I hadn't run out to go phone Tina.

Four o'clock: the supervisor called me in. He said I don't concentrate enough on my work and if I don't improve, he'll fire me. I said it was not my fault, it's all because I don't have a good memory. In the end he said I'll never have a career, but I already know that. He complained he can't trust me with delicate tasks, that I'm able to do only simple things but nothing important. He repeated that three times and I had to bend my head, unable to reply. I'd be happy if he did not fire me. But with the money Carmelo makes as building manager we certainly couldn't support the two families, ours and Tina's two children.

Six o'clock: Mr. Martelli handed me a beautifully wrapped package with ribbons. Once again I was deceived. I thought, 'This man Martelli is really nice; it really could be that he's secretly in love with me.' He kept looking at me with his blue, sly, and tender eyes. Fixing his eyes on me, he sighed, and untying the bow I thought I liked him a lot, even if he is fat. Who cares? He's got very delicate skin. I felt I'd love him as I'd never loved anyone in my life. I also thought we'd rent rooms in hotels and leave the office for hours on end in order to be together, to kiss and have sex. The thought of his fat, pale body on top of mine somewhat frightened me, but I liked the idea just the same.

I was so excited I couldn't untie the bow on the box, so I took a pair of scissors, snipped it and removed the tissue paper. At the bottom of the box inside a bundle of papers I found... I can't even think back on it... a gigantic rubber penis. I felt my whole face turning red like it was on fire and all the office staff, including the supervisor, just stood there, staring at me. Mr. Martelli had vanished. Everybody burst out laughing. Then Mr. Martelli came in, his face covered with laugh lines and his eyes puffy with tears.

Strange thing is, I didn't get mad at him. There he was, standing next to me. I could feel his stomach convulsing up and down against my shoulders; I didn't know what to do, but luckily the others did. The supervisor seized the penis and took it away, to put an end, as he said, to the obscene jokes. But the others maliciously joked that he took it to his office to have a good close-up look. Mr. Martelli received some friendly pats on his stomach from his coworkers, while fortunately everybody soon forgot all about me. He was the hero. They kept saying it took real nerve to bring a thing like that to the office.

Eight o'clock: home alone. Carmelo isn't back yet. He may be at Tina's. I thought again about Mr. Martelli and his huge rubber penis. I don't know what to make of his joke. Was it a proposition? an insult? a declaration of love? an obscene gesture? a childish joke? I'm curious to see his face in the morning.

Nine o'clock: Carmelo's home. Again he brought up the matter of the soap. I'd forgotten about it. I couldn't understand what he was arguing about. To change the subject I asked him about Tina. He said I should mind my own business. We didn't talk at dinner, but halfway through he began to complain about the string beans being cold, the bread hard, the eggs stale. I said we haven't the money to eat better, besides, I haven't got time to cook all the meals because I work just as much as he does. That kept him quiet.

To cheer him up I told him about the joke my colleague Martelli had played on me. I was eating bent over my dish when I felt a sudden stabbing pain on the back of my hand. As I lifted my eyes I realized Carmelo had tried to stab my hand with his fork. I pulled my bleeding hand back and hid it under the table. He shouted, 'You rotten bitch!' kicking the wall and left, slamming the door.

Midnight. I was already sleeping when I felt Carmelo's leg sliding between mine, and his tongue kissing my ear. We had sex for the first time in three months. When we finished he rested, stretched out on top of me, and apologized for stabbing my hand with the fork. I said I'd already forgotten about it. He said that didn't console him, that he was an animal and wanted me to forgive him with all my heart. I said I did forgive him. He insisted I must add 'with all my heart.' So I said it. He said he'd been very irritable lately. I asked whether it was on account of Tina and the children. He said it wasn't their fault. Tina and the kids were fine, but he worried just the same. So I asked him if he was concerned because we hadn't enough money, but that wasn't it either. I said that if he wanted to go and live with Tina I would not hold him back or blame him. He started to scream that I was his wife and we must stay together forever, no matter what happens. Then he started kissing me again and fell asleep still on top of me."

So this is what happened on September 3rd. And what about the 4th and 5th? I don't know. I can't remember a single thing and probably lived the following days doing the same things, feeling the same feelings. But maybe not. If I did the same things I would have recorded them in the diary. Instead there are those two blank pages to suggest maybe something happened that I couldn't or wouldn't write down. But what?

I think about it so hard that my facial muscles hurt from the tension. I try to concentrate in a real effort to remember, but the more I strain my memory the more it goes blank.

At times, when I'm very still and relaxed, I'm able to recall sensations associated with an experience, but all the while the past drags me down like a sack of potatoes, leaving me breathless.

And so I allowed myself to relax, trying to have fun, to void my mind, not forcing the process of remembering. Then I tried to think of completely unimportant things, but this method didn't help either. Like the birds in Plato's tree, my memories have flown away from fear and maybe will come back only when they want to, who knows when.

I feel rather hopeless. This sadness has even affected my sight, so that I was literally scared blind. I called the office to say I was sick. All day I just sat on a chair, staring at the wall in front of me.

At about eight in the evening the doorbell rang. Unable to focus, I felt my way to the door and opened it, expecting Carmelo. Instead I heard an unfamiliar voice asking if I'd be interested in buying some household detergents. I said I wasn't and quickly slammed the door.

Only then did I really notice that Carmelo wasn't home. He had not come back for lunch or dinner. I thought he must be at Tina's with the children. But why hadn't he come home at all? This question prompted others that somehow could be connected to my blank pages.

The more I questioned my memory, the more my mind recoiled in pain and silence, making it impossible to see clearly into the past.

I went back to sit and stare at the wall. It's strange that though I was nearly blind with fear, what frightened me most in that precise moment was not my potentially going blind, but the reality of the two blank days. Those two empty pages in my diary, otherwise filled with writing about actions and events, made me feel disorganized and uneasy. This was quite absurd and worrying because it confirmed the degree of confusion and uncertainty that had come into my life.

I sat on that chair through the entire night, unable to see, crippled by extreme panic and inertia. Nothing would emerge from my memory, not a spark of the past that needed piecing together, no identity.

The following morning, feeling the warm sunshine on my legs, I got up and automatically moved toward the bedroom with the idea of making the bed, which in fact had not been touched.

My mindless gaze caught sight of something irregular: one of the two closet doors was ajar. I drew closer to shut it, but spotted a shiny white thing among the hanging clothes. I opened the other door and crouched down to take a closer look.

Some time must have passed before I realized that what was there, bent in front of me, was Carmelo's body, in a fetal position as if in his mother's womb.

I passed out. I lay there on the floor in shock. I searched furiously in my memory, desperately trying to find a clue, some detail that would jog my memory.

Carmelo was dead. But why? I was sure the two blank pages explained this one secret. Try as I might, though, I was unable, totally incapable, of remembering anything.

I called the police. Several people with heavy shoes invaded my apartment, talking loudly, giving orders, asking questions, taking measurements and fingerprints. They took the body away immediately.

Meanwhile I regained my sight. I felt better because I could see the face of the man in front of me questioning me. My mind was still vacant, like an empty box.

The commissioner said it was suicide: Carmelo had stuck his head inside a plastic bag and died of asphyxiation.

At the funeral I saw Tina and the kids all dressed in black. The two children look like Carmelo. They're slight, pale, and stoop a little. Tina is petite, but fat and flabby. I can't imagine what Carmelo saw in her.

The children stood still, well behaved, and didn't move their legs, which were red from the cold air. Tina then came toward me. She hugged and kissed me, wetting my coat collar with her tears.

Now everything is settled and I should be happy. But I'm not. Something bothers me. I know that if Carmelo had really committed suicide I'd have written about it in this diary.

Now I ask myself, did Carmelo really kill himself and why? Or did I kill him?

I'm unable to come up with an answer. So long as these two pages remain blank, something crucial will stay hidden in my past, and I don't know whether I'm innocent or guilty.

I'm waiting for my diary to tell me the truth. Everything about my conscience and my awareness is recorded here, in these pages. Nothing and nobody could say more about me than this diary, which has a life and a body of its own while my consciousness does not. This diary records the past and the present, whereas my memory lives outside of time. This diary is full of memories and evidence, whereas my memory is empty and lifeless.

I'm sure some day something will suddenly jog my memory, something that will finally free me from this blank torture.

Maria

When I get up to go to work in the morning, Maria is still sleeping. I slide off the bed without making a sound so she won't wake up. I pick up my clothes from the chair, go to the bathroom, and get dressed, shutting the bedroom door behind me slowly without letting it click. Then I go down the very cold hallway. Our apartment has no central heating. Our gas heaters unfortunately warm up just one area of the room at a time and so our apartment has areas of warm and cold air that never mix.

By nine I'm at the office. In the first few minutes the loud noises startle me, and I wonder how I've been able to put up with this since I can't get used to it. But my surprise and inertia last only briefly, because the noise from the machinery on the other side of the glass divider soon becomes something familiar, like the rumbling of a waterfall broken at regular intervals by something like a drum roll. Searching among the filing cards, I turn on the automatic key puncher, keeping the adding machine close at hand.

My office is actually a glass cubicle set right in the middle of an enormous room in a car factory. Five other people work with me, three men and two women. I've been with them now for over six years, but still I can't say I know them well. I don't talk much, but they're always chatting, even though I can't hear them because the noise from the machinery drowns them out. If you want to be heard, you have to speak right up against the listener's ear and I myself never have to say anything so important to make me want to place my lips against anyone's greasy ears.

At noon when we hear the siren, the workers and the noise stop immediately. Then and there the silence provides relief, but it soon becomes unbearable. I am suddenly upset by a number of things I hadn't noticed before. My eyes sting from the neon lights, my fingers hurt from repeated use of the machine, and the warm air has a stench of human sweat.

Today, for the first time since I came to this factory, I lifted my eyes to take a look at my co-workers. They gladly go sit in the courtyard at lunchtime. Some carry wine flasks, others bring small tins of spaghetti. They go by without noticing me. Though the cubicle where I work is well lit and you can easily see inside, the workers never take the time to look in. They're so used to us being in there that we might as well not exist.

Whenever the office girl goes by, my eyes follow her; a black unbuttoned lab coat hangs over her miniskirt and strong, muscular legs covered by red-checkered knee socks. I look at her because she looks like Maria: high cheekbones, a wide jaw, slanted, close-set eyes, black eyebrows, and an air about her that brings to mind the face of a child with Down syndrome.

I get up, slip on my coat, and go out to look for the girl in the courtyard. I glance over the group of women eating and sitting on the ground by the flowerbeds, but I don't see her. Maybe she likes the crowded racket of the cafeteria.

By the time I reach home, Maria has just got up. The apartment is a mess: the bedroom smelling of cigarettes, the bed unmade, the bathroom with water splashes all over, the kitchen icy cold and full of smoke.

As I begin to straighten out the mess, Maria walks around the house, chainsmoking in her Japanese kimono, following me, chattering as I go about the chores.

Maria's voice is lovely. At times, whenever I do the housework, dusting, or straightening up, Maria sits on a stool in the bedroom by the window, warming her back in the sun, talking to me as if I were not there at all.

I cannot follow her chattering, which is too involved and serious for me. But I'm charmed by her clear musical voice, light like birds in flight.

We eat together in the kitchen. Maria sits across from me, gulping down with pleasure whatever I put on her plate. She actually doesn't notice what she's eating because she is absorbed in her own thoughts. Then suddenly a strange but familiar frown of concentration clouds her face.

"You ever wondered what love between two women is like?"

"No, why?"

"There must be a reason you haven't, don't you think?"

"I don't know."

"Why should I love you or have sex with you instead of a man?"

"I don't know, maybe because you like it."

"But why do I like it?"

"How should I know? Because you love me?"

"Big discovery, silly! But why do I?"

"I have no idea."

"I think men and women don't want to have sex anymore because they don't want kids. There's already too many of us."

"More salt fish?"

She nods and puts in her mouth a piece of the cheapest fish I can find, the kind that's fattest and stringy. But she doesn't taste it; I can tell by the movements of her jaw chewing mechanically, staring out in space, quickly wolfing down piece after piece.

"Whenever they talk about non-violence they make me laugh. Everybody performs violent acts from morning to night."

"I bought some giant grapes for you, want some?"

"We get up in the morning and start the day by killing three thousand cows."

"Cows?"

"Of course! How many cows, calves, and sheep do you think they kill every day in a city like this?"

"How should I know?"

"And what about you, don't you feel the violence of your superiors?"

"No, I don't. They don't bother me."

"But I'm not talking about physical violence. How much do they pay you a month?"

"Just enough to live on."

"Do you know what their profit is on your wages? At least 200 percent a month—that's all money stolen from you."

"So what?"

"And what about when they oblige you to stay in that glass cubicle, with the loud noise, under those awful lights, for eight hours a day."

"So what? I work and they pay me."

"You silly fool, don't you see that you work and they steal from you. That's the reality—they rob you every day and every hour. Not only do you let them, but you're even glad they do it. It's crazy, isn't it?"

I laugh. Her face is so serious and angry that I feel even more like laughing. I don't feel like talking because soon I have to go back to work and I'd like to lie down and rest a while. But Maria doesn't allow me to cut through her chatter; she wants me to stay seated, facing and answering her any way I please.

I go to make us coffee and find the espresso machine full of old coffee with two floating butts.

"Why do you throw your butts into the coffeemaker?"

"Know what, you're dense as a doorknob when it comes to political smarts. You get lost in useless everyday stuff, coffee grounds, the laundry, salt fish, giant grapes, dirty linen. You never think about issues that concern everybody besides yourself. You don't care about the world and all the injustice in it. You refuse to pass judgment because for you everything is fine, so you're worse than an animal."

Whenever she talks like that I become sad, suddenly tired, and no longer feel like doing anything. I look at her hard but beautiful face, its paleness that almost frightens me.

I go to the bedroom, lie down, and close my eyes. Soon I feel her kissing my forehead, my chin, my lips, and all my sadness vanishes.

I spend the afternoon writing, shut up again in the glass cubicle, beating down on the typewriter, operating the key punch, answering the phone. Now and then I lift my stinging eyes to the glass wall that separates me from the rest of the department. I can see bent backs, car body parts hanging from heavy cables, and black lab coats moving about. The girl with the muscular legs and disabled child's face works in another department at a plastic-printing press. I see her only at noon and at closing time when she goes by my cubicle without looking in, swinging a small, light blue cloth pouch.

One day Maria greets me with an expression of utter exasperation. "What's happened?" I ask her as I begin to tidy up the bedroom—like moving around the house a bit after being shut up inside the cubicle all day.

"You know my Dad is a farmer."

"Yes, you told me."

"He lives in Urbino."

"Yes, I know. So?"

"Can you possibly imagine what's in the head of a farmer without political smarts?"

"Your father's your father. You should love him."

"Don't talk nonsense. My father's a poor farmer who should prefer a revolution. Instead, he's more conservative than the landlords he works for. You understand that? He's a stupid self-centred fool concerned only with saving money."

"But he's your father."

"I don't give a damn!"

"A father's a father; you can do nothing to change that."

"Fathers and mothers are a sickness that we should destroy."

"What's happened to you?"

"My father has come to know I'm living with you and he wants to have me committed to a mental hospital."

"Why?"

"Rather than see me as 'abnormal,' as he puts it, he'd rather have everybody think I'm crazy."

"Did you see him?"

"Yes, he came this morning while you were out."

"And what did he say?"

"He says he's ashamed of me, that in the village everybody says I'm abnormal. Instead, he goes around explaining to them that I'm crazy and he'll have me locked up in a loony bin."

"But he can't do that, can he?"

"He's got a policeman friend who's ready to help him."

"But you're not crazy, who would ever believe you're crazy?"

"My father's got a hard head."

We stop talking about it because Maria's father never did come back and, after three months, I think his threat is a thing of the past.

One morning I go out to work as usual. I shut myself up in the cubicle because I have a series of calculations to verify and I work steadily at the adding machine for the entire Saturday morning. At a quarter to twelve I see the workers pass by the cashier's window to pick up their paycheques. I look for the girl with the odd face, but she's not there. Her envelope was picked up by a young blond who claimed to be her cousin.

At noon I lock the drawers, cover the machines with black cloths, and head for home. The bus was so crowded I could not get off at my regular stop because people's bodies blocked my way, and by the time I reach the exit, the bus is already on its way. So I'm forced to walk back a distance. When I reach home it's already one.

Nobody home. I imagine Maria's out shopping. I wait for her until two-thirty, when it's time for me to go back to the office, but Maria doesn't come back.

I hurry to the office, work till seven, and then go home. Maria is not there.

Two days later I find out that she's been taken to the mental hospital. I go to visit her. She is paler and frowns more than usual.

"Don't worry about me because I'll be out of here in no time. Everybody knows I'm all right."

"When are you coming out?"

"Soon. But it's not the doctors that drive me nuts."

"Who then?"

"The patients."

"How's that?"

"They just let the nurses do whatever they want. They don't protest, they don't argue or organize a protest. They're tied to things just like you are. They live for soup, rationed meat, TV."

"But they're mentally ill."

"No, they're just objects."

"They're sick."

"They've given up understanding things, just like you."

"When will you get out?"

"Soon."

But I cannot talk with her much longer because the nurse comes to shut the door. Only then do I notice that a very strong odour, an animal stench, pervades that big room. My throat contracts and I'm unable to breathe because of my increasing revulsion.

A week later I go back to visit Maria, but they tell me she's left. I am about to turn around and go home, glad of her escape, when a fat, blond boy walks up and tells me that Maria killed herself. Finishing his story, he lets out an anguished, senseless laugh. I don't know whether I should believe him. Then, by the way the nun grabbed his wrist and dragged him away scolding, I realize that what the boy just said about Maria is true.

~

These Hands

November. Wednesday

Boiled potatoes and hard boiled eggs. It's mid-week and I have no money. Last night I dreamed about a flying turkey flapping around. Then its stomach split open and chestnuts rained down. I kept my mouth open wide, but couldn't catch a single one. After trying for half an hour, my jaws ached and something dropped just between my teeth, a blob of bird shit.

Friday

I had macaroni boiled in a clear, tasteless soup mix. Nothing else in the house. Tano says he needs fat foods because it's cold. Tomorrow I'll make him tripe with tomato sauce. Giorgio says Tano's a turd. Tano says Giorgio's a pest. Meanwhile Marta phones: We going to the movies? I can't imagine what she wants, but I know she wants something.

Saturday

Payday. I bought lamb and tripe for Tano. Paying the butcher, the baker, the light and gas bills, leaves only a small amount till the next Saturday. Marta calls again: Where's Giorgio? How should I know? I'm not his wet nurse. Maybe he's out with Tano. Luckily the factory is nice and warm, but it stinks too. But after five minutes you don't notice. I've got to get myself a new pair of shoes.

Sunday

Slept in late. As soon as I'm awake Tano wants to have sex, but in the morning I don't feel like it; then in the evening when I do, he's the one who doesn't want to. Beans and potatoes with a bit of tuna in oil. Tano says he's cold. He wants fat meat. I've got a ton of shirts to wash, but on Sunday, my day off, I just want to sleep. After lunch, while Tano's out, I go back to bed. I fall asleep. I must change those stinking sheets.

Wednesday

Giorgio phones to say he and Marta are tying the knot. Good for them. The factory's a mess because they want to strike. But who gives a damn about the strike! Anyway, I heard the union boss say this isn't the right time to strike and that they're all crazy. The Workers' Committee passed around a flyer. I didn't even bother to read it.

Friday

Giorgio rings up to say Tano is not a friend because they had a fight. How can there be friendship between a shopkeeper and someone out of work? For three days we've hardly eaten anything. Tano keeps bugging me to buy on credit. But who'll give me credit? The butcher said no, that first I should pay last month's bills.

Sunday

At the factory the endless gossip about a strike gives me a splitting headache. What on earth do they want? Monday's the meeting of the Workers' Committee. Meantime I haven't had a crap for two days; no wonder, all I eat is potatoes.

Tuesday

We got a letter saying Tano's father was dying. Tano left for Calabria after Giorgio loaned him the money. When will you come back? No idea. Well, who works around here, anyway? Not him, that's for sure. Says he can't find work, that there isn't any. Meantime he lives off me, his wife. Yesterday I had half a pound of boiled zucchini. Still nothing. My belly's hard as a drum.

Wednesday

Finally, I had to sit on the john this morning. I felt I'd unloaded a ton. Everything's going wrong at the factory. They can't reach an agreement so the unions fight and we just look on. One guy called me a scab so I told him to fuck off. He sat next to me in the cafeteria. He's new, fat, blond, and he's sixteen. Who did I see on my way out? Giorgio. He gave me a record, a 45—the song's called "I Always Loved You." Is he trying to tell me something? I don't even own a record player. He said I could use his at the shop. No word from Tano and nobody knows when he'll be back.

*D*ecember. *Monday*

Marta phones to says she's coming for supper at my place, but I don't know what to feed her since I haven't got a scrap of food. She says she'll bring everything. Well, okay. So she brings three eggs, a little tube of mayo and three rolls. She really went out of her way! Giorgio arrives right at her heels. We three sit down to eat what's hardly enough for two. After supper the two of them sit there drinking Sambuca. I hate Sambuca. Then to bed. All three of us, of course. I knew it would end up like that, but I got no pleasure out of it. Marta lies stiff as a board and Giorgio plays the macho man. I kicked them out before midnight.

Tuesday

At the factory they make me laugh, still talking strike. Anyway, I'm quitting at the end of this year. Where the hell will you go? Tano always asks. He's afraid I'll lose my job and won't be able to feed him. I want to be a manicurist. With these hands! If my hands are in bad shape it's not my fault. I'll just wear gloves. Tano says I talk too rough to be a manicurist. Who gives a fuck? Manicurists aren't professors, are they?

Wednesday

Tano's back; he's angry because his father didn't die. What were you looking for? You know he hasn't got a cent to his name. He's furious and won't even answer me. But he's right: they called him down to Calabria because his father was dying and it's not true. Tano says his father has some savings. How much? He hasn't got a clue.

Friday

The sink I was fixing today was missing six washers. The foreman looked at me as if I'd stolen them. Go see Lanfranconi, he tells me. I go, and he says that stuff doesn't come from his department. Who placed the order? So it goes, they send me from one office to another. Finally I go back to Nino, who meanwhile had found some other washers. I wasted forty-five minutes and it'll be taken off my pay. Shitheads!

Saturday

I got paid. After deductions there's hardly anything left. They said we all agreed to take up a collection for the director's daughter's wedding. I don't give a fuck about the director's daughter and I never agreed to it, but they took the money just the same. Worker initiative. Bull! I've got to pay the butcher, the delicatessen, and last month's rent. Giorgio calls to ask if Tano will leave again. He's not staying just to please you, stupid! If I didn't hate asking for favours so much, I'd ask him to give me a job in his shop, because factory work isn't for me. Marta, for instance, does manicures. And I know how incapable she is. So, giving manicures can't be that difficult!

Sunday

I made spring lamb with fresh onions. Tano wolfed almost all of it and there wasn't enough for me. Giorgio and Marta came later. We talked about recipes and the best way to cook dried cod.

Tuesday

When I leave the house Tano is asleep. He gets up around eleven and later goes for a walk, supposedly hunting for a job, but he doesn't lift a finger and just wanders. He thinks somebody will stop him and say: Pardon me, you want to work for me, make loads of money, and not lift a finger? No news from Calabria or from the father who's had cancer for two years and has no intention of dying. Giorgio comes to me at the factory exit. What do you want? I ask. He gives me another record, another love song, but I know what he wants.

Thursday

Marta phones to say Giorgio's eaten spoiled shrimps and is in bed with a high fever. Tough luck! He's a nuisance. Marta sobs.

Friday

At the factory my time passes in a flash. I just get in and already it's time to go. As long as I'm there I don't feel tired. Then, when I'm out, my hands shake, my head spins, my eyes burn. When I get home I don't have the strength to do anything.

Saturday

After work I go visit Marta at the shop. She's worried about Giorgio, seems his fever's up. I see the renovated shop for the first time: new mirrors with gold frames, three brand-new hairdryers, and they've hired a girl to heat the wax for the clients' legs. Marta wears nothing under her smock. Aren't you cold? Heck no! She worries about Giorgio, who's sick. I take advantage and get my hair washed for free. Giorgio's sister eyes me, disgusted.

Sunday

Tano comes home with a change purse full of money, says he found it on the ground, near the Ariston cinema, as if I'd believe a lie like that! We go immediately to a *trattoria* to eat pasta and rare steak. I haven't been in a restaurant since I got married. After dinner, home to have sex. Tano complains that I come too soon. I don't like him on top of me so he didn't have time to get worked up.

Tuesday

Complete chaos at the factory, a general strike. It turned sour when no agreement was reached between unions. Two members of the CGL got fired. Didn't I say it was better not to strike? Those losers! First they act macho, then get scared and shit their pants. No funds in reserve. So what? The workers go their own way. So what? Our Workers' Committee stinks.

Thursday

Giorgio's back at the shop. He rang to say he was better. I knew it. I know about food poisoning. I've had it. It goes after three days. It would be better if it didn't weaken the body so much. Marta cut her hair, looks like another person. I don't like it and told her so. She started to cry.

Sunday

Yesterday was payday. Today I'm already out of cash. Didn't buy shoes this morning either. Tano didn't show for lunch or dinner made from our neighbour's flat noodles. He dried them on top of his radiator, so they tasted like paper.

Tuesday

Terrible day: my cold won't let me breathe. Marta whines because she caught Giorgio locked in the storage room with the girl hired a month ago to do hair removals. I eat only beet leaves. I bought about eight pounds and now my shit is green.

Wednesday

Tano found some more money on the ground. This time I told him to his face that he's a liar. You stole it! He denies it. He gives me a lot of bull. But it's nice having money without working for it. Again we went to a family restaurant and then to a movie. I ate mushrooms sauteed in onion and garlic and veal Milanese with beans in oil. The neighbourhood cinema was showing a war movie. Tano fell asleep and at home he didn't even want to get undressed for bed. But I forced him and we had sex for an hour straight. There are still some beet greens in the kitchen. They're a little spoiled but still okay.

Friday

The beet leaves are mouldy. I had to flush them down the toilet, which clogged up. Giorgio calls to say he wants to see me. What can he want? At his shop? No, he says, some other place and I go meet him after work. Tano's always out these days and gets back after ten. What does that fool want? To play threesome with Marta and me. I tell him nothing doing. Why not? Does it revolt you? Yes. But it's not true. He's the one who disgusts me. But I dare not tell him to keep him sweet with me. Sooner or later I'll leave the factory and ask him to hire me as a manicurist at his shop, called "The Libellula." The name brings to mind the country. He found it in a detective story. I'd like to work at The Libellula.

Saturday

Marta is happy. The girl who did the hair removals went away because she found a better-paying job. She phoned me at night just to tell me. Tano woke up and just started spitting on me, on the pillow, on the phone. I had to change my nightgown; it was that spattered. I'm married to a nutcase.

Sunday

I spent all morning in bed and the afternoon washing and ironing. What a shitty Sunday!

Tuesday

The blond man who called me a scab sits near me at lunch, but I don't like him. He has yellow teeth, always talks politics, and is a member of the socialist party. He carries his paper folded in four inside his overalls and eats while reading, or he talks to me. He says workers have lost faith, and they're all rotten, useless bourgeois who think of nothing except buying home appliances and new clothes. I like to talk with him because he's got enthusiasm, but when he squeezes my hand under the table, I tell him to get lost. The only nice thing about him is his straight blond hair.

Wednesday

For two days I've eaten nothing but pasta. I'm broke and still owe money to the delicatessen, the butcher, the phone company, and the milkman. After paying them, I'll be paid-up.

Thursday

Tano stayed out all night. I don't see him anymore. He seems more like a ghost than a husband. He's losing weight. After our wedding he got fat; now he's losing again. He makes a silly face that gets on my nerves and when I ask what he does or where he goes, he starts to spit.

Saturday

I got paid and already it's all gone. I can't see myself staying on at the factory. I don't talk to anybody. I even told the blond hunk not to bother me anymore. He got offended and took off. When I work I think of nothing else, so I work and that's it. I don't even have time to look up from the tubs. As soon as I finish, I dash home. If Tano isn't there, I don't eat. I suck a raw egg and go to bed.

Sunday

One of these Sundays I want to go dancing. But I always have a ton of clothes to wash. Marta rings to say the shop is a mess. Someone broke in the other night. Two women helpers are sick. Giorgio had to sign two loan drafts for the rent.

Monday

I got a stomach ache. I'm tired of eating spaghetti with tomato paste that's spoiled and bitter. And anyway, I need meat for strength so I can work. Giorgio comes to the factory door to meet me after work. What does he want? Nothing, he just came to say hi. We walked, and he put his arm around my waist. What a slimy guy. I promised to play threesome with him and Marta again just to keep him sweet with me. I wouldn't put it past him to deny me the manicurist job if I didn't play along. I know him.

Wednesday

Tano came back with a new brown leather jacket lined with sheepskin. Where did you get it? If they catch you and put you in jail, it's your problem. He doesn't give a shit, and he doesn't talk anymore but spits constantly. Okay, be a thief, I tell him, but at least bring money home regularly so I can quit the factory. He gives me a kick that almost cracks my knee.

Thursday

The factory will be the death of me. Constantly breathing those acid fumes has brought on a devil of a cough. When I put on cream and oil, the skin peels off my hands like an onion. They're swollen and eaten by the acid. Gloves are useless. The acid eats through the gloves, the skin, everything. I asked to change departments. Okay, he says, we'll move you. But when? Meanwhile, time goes by and my face is always over those fumes. My cough is killing me and my hands get uglier by the day.

Friday

Went to Giorgio's house to have sex, with Marta melting as soon as he touches her and me cold as ice. I don't like Giorgio, or Marta for that matter. After a while I got up and took off. They were going hard at each other and didn't even notice I left. They use me to get excited. That's the idea. But I don't give a fuck about them. I dislike them both. I do it just because I want the manicurist job at his Libellula.

Saturday

The usual upsets. I fill my belly with spaghetti. The dried cod is hard as a board. Tano comes home just to sleep. I leave him cold stuff but he doesn't eat it. He eats out, who knows where. And, like an idiot, I keep going to the factory where nothing works well and they won't change my department even if I die. Some day I'll pick up all those tubs of acid and throw them to their faces. They say I'm hard to get along with, that I don't talk and don't make friends, and that I don't cooperate to promote workers' rights. Who gives a shit about the workers! I'm not a worker. I'm leaving at the end of the year. I'll be a manicurist, just like Marta.

Sunday

Tano comes home happier than I've seen him in a long time. He puts a big 5,000 lira bill in my hand. Immediately we dash to a *trattoria*, lean prosciutto and olives, fettuccine with meat sauce, roast lamb and fresh onions with sweet and sour sauce, radicchio salad, fresh cheese, custard, bananas, dried figs, and coffee. On top of it all, a litre of rich, sparkling red wine. We ate from nine to midnight. I was so stuffed. At the end I belched, and since I was full up to my neck, a bite of roast lamb came back up. We went straight to bed. But no sex. Tano began to snore while still sitting on the john.

Thursday

I haven't seen Tano for two days. Marta called crying: Giorgio doesn't know what he's doing. He isn't thinking. In two days the first rent comes due and they haven't got the money. Marta says she'll borrow from her mother. Don't let him cheat you, I say; it's his shop. You're not married to him, you know. But she keeps sobbing. She's an idiot and only thinks about sex.

Friday

No news from Tano. Marta says to call the police. But I don't give it a thought. If something has happened, we'll find out.

Saturday

I ate well this evening by myself. A steak big as the palm of my open hand. Fried spinach with mozzarella. Tano didn't get back last night.

Sunday

Went with Giorgio and Marta to the country, to Scrofano to eat wild game, stewed hare, then fried sweetbreads, pork in oil, garlic, red peppers, and sauteed mushrooms. For dessert, cream pastries with red cherries that coloured the whipped cream. And those two always necking. I kept my distance and just kept eating. Tomorrow, with the rest of my pay, I'll buy myself a new pair of shoes.

Monday

Marta got her mother to send the money and Giorgio made the rent payment. Now he's good to her, after he's taken all her mother's savings.

She says the shop is doing better. They've replaced the broken stuff. Now they have more clients.

Wednesday

Tano is in jail. A policeman came to tell me. It seems he almost cleaned out a fabric store and they want to give him six years. Giorgio and Marta show up at my house in the evening. But now even if they try to bribe me I won't go along with them. Not even dead. Giorgio brings me an L.P. He can go to hell with his records and his Marta. He says he can't come if he doesn't have two women at the same time. I don't give a shit. Marta looks for the Sambuca. But it's finished, she drank the bottle dry. At eleven I throw them out because I'm sleepy. Anyway, who gets up at five in the morning? Not them. They don't go to the shop till after nine.

Thursday

I go visit Tano. As soon as he sees me on the other side of the bars, he starts spitting at me. I take the stuff I brought and go. He calls after me. I turn around. He gives me the name of some lawyer he thinks can work miracles, then I go. At the door I meet Giorgio and Marta. They say they're getting married. All the better. They want to say hello to Tano, but they're too late. It's closing time. They give me a ride home. It's obvious Giorgio's making money. He's getting ugly and going bald. I ate almost a whole chicken by myself, but I don't like eating alone. I drink a glass of hot wine with sugar and am off to sleep. I feel a flu coming on.

Friday

I woke up with such a pain in my kidneys I nearly fainted. Thought I should go back to bed. Instead, I go to the bathroom to wash, sweating from pain. I need money. My pay isn't that bad, but if I don't keep up my average of four hundred pieces a day, I'll get fired. The pain's back: just today I had a draft right on my back. I yelled at the people standing under the window. They shut the window for a minute and then reopened it, saying they couldn't breathe for the stench. At this rate I'll get arthritis in no time. Up and down, over the tubs with pieces of rubber on my arms. There came a point when I felt no pain or anything else. I was numbed by acid fumes. I didn't even notice the timekeeper standing behind me like a guardian angel.

Sunday

Slept almost all day. In the afternoon I get up and look around in the kitchen. There's a chicken wing from the other day and nothing else. I eat the chicken wing and hot broth made with clear soup mix, which I hate.

Not even a breadcrumb. I slip back into bed and sleep a bit. I dream about Tano and come in my sleep, like a nut. I wake up all soaked.

Monday

I did buy the shoes, but they were a bad bargain. I was trying to save a little, as usual, and after just one day they're already looking old. But they're pretty, black with high heels. There's this guy I like at the factory. He's been working with me at the tubs for two days. He's calm and slow, but doesn't know how to handle the pieces. He started just a few days ago, isn't even twenty. He's so thin he seems like half a man. He's handsome, though, too handsome. I notice everybody devouring him with their eyes. But he doesn't notice because he's so full of himself. Whenever he can, he stares at himself in a hand mirror he takes from his pocket.

Wednesday

Nothing but rain since yesterday. Many women come to the factory wearing mountain socks up to their knees and red and yellow boots I like so much I could almost eat them up. I'd like to get myself a pair as soon as I put aside some money.

Thursday

Still raining. I keep my new shoes in the closet, wrapped in one of Tano's old shirts. For the first time at the factory, I realized I don't have time even to look up from my work. I haven't time to look at the young man working with me. Only in the cafeteria can I feast my eyes on him in peace, but he sits apart by the window and eats while reading the paper, never looking my way.

Friday

I get home and go right to bed. I'm afraid of getting a backache again. But I feel better. Even my cough is better. Only my hands are revolting as usual.

Saturday

Swiss chard and hard-boiled eggs. Hard to digest. Heartburn all night, and in the morning I wake up tasting metal. Finally, today, I talked to the young man. His name is Romolo. Says he's tired of the work. Imagine him telling me that! I invited him to supper tomorrow. Now I have to clean the revolting mess in my house and buy something to eat. Do you like lamb? He nodded. So I decided to make him lamb with vinegar and rosemary. Luckily I just got paid.

Sunday

I was so excited I woke up at seven. I cleaned the apartment, washed the floors with soap and shined them up with wax, so now I could slip and break my ass. But at least it's clean and there's a good scent of wax and sawdust in the rooms. In the afternoon I go to see Tano. Seeing him behind bars turns my stomach. Now that he's growing a beard like Saint Joseph, he's more handsome. Says they've taken all his money. Who? His friends. And you just let them rob you? He's such an ass, good only at being taken. He says he doesn't eat and at breakfast they give him milk and coffee that tastes like piss, overcooked beans and rotten-smelling meat for lunch, and in the evening a soup he gives away because the mere smell of it makes him want to throw up. Bring me something to eat, he says. But I haven't got the time or the money. After leaving the prison I get groceries and go home to cook. At nine the doorbell rings. I run to the door and peek through the peephole. It's those two asses, Giorgio and Marta. I pretend no one's home. So they keep ringing. After a while they start to pound at the door with their fists. I open and tell them I'm on my way out. I persuade them to go home. I go along to show them I'm really leaving. When I return home, Romolo's already gone and I find a note under the door. "Why did you play this joke on me?" Blast those two! I eat the lamb all alone. But I'm not hungry. My stomach hurts. I go to bed with a hot water bottle and I'm so furious I start to cry.

Monday

I haven't got a chance of talking with Romolo because they've moved him to another section. I worked badly and damaged about ten pieces which I held in the acid so long they were half corroded like stumps. The department manager gave me a real lecture in front of everybody. Anyway, I have to pay for those damaged pieces. So why chew me out? Isn't losing the money bad enough?

Wednesday

Marta phones to say I must go to the shop. Giorgio's sick. What's wrong with him? Nothing. Well then? He yelled at everybody and doesn't want to marry her. Why not? How should I know? Those two are such a nuisance, they give me a headache. Tano writes me an insulting letter because I don't bring him food and because they're ruining him in there. What can I do about it? At the factory I look for Romolo in the cafeteria. Now he works at the assembly line and is radiant in his white overalls. I ask him why he didn't wait for me the other evening. He looks at me and doesn't say a thing. Is next Saturday okay? He nods. I go home happy. I talked to him with my hands in my pockets so he wouldn't see them.

Saturday

He came over. We ate and drank, then we slipped into bed. He has a white body with countless blue veins that make patterns under his skin. I forgot to take off the receiver. At the peak moment the phone rings and rings. Answer it, he says, it's irritating. I answer it. It's Marta complaining that Giorgio's having sex with a client. What an idiot! She says the woman is in the movies, lives at the Excelsior and has him come over to her room. Are you sure they have sex? Sure I'm sure. I found his jacket smeared all over with lipstick right down to his pocket flap. Seems she's not even young. She gave him a gold watch with a gold band. I'd love to eat at the Excelsior some day, I think to myself, at a table with silver dishes, a whole roast pig with the skin crisp as a cracker, a lobster with all the claws to suck, squid cooked in ink, macaroni pie with white sauce. I almost forgot about Romolo. He makes love like a puppy, so sweet and shy.

Sunday

Tano mumbles and spits. I brought him some food. He threw it to my face. He wants to get out. But how? Marta's always in tow, lamenting. Giorgio is so mad he throws the dye on the floor. Will they get married or not? Who knows. One day it seems they will, the next not. Chicory and potato soup again. I'm broke and still owe a lot to the butcher, the baker, and Marta.

Tuesday

The actress from the Excelsior left. With a kick, Giorgio broke a mirror into a million pieces. He'd paid quite a bit for it without the frame. A week's pay. Marta burned her face with hot wax. She says it will leave a scar. She's always crying, and calls me up to say she wants to end it all. I can understand why Giorgio doesn't want to marry her. She's always complaining.

Wednesday

I eat only bouillon soup, potatoes, and hard-boiled eggs, hungry like a wolf. Last night Romolo came over. What could I offer him? Nothing. Not even a drink. He asked how old I am. Twenty-seven. He's nineteen. I show him my hands, I'm so ashamed of them. He said my hands don't matter to him, and spent all night with me.

Friday

Marta calls to say they're getting married. She'll cover the scar on her face with a wig. Fine. Meanwhile, they keep Tano locked up without a trial. His mother comes from Calabria and wants to sleep in my double bed. We'd both fit in it, she says. But I don't intend to sleep with her, so I give my bed to her and I sleep in the kitchen on a mattress that my neighbour lent me.

Saturday

When I come home the good aroma of fresh onions in a sweet and sour sauce brings me back to life. Tano's mother is fixing dinner. Fresh onions, beets, mild cheese, and some tender goat's meat she brought up from the farm. I sit down and don't even get up to set the table. I let her work. It's great to have someone else working in the house for me!

Sunday

We took Tano a basket full of food, but he wasn't happy, complaining that he wanted cigarettes. His mother went to the tobacco store and bought him ten of the strongest brand, Export. Tano threw them in her face. Then they locked the gates because it was already late. Seems those two are really getting married. Marta is happy, even with a burned and scarred face.

Tuesday

They're starting to talk about a strike again at the factory. I don't pay attention to anything or anybody. As soon as those two get married I'm going to ask them to give me a job in their shop, The Libellula, as a manicurist and bye-bye to the stinking factory!

Wednesday

I'll have goat's meat every day till it's completely gone. It keeps beautifully with just pepper and garlic. My mother-in-law even brought some pears, long and narrow like fingers, and they're sweet like honey. Her olive oil is thick and bitter like motor oil.

Thursday

I slept badly. My mother-in-law snores so loudly that even with the door closed I could hear her. I whistled and shouted. Then I threw a pan on the bed, but she didn't even wake up to say ouch! Tano's going grey and keeps asking for cigarettes. I left him the last of my money.

Friday

A girl is chasing after Romolo. She works in his department and is as strong as an ox, with neck muscles like a man's. She's always laughing and touching Romolo. Piece of shit! Her name is Tunica; never heard it before.

Saturday

I got paid. I paid the butcher, almost paid him off, paid the phone, the gas, the cobbler. That leaves me owing much less, first to the butcher, then to the delicatessen, the grocer, and the milkman.

Sunday

Tano says everyone jerks off in that jail because there aren't any women around, and after a while they just can't stand it. Too bad he let himself be jailed like that. I brought him the goat's meat that was left, but he says he isn't hungry. He wants cigarettes. His mother has no intention of leaving and continues to sleep in my bed, searching through everything and eating all she can find, a crumb, a crushed bean, a crust, even coffee grounds. Anything. Then sleeps and snores.

Wednesday

Romolo wants to come home with me, but Tano's mother's still here. So we have to meet outside, on the street, and can't even touch. Shall we go to the movies? What for? Just to waste money? So we walk and get tired for nothing. We walk and we talk and he tells me I must leave my husband so I can live with him, but I won't because I'm really not in love. I like him, and that's all.

Thursday

Tano's mother is still here. She took out another large bill. I don't know where she'd hidden it. She told me she had no more money. We buy some things for Tano, but he only wants cigarettes. I realize he gives away food for cigarettes.

Friday

There was an accident at the factory. A new hire lost his arm. Toward 9:30 we heard a cry. Three people stood around the old model TTO machine. We dashed there. The boy's arm, right up to the shoulder, lay there on the floor. He looked at his arm, just like an idiot, and fell to the floor too. When I told Marta she began to sob. Marta always cries. Good thing she's getting married. I'm waiting for the right moment to ask Giorgio for a job in his shop. If things go on like this, the factory will rob me of all my youth.

January. Tuesday

Romolo and I are always together in the cafeteria with Tunica usually hanging round. Romolo says he can't stand her, but then he lets her stroke, pat, and admire him all over. He's so vain.

Thursday

Marta tells me she saw Tano's mother begging at the corner of Piazza del Gesú. I don't believe her. Meanwhile it seems Giorgio has grown kind and affectionate. He thinks only of the house they'll have after they marry, and saves money for the furniture. She wants him to sell the gold watch he got from the client at the Excelsior, but he won't do that. He says they'll marry in April.

Sunday

Sunday again. I never know what to do on Sundays. Aside from visiting Tano, who doesn't say a word now except to ask for cigarettes and more cigarettes. Romolo goes to watch soccer. At six he asks me if I want to go out. But where? Once we had sex on a park bench in the Borghese Gardens, but the police almost spotted us. Later on it poured. The grass was all wet but fortunately Romolo spread out his raincoat. Then we saw we were lying on a heap of shit. Giorgio and Marta came to dinner. They brought a tray of sweets filled with ricotta. Delicious. But the ricotta was a little rancid, and the pieces of candied fruit stuck to my teeth.

Tuesday

Looks like the trial will take place next month. By now, Tano has grown yellow because he chainsmokes and doesn't eat. He has a bad cough, like me, with the difference being that mine comes from the poisonous vapours at the factory and his from smoking. His mother brought him a carton of an American brand that she got who knows where. I told Tano that Marta saw his mother begging in front of the church of Gesú. He answered that he didn't give a damn. How much does she make? How should I know? Marta says that a beggar can make a good deal of money in one day. So she says. But how should I know?

Wednesday

After the accident of the amputated arm they came to a decision at the factory: the strike is on, even if the workers' representatives are not in favour, even if the unions can't reach an agreement. If there really is a strike, I'll take two days' vacation and go with Romolo to have sex in a hotel. It'll cost a lot. But who cares! We fight constantly because we don't have a place and we can only hold hands and kiss in the rain.

Friday

Yesterday I went to the doctor because I'm dizzy, my kidneys hurt, and my hands are a total mess. I know it's the fumes from the acid and there's no cure unless they put me somewhere else. But in the meantime I went to the doctor and waited forever. There was a line that went almost outside the door. Anyway, after an hour and a half my time permit ran out and I went back to the factory without seeing the doctor.

Saturday

Romolo says he wants me to move in with him. But he still lets Tunica touch him all over. One day I'm going to grab her by the hair.

Sunday

Tano has grown so thin that he looks like a sardine. He's lost two side teeth. When he talks there's a black hole on the right side of his mouth. He doesn't say a thing to me. He only wants to smoke. He'd sell his mother for a drag.

Tuesday

The strike has failed again; we were ordered back to work. Everyone has a different explanation. I knew it would end up like this. I didn't go to the factory. Not for a strike. I couldn't care less. I take advantage of it so I could sleep for two days in a row. I'm always sleepy because my cough and my mother-in-law's snoring keep me awake. Once I'm awake I can't fall asleep again, and at 5:30 a.m. I have to drag myself out of bed to be at the factory by 7:00.

Saturday

Giorgio and Marta got married, but already they're not getting along because Giorgio's in love with a client who's a champion diver. He'd like to have sex with both women. I've seen the champion, who's short, strong, tanned even in winter. She moves like a hare, wears her dyed blond hair very short. Marta says she hates her. But meantime, the moment she says, do my hands, she does it immediately without a word. She has never even stuck her scissors under her nails.

Tuesday

Romolo insists I go stay with him. When I tell him no he pouts. My mother-in-law finally left. The stench from dried piss on the bed takes my breath away. My mother-in-law is incontinent and every night some piss leaked onto the bed. Now the mattress is full of the stench. I aired it on the balcony for two hours, but it didn't help. Tomorrow I'll have it redone, even if it's going to cost me a bit. What can I do? I can't sleep with the stench of piss.

Thursday

Marta phones. They have postponed the honeymoon on account of the shop. They'll leave in August. Perhaps now is the time to ask Giorgio to give me a job. I'll do it tomorrow or next day. But first I should have them over for supper one evening.

Saturday

I had my neighbour lend me some money. I made oven-baked pasta, meat with tomatoes, a pudding with lemon and vanilla cream. I even bought Sambuca for Marta. The two of them downed it in half an hour. Then Giorgio began to feel around. He's an ugly, slimy man. I don't like him. But I didn't let him see that in order to keep him sweet. I tried to send them away. I knew where they were headed—straight for the double bed. I knew it. The stench of the mattress, my coldness, nothing deters them. Giorgio and Marta both on top of me. I shut my eyes and decided I'd go through with it for the job. So I talked to him beforehand, asking if he'd hire me at the shop as a manicurist. He said fine, fine, and that's it. And so we had sex. After a while I got hot and I came. I thought I wouldn't be able to make it. Then I only wanted to sleep. I tried to kick them out, but I fell asleep in Marta's arms, my mouth on her bare breast.

Sunday

Tano lost another tooth. He also spent ten days in the recovery room. He was fed intravenously and put on ten pounds. Then he was put back in his cell. He's already begun to lose again.

Wednesday

I talked to Giorgio and reminded him of the promise he made me the other night. He looked at me with a blank stare, didn't say a thing. Why? Is something wrong? But you don't know a thing about manicuring, he says. But I can learn, can't I? And where would you hide your hands? You can't do manicures with those hands. Then I'll do shampoos. No. I can't even pay my two helpers. Well, what can I do?

Sunday

I told Tano that Giorgio is a turd because he has denied me a job now that he makes good money. He asks whether I brought him cigarettes. Nothing matters to him except his cigarettes.

February. Wednesday

Marta calls to invite me to supper. I said no. I've decided not to see them anymore. They can go fuck themselves.

Thursday

I went back to the doctor. This time I waited even after my permit ran out. After two hours and fifteen minutes they showed me in. The doctor says I must look after my hands and lungs. Now, I know that, but how? He gives me a prescription and a request for the manager to change my department. I went to the department head with the prescription and the doctor's request. He stuffed the request in his pocket and that was the end of that.

Friday

Tunica's sick. Romolo came to sit next by me. He says if I don't leave my husband he won't see me anymore.

Sunday

I took Tano three cartons of cigarettes. Now my week's money is gone and I have to start asking for credit again.

Tuesday

I left Romolo. He'd become a big nuisance. I got a letter with some money from my mother-in-law.

Thursday

My department got changed. Finally. Now I work on the assembly line and I don't have to bend over, or lift heavy things, put my hands in acids, or breathe poisonous fumes. But doing the same movements five or ten thousand times a day makes me sleepy. Can't keep my eyes open and at times I sleep with them open. My arms go on working, but I sleep.

Friday

The lady working with me on the assembly line can eat a sandwich and work. I don't know how she does it. She's so good that for half a minute she uses only one hand to do the work of two while she eats with the other. With tiny bites and rapid chewing she manages to eat two sandwiches in an hour and a half. If I move one hand just to scratch my nose, I'm immediately four movements behind and to catch up I have to hurry so fast I'm drenched with sweat.

Sunday

I took Tano three cartons of cigarettes. He says they aren't enough. He's become yellow, dry and wrinkled. I don't recognize him anymore.

Tuesday

I met another man, Liberio. He works in a bar and owns a scooter. He promised to take me for a ride to the country on Saturday. Truth is, I'm ashamed of my hands.

Wednesday

I bought myself a pair of wool gloves. Liberio says he doesn't give a damn about my hands. His hands are swollen too from keeping them in the freezing water. But mine are revolting. Besides being swollen they're red, peeling, and cut. The cuts don't heal and they ooze a watery liquid that hardens into yellow crusts.

Thursday
Romolo keeps his eye on me. He talks to Tunica and looks at me. I pretend not to notice. Now and then, when he isn't watching, I look him over and think he's really a handsome devil, with his light blue eyes and white skin so close to his bones and hair parted on one side covering his head like a crown. He's really the most handsome guy in the factory. And I'm a bit sorry he's not mine anymore.

Saturday
This is the first time I have some money left over from my pay. I bought myself a hand cream with vitamins. It cost quite a bit, as if it's gold. A tiny little jar, after all. With some more money I bought a carton of cigarettes for Tano on the black market.

Sunday
In a few days the trial. Seems I also have to go as a witness. But what can I say?

Monday
Today a girl who works on the assembly line with me said that Romolo and Tunica got engaged. As usual, they were sitting together in the cafeteria. She laughed and he was busy talking in a low tone.

Tuesday
Liberio's face isn't that handsome. He has a pug nose and his eyes are too close together. But he's got the most beautiful body I've ever seen and his skin is like resin. When he sweats he lets out a good scent, a bit acid, like crushed roots.

Thursday
The trial is this morning. I got time release from the factory. They made me wait for five hours outside the door. Seems witnesses can't enter the courtroom. Seven other people waited outside with me, whispering with some lawyers in long black gowns. At 2:30 they let me in to testify. I was so hungry I couldn't see straight. Are you his wife? What do you do and not do? Where do you work? Did you know your husband steals? And why? And where and when? Et cetera, et cetera. They gave me a headache with their questions. I tried to see Tano, but didn't know where they had put him. No sight of him. Then I saw him right behind me before leaving.

Saturday
Marta called to ask about Tano and the trial. I told her they gave him four years. She immediately started to cry. Giorgio grabbed the

phone from her to say it's a shameless disgrace. I slammed down the receiver.

Sunday

Tano's eating again. He even cut down on smoking. He was happy to see me. It's the first time I've seen him happy.

Tuesday

Last night toward nine I was already in bed and Romolo came by. We had sex. I realized I still like him.

Wednesday

At the cafeteria, Tunica and Romolo are always next to each other, laughing together. But Romolo looks in my direction, moving his fingers as if to say he'll phone me.

Friday

Now I have two lovers: Romolo and Liberio. With Liberio I go out to dance and have sex. I told him I have a husband at home. Romolo comes to the house two or three times a week and stays all night.

Sunday

I wasn't able to see Tano because he's in isolation. The guard told me he had committed indecencies. But what? You can find out from somebody else. I asked around. Seems that in the cell where Tano stays with some others, a boy went in to get their clothes for washing and all four of them jumped him and raped him. The boy had to be taken to the hospital and they were locked up in isolation. I left some cigarettes for him with a man in the next cell called Mario.

Wednesday

I fell asleep in my chair yesterday at the factory. Luckily, the lady next to me, the one who eats mortadella sandwiches while working with just one hand, gave me a sharp pinch. I jumped up, startled, and resumed working. But some pieces had piled up for the girl after me who was already shouting son-of-a-bitch at me. The department head came over and fined me.

Thursday

Liberio says I must leave my husband and go live with him. But I'm already tired; he sticks to me like glue and sulks.

Friday

I split up with Liberio.

Saturday

At night I can't sleep because of my cough. Though I'm in another department the poisons have stayed in my lungs. Romolo was waiting cheerfully outside my apartment building, wearing a new red shirt and a pair of thick, white wool socks that made you feel hot just to look at them. I was so tired that I fell asleep in his arms before we had sex. But he let me sleep. In fact he too fell asleep.

Sunday

Spent all day sleeping. Once in a while I woke up with the phone ringing, but I never answered. It's Liberio looking for me. Again yesterday he waited for me at the factory exit. Romolo saw him and got really mad. I had to make up some excuse.

Monday

Mondays are awful. I just can't wake up. I'm cold, my head aches, and the mere thought of starting another week makes me want to puke.

Tuesday

No money left. Tano's still in isolation. I left him some more cigarettes. My neighbour lent me some money. I bought some eggs and four kilos of potatoes.

Thursday

Potatoes and eggs. I eat one fried egg a day. They must last till Saturday. In the cafeteria, a bit of money got me a plate of fettuccine that was tough as cardboard, and a glass of beer with water. Tunica got married. I heard it yesterday from a lady who works on the assembly line. Seems she married a police officer. Romolo eats alone, reads the paper, and looks at me.

Friday

The eggs are finished. I ate potatoes boiled in a clear soup mix. I bought some milk on credit. I must pay the grocer for the laundry detergent.

Saturday

Payday, finally. I've got to get Romolo a present; tomorrow's his birthday. Liberio phones me all the time.

Sunday

Slept all day. Romolo went to the soccer game. Toward evening I felt like going dancing. I was just about to call Liberio to take me some place with him. But then he'd just stick to me, and how could I get rid of him? All the same, he's got a great body. Yesterday I spotted him waiting for me at the corner. He's slim but looks strong, long neck and legs, beautiful skin colour, like barley candy.

Monday

Marta is expecting. She called me, sobbing. I didn't have the courage to scold her. She's silly. Always crying. But I was glad she phoned. I think she's better than Giorgio, who's a shit. She would have given me a job as a manicurist at the shop.

Thursday

Liberio left for Germany. He took on a truck-driving job. Seems he gets good pay. Came to say his goodbye outside the factory. I got on his scooter behind him. Before turning the corner I saw Romolo come out, looking at me with two eyes black with jealousy. I took Liberio home with me. I let him tell me about his new job and his upcoming trip. And all the while I was looking him over. I kept thinking I wouldn't see this beautiful, healthy body anymore. And I wanted to have him for the last time. We had sex on my bed for the first time. And so I was able to see him all naked with his caramel skin. Usually while outdoors we have sex in a rush, wearing our overcoats and sweaters because of the dampness of the ground, and for fear of being seen. This time we took it slowly. But he can't fuck like Romolo. He simply owns that handsome blond body, and the more I look, the more beautiful it is.

Sunday

Now Tano struts around the prison like it's his own house. He's jolly; he talks continually, smokes less, and eats everything they give him. He wants money from me, nothing but money. He says he'll buy things for himself. Inside he's become friends with a man they call Manine because he has busy little hands like a monkey. He said they love each other like husband and wife. And what about me? You're my wife on the outside, Manine is my wife inside. That's what he answered, and started to laugh. When he laughs he twists his mouth to hide the hole of his missing teeth.

Tuesday

Liberio has written me a letter from Hamburg. He says it's freezing, below zero, and that the Germans are all shits.

Wednesday

Romolo's jealous. Every evening he comes to make sure I'm alone. Each time he says I should go live with him. He's lost weight. Looks like a skeleton. I told him if he goes on like this he'll lose his sex appeal.

Thursday

Marta came over to show off her belly. She took my hand and placed it under her skirt. Feel how big this is, feel it. As for me, I find pregnant women revolting.

Friday

Liberio writes that he lives in a room with eight other Italian workers. They sleep in bunk beds like on night trains. He says he hasn't even learned to say good morning and that German is a shitty language.

Sunday

Tano has grown fat and happy. He laughs, chatters, and asks me for money. But I'm completely out. I spent all my week's money on a quilted wool jacket for Romolo. It's Sunday and I have only a little cash left till Saturday.

March. Monday

Another month. Liberio writes to say he's met a girl named Christa, that when he has sex with her he thinks about me. I think about him too, about his body like a giraffe with its scent of dried figs.

Thursday

Yesterday they changed my department again. They put me on a lathe. I started the motor and zap, I cut off a finger and fainted. I woke up at the First-Aid with someone injecting me in my vein. They've given me ten days of recovery leave. But who gives a damn? I don't need rest, I need my finger back. I'm already really unlucky with my hands, but I always get into more trouble.

Saturday

I haven't eaten or slept because of the pain. Romolo comes over every evening. But I don't want to see anybody. I take a ton of pills and so I'm always in a daze.

Thursday

I could write if I wanted, but I don't feel like it. I don't feel like doing anything. I'm sick and tired of everything. I'm fed up.

The Life and Prose Works
of Dacia Maraini: An Afterword

Dacia Maraini was born in Fiesole, near Flo-
rence, on 11 November 1936. Her mother, Topazia Alliata, was a painter
from an aristocratic family line that dates from the early seventeenth
century. Her father was a renowned anthropologist and professor of Ori-
ental Studies. He emigrated to Japan with the family in 1938 to continue his research on the Ainu people. After Mussolini and Hitler signed
a pact, Italians living in Japan were asked to swear allegiance to the Fas-
cists; her parents' refusal to pledge allegiance led the family to be interned
for two years in Khobe, a Japanese concentration camp. In an interview
Maraini told Adele Freedman that the camp was "like a German one
without the gas."[1] Maraini remembers that she and her sister were the only
children, and that everyone suffered from hunger. In 1947 the family
returned to her mother's native city, Bagheria, in Sicily, but the trauma of
camp life and the severe post-war poverty she experienced with her family in Sicily remained with her for decades. In the Freedman interview
Maraini elaborated: "I was paralyzed for many years.... I couldn't speak
because I was in shock, I was afraid of everything....They took everything
from us. Really, I only started to come out, to feel well with myself and
my body, when I turned 40." In her teens, following her parents' separation, Maraini moved to Rome with her father and sister. The separation,
and the stay in the big city, introduced an additional element of insecurity but also a degree of freedom for her to explore urban life: "I walked
a great deal because I had no car, nothing. I'd take the bus to the city centre, and then I'd walk, so I got to know city squares, museums, foun-
tains....After two years we went to live by the Tiber....I was eighteen
then...and I began to notice the typical problems of a city, also because

I was becoming more aware politically; I read newspapers and was no longer subject to the ghosts in my imagination."[2] Maraini acknowledged to Freedman, and subsequently, that her development as a writer has been deeply marked by her urban experience as well as by her struggles till her early twenties: "I had never felt free in my life, I never felt free in school. Writing was like self-analysis for me." To Liberato Santoro she has spoken about her work in depressed areas of Rome: "My fuller encounter with the socio-political dimension coincided with and was mediated by my sharpened awareness of the condition of women in our society. I worked, for years, in Centocelle, a poor, depressed and underprivileged suburb of Rome. I observed the humiliating conditions of women in slums, prisons, precarious marriages, unhappy families. I studied the social problems of abortion, rape, prostitution. I began to see more clearly the problem of sexual difference as part of the division and conflict of social classes. My novel *Memoirs of a Female Thief* recounts those experiences." The love of writing seems to have been a natural part of the Maraini family, which she indicated in her entry in *Autodizionario degli scrittori italiani* (1990).[3] At sixteen she started a school newspaper, and at eighteen she was "passionately engaged in producing, with a group of friends, a small journal, *Tempo di letteratura* (Literary Times). It was a useful exercise in expressing critical and political ideas"[4] about Italy, a country still beset by the ravages of a lost war, poverty, and an unclear vision for the future.

A very private person, Dacia Maraini's own life was in part influenced by the times. Her marriage to painter Lucio Pozzi lasted not more than four years, in the course of which she experienced a painful and devastating miscarriage. But although she has no children, she has been and continues to be an intellectual "mother" to women of all ages. Through her plays and by founding and developing Teatro Maddalena in Rome (1973-90), Maraini has brought new life to Italian theatre, and has helped place feminist issues on the international stage.[5] All along, her many radio and television appearances, newspaper and magazine articles, and interviews on Italian society and the purpose of art and literature have brought Maraini's name and views into the average Italian household. In the past two decades, the abundant translations of her works and her frequent visits abroad have brought Maraini, the person and the writer, in contact with women internationally. In an interview with Karin Fleischanderl, she mused: "I have countless daughters, who want to make out of me their generous mother, forever at their disposal. Sometimes they are so persistent that they almost frighten me.... But since I need to be needed by others, I find myself almost unwillingly placed in the situation of being mother to so many children, most of whom are daughters. They encourage me to play the pipe that lures them out on the streets."[6]

The publication of her first novel, *La vacanza* (1962, *The Holiday*, 1966), launched Maraini's career as a writer concerned with women's condition in the family and in society. The novel is subtitled "l'adolescenza di una donna oggetto" (the adolescence of a woman as object). Although it is difficult to identify with precision the stages of Maraini's literary development and production over the past four decades, with respect to the novel, we will nevertheless attempt in this overview to trace stylistic changes and thematic concerns as they are displayed in the landscape of her corpus. Some Maraini scholars (Sumeli Weinberg 1989, 68–69; Lazzaro-Weis 1994), speak in general terms of three stages or periods. Here, we are interested only in Maraini's prose works, because thematically and stylistically they have characters and characteristics that are reminiscent of the stories in *My Husband*. Our review of the prose is necessarily located within the sociology and economy of the times, in part because Maraini has come to view the predicaments and dilemmas facing the contemporary Italian woman as gender based and as emerging from centuries-old traditions and practices that have not kept pace with changing times due to the influence of the Church, the economy, and social forces. In a 1981 interview with Adele Cambria she stated, "Feminism has made possible a closer identification between literature and life," and "I no longer see literature as separate, as external to life." Thus, for Maraini's women understanding and comprehending the self—their fundamental quest—requires first and foremost an understanding and evaluation of society, the world they inhabit, and of the life conditions surrounding them and the family structure.

Maraini's initial phase as a writer spans, in our view, approximately the first decade of her activity, from 1962 to 1971. The prose of this period is characterized by a degree of stylistic experimentation and influences from major contemporary Italian and European writers. Maraini has stated that in these early years she was seeking her writing voice. In the Freedman interview she acknowledged that, at the beginning of her career, writing as a self-expressive act allowed her to overcome the sense of human and cultural separation that resulted from acute hardships during and following World War Two: "It became so important I couldn't stop writing, when I did I felt empty." In addition to *The Holiday*, a number of successful works were published in the first decade or so, a time when Maraini was also very concerned with the abject condition of the

Italian theatre. Three novels, one collection of poetry, and a collection of four plays, as well as the short story collection *My Husband*, belong in this early phase, which is immediately concerned with the search for identity, and with examining the life conditions of women of all ages in Italian urban settings. The dynamics of family life and values as well as social infrastructures are brought into question in the early prose, which uses the internal monologue of a first-person narrator, a device that Maraini has employed throughout her career, with the exception of *Isolina: la donna tagliata a pezzi* (1981, *Isolina: The Woman Cut to Pieces*, 1993) and *La lunga vita di Marianna Ucrìa* (1990, *The Silent Duchess*, 1992), which are presented in the third person. As is often the case in *My Husband*, the protagonists of her first three novels range in age from their early teens to their late twenties, young women subject to numbness of senses and intellect. Lacking critical subjectivity and interest in life, they are unable to act or react against oppressive and possessive male attitudes. Theirs is an existence predicated entirely upon the physical needs and material values dictated by the men in their lives—be they fathers, husbands, lovers, brothers—who espouse the discourse and lifestyles of the materialist and conservative political establishment of the 1960s. Lacking independence and critical perspective, these early protagonists, such as Enrica in *L'età del malessere* (1963, *The Age of Discontent*, 1965), Maria in *A memoria*, and several nameless narrators in *My Husband*, lead purposeless, undisciplined, and alienated lives, as if waiting for a moment of fulfillment, which never arrives. Viewing marriage as a ticket to a better life, and yielding to men's wishes and whims with masochistic condescension, they are at times rewarded with unwanted pregnancies and dangerous abortions. In their manifestations of fragmentation, alienation, and vacuousness, Maraini's early women can be said to "characterize certain conditions of postmodernism" (hooks 136). Often Maraini creates women's identities in terms of "otherness," that is, in relation to the central male position of "normality" as socially perceived. Stories like "Dazed," "Suffering," and "The Linen Sheets," from *My Husband*, show that women are not able to break out of their inertia. Subject as they are to familial, social, and economic entrapment, they seem to carry the burden of centuries of passive acceptance.

Maraini's second novel, *The Age of Discontent*, recipient of the prestigious international Formentor Prize and immediately translated into several languages, illustrates in the protagonist, Enrica, the traits of the women of this first phase of Maraini's writing. Like some of the young narrators in the stories in *My Husband*, the seventeen-year-old Enrica is the only child of a dysfunctional couple: her father is a disillusioned recluse whose only activity is to build birdcages that no one buys, while her mother, on becoming pregnant, abandoned her youthful dreams to marry and work in an office. The title, also translated as *The Age of Malaise*, immediately conjures up Sartre's existential novel *La nausée*, and Moravia's then very popular existential works: *La noia* (1960, *The Empty Canvas*), newly translated as *Boredom* (1999), *The Age of Indifference*, and *The Conformist*. Beginning with Enrica, Maraini shows how the battle of sexual politics is waged on the female body. By having Enrica narrate her experiences in a stream-of-consciousness fashion, and at the same time with an attitude that distances the reader's emotional involvement, Maraini is expertly able to elicit empathy with the narrating voice while maintaining her as the sexual object she has become. One not only reads but also senses Enrica's exploitation, repression, and segregation: her male friends are either young with no promise or too old and debauched. When she becomes pregnant from Cesare, the perennial student dependent on his parents, he urges her to have an abortion, because his father wants him to marry a woman of means. Fear mixed with shame prevents Enrica from disclosing her pregnancy to her parents or friends. She risks her life with a secret, and at that time illegal, abortion. Ironically, her mother keeps reminding her that her virginity will win her a man of means. Traumatized by the abortion, revolted by her mother's naivety and her lover's callousness, Enrica comes to realize that her present environment offers her no future, that the course of her life can improve only if she is financially independent and free to move away from the fetters of family, tradition, and self-centred men. The open-ended conclusion has Enrica determined to leave all abusive attachments behind: "Before going out I turned around and saw him sitting midway down the staircase holding his head in his hands. 'Good-bye,' I called back.... Summer is just around the corner, I said to myself, and then I'll start a new life. Meanwhile I must go back to the villa. The next day, I promised myself, I would get up early and go look for another job" (220).[7] The women speaking and suffering through the traumas, conflicts, and realizations of the first three novels, the short story collection *My Husband*, and the early plays, call attention to injustices to women in and outside of the family. Caught within their isolated existence, in the finiteness of their insoluble predicaments, women are shown as subalterns in relationships where they experience no complementarity with their male counterparts. Of Maraini's early men and women we could assert what Bryden says of Beckett's early characterizations, "Women 'don't' and 'can't,' for they are here measured against a yardstick invented and operated by a male—a male, moreover, who, contrary to their hopes, is not open to persuasion" (38–39).

To this first phase also belongs *A memoria* (1967; Memory),[8] a non-traditional novel which, as Lombardi correctly notes, "has been consistently avoided by the critics because of its utmost obscurity. Impossible even to summarize, this work seems to reject critical exegesis" (152). In his extended study, Lombardi refers to the several influences visible in this avant-garde work: Robbe-Grillet, Sarraute, Beckett. With respect to the latter, speaking with Anna Camaiti-Hostert about her early readings, Maraini has stated: "But the author I particularly enjoyed was Samuel Beckett, who influenced my writing at a very early stage. The first story I published, 'La mia storia tornava sotto l'albero carrubo' (My Story Came Back under the Carob Tree), was completely Beckettian" (*The Silent Duchess* 240). The relationships that *A memoria* bears to the works and characters not only of Beckett but of the avant-garde in general are too numerous to explore here. However, some salient traits ought to be noted for their unusual character in the Maraini prose corpus. The mothers in *A memoria*, for example, are portrayed as animal-like creatures, widows, whose aggressiveness and voracious appetite—for food and sex—emasculate the men close to them: at times they are worse than female animals, because instead of giving they take food from their children's plates. In addition, Maria's own features are like those of a "rapacious bird," and her friend's sister is presented as a "leech." Mary Bryden notes this human-animal trope in Beckett, where "animal species are often used to sub-divide and describe women" (34). Maria—like some of the women in *My Husband*, and to a lesser extent, like Enrica and later Teresa in *Memorie di una ladra* (1972, *Memoirs of a Female Thief*, 1974)—is a woman who lives mainly by instinct, devoid of social history or consciousness. We can say that, like the female characters in Beckett's early prose, the women in Maraini's early prose "are seen as apprehending reality by means of the evidence supplied by their senses alone: any wisdom accruing to them…amounts to stock responses to known experiences, and not to abstract reasoning or creative thought" (Bryden 22). The very emotional and sensual Maria and her "intellectual" husband Paolo are indeed two individuals at the margins of society. Their fragmented characters and consciousness are reminiscent of Beckett's human caricatures who fail to communicate and connect, speaking through empty, repetitive tirades. As in Beckett, fragmented sentences and nonsense repetition are abundant in the "conversation" between Maria and Paolo: "You know how many years we've been married?" "Eight. Why?" "We've been married for eight years." "How long?" "Eight years." "It's a lot." "Too long?" "No. It's right." "What does right mean?" "It means what it means. Neither too short nor too long." "We've been married for almost six years." "Is it six years we've been married?" "Almost." "It's a lot." "Too long?" "No. It's right." "What does right mean?" "That it's ok as it is." "Next month it'll be ten." "Ten what?" "Ten years we're married" (*A memoria* 19–22). This "dialogue" is repeated three times over the first four pages, with slight variations that aggravate the absurdity.

Seeking to contextualize it in the avant-garde literary landscape of its times (Poggioli 230), Lombardo regards this novel as a "work of art that stems from profound existential despair" (153), while Pallotta, judging from a "feminist viewpoint," finds it "a disturbing, ambivalent work permeated with contradictory notions" (194)—referring to it en passant, as "one of the more interesting experimental efforts of the post-World War II avant-garde in Italy" (193). We propose that although Maraini may have intended to try her hand at an experimental avant-garde novel and produced what we prefer to call an anti-novel, its value for Maraini the writer consists, in part at least, in the writing experience it afforded her for her future work. That is, as a piece of writing, *A memoria* was more important for the writer than for the almost indifferent reading public. We conjecture that for Maraini the artist, five years into her writing career, this piece of writing proved to be a most formative experimentation, a sort of "writing laboratory," an open and unlimited field where the young writer could discover the possibilities of different styles and test their limits as well. Published just a year before *My Husband*, *A memoria* eschews conventional narration. It is, in fact, presented in three different writing styles: epistolary, journal entries, and continuous conversation. This mixture and confusion of styles together with the erratic punctuation and sentence structure serve the requirements of the *nouveau roman*: to mirror the fragmented identity of the protagonists as well as the formative purposes of the writer. Some of the techniques tested in *A memoria* were immediately implemented in the stories in *My Husband*. The story "The Other Family," for example, uses, almost exclusively, continuous conversation. The robot-like husbands and children in the two dysfunctional families bandy about the uninterrupted, repetitive, and empty chatter of the Beckettian mode, failing to engage and listen to one another as a family.

Stories such as "Maria" and "Plato's Tree," which deal with the loss of social memory, and others concerned with elements of hypersexuality, social alienation, and madness, refer back to *A memoria* and recall the absurd emptiness of Beckett and the inert or absent humanity in Ionesco. The experimentation found in *A memoria* in relation to both concept and style represents, in our view, a necessary and very real intersection in Maraini's career. Shunned for over thirty years by critics and translators alike, this anti-novel marks, it seems to us, a crossroad at which Maraini the writer was able to work out her art with respect to genres, themes, and styles. That is, having experimented in order to discover what was for her the substantial character of *la scrittura*, the act of writing, with its infinite facets, Maraini could now better determine what themes, extremes, and styles worked well for the theatre, and which could work best in prose. We venture to suggest, then, that Maraini applied the epistolary style, the journal narration, and the flashback technique to her novels and short stories—the latter two immediately and abundantly put to use in *My Husband*—while reserving for her theatre the more extreme expressions and exemplifications of revolt and the absurd that are central in the ideology and style of *A memoria*. About her early theatre Maraini has said, "We started out with a theatre that broke with the past, attacked, set up barricades....We wanted to spread ideas that very few people held and very few people agreed with" (Bassnett 455). It may be of interest to note here that, while Maraini was a prolific playwright in her early years, only after *A memoria* were her plays produced and published. In the same year of the novel's publication, Maraini, along with Pier Paolo Pasolini, Alberto Moravia, and Enzo Siciliano, founded Il Porcospino, the Roman theatrical company whose purpose was to stage plays by contemporary writers. When a year later it folded, she founded the Compagnia Blu, for which she developed several plays. In 1973 she went on to found the Teatro Maddalena, by and for women, which enjoyed almost two decades of productive activity. For this stage Maraini wrote abundantly and successfully: "Virtually all social questions engaged by feminists, from abortion to patriarchy, are present in her plays, given voice by assertive women on stage" (Pallotta 192). Along with allusions to alienation and madness, *A memoria* introduces a number of features, such as contradiction, despair, verbal violence, subversion, self-effacement, excesses of the senses, the absurd, and shock, which Maraini later brought to the stage. We can confirm this through Maraini's own words, when she stated in an interview with Anderlini: "Madness is not adjusting to the world....My play *Clitemnestra* is the story of female madness, of rejection, incongruence, non-relationship with the male world" (150). Maraini's theatre combines stylistic and ideological elements of Beckett, with a didactic subtext that is often reminiscent of the theatre of

Berthold Brecht. Thus, the writing "experiment" that is *A memoria* is for us a most interesting work, not only because it broke away from national literary models but also for the artistic experience and freedom it afforded its author.

The works comprising Maraini's next two phases are substantially informed by the literary experiences of the formative first decade. As stated, the four styles comprised in *A memoria* are flashback, journal narration, epistolary correspondence, and dialogue; Maraini's prose since *A memoria* is a manifestation of the very successful application of all these, especially dialogue. Flashback becomes an important manner of narration as evidenced by three major works, *Memoirs of a Female Thief, Il treno per Helsinki* (1984, *The Train*, 1988), and *The Silent Duchess*, where memory is central to identity. *Donna in guerra* (1975, *Woman at War*, 1988) is presented as a diary, while epistolary correspondence is the technique that gives life to two novels, *Lettere a Marina* (1981, *Letters to Marina*, 1987) and *Dolce per sé* (1997, *The Violin*, 2001), where a renewed sense of identity surfaces in relation to an empathic corresponding "other." In each case the act of writing is fundamental to discovery: Giovanna (Vannina), in *Woman at War*, maps her transformation from a compliant and complacent housewife to a self-conscious, assertive, socially and politically aware woman, able to question and reject conventional role-playing as it has been made to apply to both women and men. In *Letters to Marina*, the epistolary exchanges afford the protagonist Bianca the possibility of reviewing her relationships, and face the pain of giving birth to a stillborn son. The written exchanges present for both corresponding subjects a period of self-analysis and reflection, which develops in them the will and strength to come to terms and move on with their lives. Since Maraini has indicated that writing was for her a form of "self-analysis," it is unsurprising that novels having writing and recollection at the centre also contain strands of autobiography (*Letters to Marina, The Train, Bagheria, The Silent Duchess*). Maraini's feminist thought posits, in part, that through the act of writing—agonizingly conveyed in *A memoria*, and triumphantly highlighted in *The Silent Duchess*—women ensure their inscription in history, not through writing alone but through all creative activities interpreting and articulating an understanding of the self, of the world as idea and activity.

Five years and five plays after *A memoria*, Maraini published *Memoirs of a Female Thief*, which introduces one of her most colourful, self-narrating protagonists in the vein of the picaresque. With the publication of this novel, Maraini entered, in our view, a second phase of writing, extending just beyond the next decade. In the prose works of this phase, Marini portrays women who reclaim their bodies and their pasts. By writing or speaking about their lives, they are able to transcend the constrictions and limitations of the present in order to forge new landscapes of possibility. This period exemplifies Maraini's central concept about women not simply as "mediators" in a male-centred world but as active agents in their own right: "I prefer to think of women as active agents capable of shaping reality with their characteristic sensibility: as endowed with autonomous creative subjectivity" (Santoro 13). The prose works pertaining to this period are *Memoirs of a Female Thief, Woman at War, Letters to Marina,* and *The Train.* Their protagonists actively confront the personal and social predicaments that stand in the way of self-recovery or discovery. In *Memoirs of a Female Thief* the writer herself, Dacia Maraini, served as an empathic "other" who permits self-discovery through self-disclosure, since she listened to and recorded the life story of the protagonist when she was released from prison. In *Woman at War,* the "other" is the diary where Vannina records conversations with the more radical people she meets, articulating also her own thoughts and realizations. In *Letters to Marina,* the addressee is the "other," reading and responding to Bianca's epistles. In *The Train,* the recollection of events over sixteen years and review of the lives of friends help Armida bring perspective to her present life. So compelling and focused is her need to retrieve the past that the entire novel unfolds in the span of her peeling a potato, deliberately punctuated at the beginning and conclusion, "I'm peeling a potato.... Here I am holding this potato...."[9] For Maraini, the act of remembering and retrieval is as important as the very act of writing—as an act of self-construction—that often accompanies it. Characters such as Bianca and Armida have lost touch with their past, and therefore their subjectivity. Psychoanalysis maintains that subjectivity is a developmental process by which human persons build or create their individual and separate history across time. To this extent, by turning to the past, Maraini's several protagonists (*Memoirs of a Female Thief, Letters to Marina, The Train, The Silent Duchess*), attempt a discovery, a retrieval, or a strengthening of a self-identity from the oblivion of time and history.

The protagonist of *Memoirs of a Female Thief,* Teresa Numa, seeks to survive in all the wrong ways since she was born as an unwanted child; moving from destitution close to prostitution, and from one petty crime to another, she is in and out of prison till her early forties. When she tires of the harsh, vicious circle that her life has become, and begins to observe others better than herself, her new perspective renders her critical of the choices she has made thus far. Becoming conscious of her extraordinary talent for communication and her healthy appetite for life, she determines to change her life and stay away from prison. The conclusion leads the reader to suppose that, despite her weaknesses, Teresa will be able to break the chain of subjection to men and women, who have always used her good nature to their own advantage. She vows that her life will no longer depend on what she steals but on what she can earn through gainful employment, beginning with the royalties that Maraini shared with her from the sales of the novel (Introduction to *Memorie* ix). In this work, which examines the tortuous life of a lower-class woman from her socialization as a child to her methods of survival as a swindler and thief, Maraini addresses the systemic problems and deplorable conditions of Italian prisons and detention centres for women, which she researched and visited in preparation for writing the novel. Within and outside the fiction, the protagonist's self-narration serves as a tool for self-knowledge and empowerment. Outside the fiction, Maraini's identification with the narrator's lived experiences enables her, after the anti-novel *A memoria*, to construct a new, richly textured human universe in the form of a picaresque novel, reminiscent of both *Lazarillo de Tormes* and *Moll Flanders*.

In the 1970s, the decade of critical reaction to Freud's positions on female sexuality, Maraini published what critics consider her feminist manifesto, the novel *Woman at War*, which traces a woman's journey to self-discovery through daily journals. It may not be by chance that here, and in her next novel, *Letters to Marina*, Maraini has two protagonists writing autobiographically. This overt emphasis on the word and the writing self seems to function in tandem with the writings of Luce Irigaray, who in this period was reacting to Lacanian theories. If, as Irigaray, paraphrasing Jacques Lacan, states, "Women are in a position of exclusion. And they may complain about it… But it is man's discourse, inasmuch as it sets forth the law… without much hope of escape, for women. Their exclusion is *internal* to an order from which nothing escapes: the order of (man's) discourse. To the objection that this discourse is perhaps not all there is, the response will be that it is women who are 'not-all'" (88), then we might say that through her novels of self-writing, and by making writing and written recollection central elements in much of her prose corpus, Maraini creates subtexts that are emblems of women devising individual discourses, and a necessary new vocabulary of self-identification.

The very title of Maraini's fifth novel, *Woman at War*, denotes the combative stance of the protagonist Giovanna (Vannina) vis-à-vis her mechanic husband and Italian social attitudes: both regard woman and marriage in the traditional manner that has persisted for centuries. Vannina embodies Maraini's perception of women's journey to self-knowledge, equality, and autonomy as one of continuous challenges, contrasts, and choices. Passive and uninspired in her marriage, Vannina goes with her husband, Giacinto, for a vacation in Naples, believing that hers is an average marriage, like most others. As a result of friendships she develops with young men and women from an underground leftist organization, she begins to realize that she is in fact submissive to and exploited by her husband. In time she understands that she is not obliged by necessity or law (as she had thought) to continue to stay with her abusive husband. She develops the conviction and fortitude to abort the life resulting from conjugal rape. Giacinto forced Vannina to have sex, hoping desperately that a pregnancy and a child would keep her by him, physically and materially dependent. In the end, however, through an act of will and anger, she leaves him in search of a new, self-directed life, while continuing her successful employment as a teacher. The novel echoes back both to *A Doll's House*, by Henrik Ibsen, and to what is considered the first Italian feminist novel, *A Woman*, by Sibilla Aleramo. Maraini criticism continues to view *Woman at War* as the centrepiece of her production to 1990, since it employs a number of effective techniques embodied in feminist literature. Among these is the diary, the first-person narration that for long has been associated with writings by women (as it was also by "marginalized" people of both sexes seeking a sense of identity, and on the way to "becoming"—to wit prison, cloister, refugee, and immigrant writings). In addition, Giacinto is aware of and acknowledges Vannina's intellectual abilities. But he resents her for this and fails to negotiate with her compromises within their marriage that would accommodate her separate and independent identity. In the figure of the husband, Ibsen, Aleramo, and Maraini all show partners who are unbending and self-centred. However, one should hasten to point out that Maraini's feminist philosophy "does not advocate separatism," as Tamburri has observed (148). Of further interest is how Maraini uses the devices of conversation and journal recording: most of Vannina's communication, written and oral, occurs during her husband's absences, when he leaves her alone in order to pursue his separate interests. Like Aleramo's protagonist, Vannina's writing and conversations take her from being a private, passive, marginal individual to one of engaged social consciousness; that is, Vannina moves beyond the protagonists of the preceding four novels. Beginning with *A memoria*, Maraini assigns the act of prolonged conversation (*Memoirs of a Female Thief*) or writing to a majority of her female protagonists (*Woman at War, Letters to Marina, The Train, Voices, The Silent Duchess*). Their use of language also assists them in the important process of transcending gendered discourse and differences, and in moving beyond their own gendered identity, beyond the models and perceptions of patriarchy; the self-affirmation that writing procures for them is not related to their womanhood alone but to them as human beings. Mary Bryden has noted that by linking authorship with emptying and self-expenditure, Hélène Cixous posits a "writing space which becomes a place of transit or fusion for all kinds of potential or actual exclusion zones, including that of gender" (Bryden 12). In relation to the importance of writing, Cixous states: "The definition of the author is linked with that circulation. It is me, I, within the other, the other within me, it's one gender going into the other, one language going through the other, life through death" (14).

In the novel *The Train*, Maraini finally does present a writer protagonist: Armida Bianchi is a playwright who, after a traumatic miscarriage and divorce, has an independent life and has fallen in love with Miele, a man she met through her husband. As is true of some stories in *My Husband* ("Plato's Tree," "The Two Angelas," "Diary of a Married Couple," "Marco"), memory is a central theme in *The Train* which, like *Memoirs of a Female Thief*, consists of flashbacks over several years. A stylistically interesting novel, *The Train* omits minor punctuation, such as commas, in order to emphasize the unimpeded flow of memory and the train's forward movement. Armida recalls and confronts the moments of pain in her life, her traumatic miscarriage, her divorce, and her mother-in-law who, concerned as she and her son were with inheritance and the family name, convinced Armida to have a child: "I hold on for her only for her who somehow has infected me with the absolute and irreversible decision to have this child at all costs" (72). The difficult pregnancy ends in the eighth month with a stillborn child: "I collapse to sleep. My muscles relax allowing my child to be taken away by expert hands which throw it into the pail without even a gesture of affection. Then they tell me it was a boy...." (74). Armida thus has not only the act of writing but also sexual and emotional unhappiness in common with other Maraini protagonists. *The Train* is the first novel displaying what might be called a choral participation of youths, representing the aspirations of a generation of Italians. Surrounded by young, idealistic friends with common leftist loyalties and political interests, after her divorce Armida goes by train to Helsinki to take part in the 1968 International Youth Festival.

Of those years, Maraini has said to Leandro Palestini, "There was the illusion of being able to change the world.... For example I myself went on that trip to Helsinki with the 'Socialist Youth' association." When this novel was first published, reviews spoke of it as a meaningful social document for all of Italy. Writing in Italy's leading daily newspaper, *Il Corriere della sera*, Antonio Porta stated, "*Il treno per Helsinki*...resonates and is more than ever alive, as if pointing to other trains to other future times." Renzo Paris had in mind the generation of '68 when he wrote: "Few writers have tried to talk about the 'new' relationships and among these, very few women. Now Dacia Maraini focuses on this theme and looks back with a close glance at this generation." Alluding to the various failed relationships among the young Italian travellers, Paris viewed the novel as a metaphor for the social conditions in Italy in the late 1960s: "The author has allowed us to glimpse, beneath the various failures, the situation of not only an entire generation, but of the entire nation, Italy, which seems to consist of aborted projects and new starts." And for Adele Cambria, the novel is "A mirror, a synthesis, of Italian society and its bad habits." The thematic interest and characters of this novel flash back to the year of publication of *My Husband*. The failures in relationships and undertakings registered in the novel often echo attitudes and failures portrayed in the short stories. Just as the protagonists of *My Husband* find no way out of their problematic "dead-end" lives, so the group of idealistic Italian youths return from Helsinki having learned some bitter realities, dissatisfied with the Festival where they became aware of the great gulf that separates ideals from reality, thought from constructive action. Karin Fleischanderl echoed the intent of Cambria and Paris when she observed about *The Train*, "Thus, the picture of an entire generation is developed, supported by individual stories of the participants."[10] As well, the long flashback over the trip helps Armida understand that she must let go of her passionate but unrequited love for Miele. At the end of the novels of this second phase, concluding with *The Train*, women protagonists realize that not marriage alone but—more realistically—individual and financial independence as well as positive human interaction can lead to personal freedom and realization. Maraini, aware that just less than half her readers are male (Palestini, 1984), invites readers to consider these notions in her subtext.

Stylistically *The Train* is interesting for the complete absence of commas. Intended to mimic the stream-of-consciousness narration, protagonist and reader are swept along by events and the train's rapid course.

With the publication of *Isolina*, which was awarded the Fregene and Rapallo prizes, Maraini was able to address the issue of violence against women as a national scandal by contextualizing it within political and juridical frameworks.[11] With this work which, in our view, begins the third phase of Maraini's writing, she provides the ultimate awakening element: surprise, shame, and sensationalism in relation to sexual violence as a crime against women. Up to *Isolina* her message was for the most part woven within the text—the lives of women, and their realizations, served as symbolic signifiers, as the subtext. However, in this third and continuing phase, Maraini deals openly and graphically with this subject: the sexual politics of power and possession are played out on the bodies of women who are irremediably damaged or destroyed through child rape, murder, and dismemberment. Both *Isolina* and *The Silent Duchess* illustrate a principle often noted by feminist theorists: whether real or fictitious, instances of male violence against women represent patriarchy's involvement in silencing and erasing women from history. By retrieving victimized women from historical oblivion, Maraini in essence creates and frames enduring emblems to represent the female condition in past and present times.[12]

For *Isolina*, Maraini spent considerable time poring over court documents and newspapers of the period and interviewing descendants of Isolina's family. The body parts of the pregnant Isolina were found scattered in the Adige River that runs through the city of Verona; the evidence was sufficiently clouded as to make the identity of the killer(s) impossible to ascertain. Her army officer lover, considered to be guilty by the citizenry who knew Isolina, was cleared at the trial. Using a the third-person, journalistic style of reporting, the narrator intimates on repeated occasions that court proceedings were less concerned with justice than with safeguarding the reputation of the military, and checking the fear and scandal that stunned the small city of Verona. At the novel's conclusion, Maraini reports the judicial perspective on which was based, in part, the outcome of the trial: "Isolina Canuti, one reads between the lines, asked for it. Her superficiality led her to her doom, pity for her" (206).[13]

The intervention of history as well as autobiography becomes all the more powerful in the novel published five years later that deals with child rape. The aristocratic origins of Maraini's family in Sicily in the early eighteenth century are the frame for *The Silent Duchess*, an instantly popular work in Italy and Europe that sold over 100,000 copies in just weeks. Marianna Ucrìa, when a child of five, is raped by her maternal uncle with the complicity of her parents. To hide the crime they arrange her marriage to him as soon as she reaches puberty. The trauma of the rape leaves the child Marianna deaf and mute for life. Too young to remember the experience, her handicap remains a mystery to her until, as a mature woman, Marianna desperately recalls the truth of her past. Flashbacks and third-person narration allow Maraini to present Marianna's life as a heroic victory over adversity: she has five children with her husband, thirty years her senior. Communicating by writing at all times, she runs a full household of relatives, servants, and responsibilities. Largely self-educated, Marianna reads voraciously from the family library works by favourite philosophers of the Enlightenment, such as the Scottish "signor Hume." As is true of *Woman at War*, where the main character, subjected and seemingly helpless at first, develops a separate subjectivity unobserved and unwelcome to her husband, so too Marianna develops an individual perspective that departs from the eighteenth-century social systems that serve patriarchy. Beyond her conventional life of wife and mother, her readings help her to develop a consciousness about human worth that transcends sex, gendered notions, and class. In David Hume she discovers notions regarding human society and nature—ideas for example, that what is perceived as natural may be simply a result of centuries of social constructs and imperatives. Marianna's different mode of perceiving becomes all the more evident when compared to that of her husband Pietro, who fully and conveniently serves the system of aristocracy in which he was born. Even when Marianna becomes aware of the atrocious act that, with her parents' complicity, her husband perpetrated against her when a child, she is able to understand that they are victims of the very system they espouse and support, "the imminent hidden barbarity" which, in Vico's philosophy, constantly threatens "every human being and every epoch" (*Duchess* 227). Thus, Marianna's comprehension of her times and human nature are such that she comes to view her aggressors not with cynicism and bitterness but rather with pity and compassion. David Hume's philosophy plays a large part in Marianna's self-education and self-liberation. At the age of forty-five she gives herself permission to have an affair with a servant much younger than herself. Later, Marianna leaves family, wealth, and Sicily behind permanently in order to discover a new and changing world in mainland Italy. Marotti observes: "In basing ethics inside personal consciousness and feelings, in stressing the importance of pleasure in evaluating virtue, and in emphasizing the role of imagination as a tool of discovery, Hume validates Marianna's own introspective experience" (172). Maraini's novel holds many points of interest as a feminist piece of writing located at a historical peak time of male-authored writings, both philosophical and fictional. Presenting the work from a female point of view, Maraini creates a protagonist who, despite her rape and attendant handicaps, survives and transcends entrapments, and develops a subjective and critical consciousness.[14]

The detective thriller *Voci* (1994; *Voices*, 1997) also examines family violence against women: the body of a woman is discovered in her apartment. Michela Canova, a radio journalist preparing a report on unsolved crimes against women, becomes involved in the investigation of the murder of her neighbour, Angela Bari. After some tortuous meanderings she discovers that family members were implicated in the young woman's sexual abuse and murder. *Voices* is a work of fiction based on general social and national realities of violence against women—violence that can take many forms, including career discrimination, as Testaferri points out: "In the role of amateur detective, Michela Canova reiterates the marginality engulfing ordinary and career women alike in present-day Italy. Michela repeatedly challenges this peripheral status by rejecting amateurism as an existential attribution of the feminine" (44).

In this context it may be interesting to conjecture that Maraini's corpus seeks in a multitude of ways to subvert traditional perceptions and attributions about women, regardless of times and cultures.[15] The protagonists she creates (Teresa, Vannina, Bianca, Armida, Marianna, Michela), are women who offer resistance to and confront the adverse structures, forces, and challenges of patriarchal systems in order to develop or refine a separate critical and thriving subjectivity and historicity. That is, history, a product of patriarchal systems, which like them has largely excluded women, sees, in the twentieth century and beyond, women speaking, writing, and engaged in creative activities—powerful indicators of their equal ability to be collaborators in generating culture, not simply its objects or consumers. As an avid reader of the classics, Maraini is aware that Aristotle has had a fundamental influence on Western culture. Her prose works seem intent upon subverting a number of Aristotelian notions that survive in the fabric of culture. For instance, on discussing his notions about reproduction in *De Generatione Animalium*, Aristotle considers the woman along with animals stating, "The woman is as it were an infertile male.... The male provides both the form and the source of movement while the female provides the body, i.e., the matter" (Bk. I, 728a 49, and 729a 51). Maraini's women in the first decade of her writing (Anna, Enrica, Maria), seem to confirm the traditional notion from Aristotle; their consciousness seems to revolve around the male universe where they are matter whose sensory life fulfils men's vision and purpose. But beginning with the second phase, Maraini's women battle to tear down the barriers of traditional perception in order to map for themselves new landscapes of consciousness, learning, and understanding. In this respect, in regarding language and writing as a critical site of struggle, as the practice of freedom, Maraini's philosophy is, in our view, very close to that of cultural critic and feminist theorist bell hooks for whom literacy is essential because "the lack of reading, writing and critical skills serve to exclude many women and men from feminist consciousness" (hooks 105). For all Maraini protagonists, writing, reading, and developing an articulate, critical consciousness are the fundamental pursuits through which they evolve to become active subjects, to subvert the long-standing notions of Aristotle and misconceptions of patriarchy. One should hasten to add here that Maraini never demonizes or degrades the male sex. On the contrary, she often demonstrates that power does not bring men happiness, that the defects of patriarchy bring harm both to women and to men, be they fathers, husbands, or lovers. Marianna's father and her husband Pietro, Vannina's repressive husband Giacinto, Armida's lover Miele, are men who are shown in their vulnerable humanity, limited within the narrowness of perspectives they ascribe to and the systems they uphold. At the conclusion of his interview Liberato Santoro asked Maraini, "What advice would you give to men, that we may learn to better understand women?" Maraini replied with one word, "Love!" (13) Maraini's prose works seem to indicate that her notions of "love" rest upon considerations, perspectives, and actions that make a full existence possible for both sexes. Looking again to Aristotle, perhaps this time Maraini would recommend that his idea of *amicitia*, friendship, should accompany love—an equal and complementary friendship among and between the sexes, not based on mutual exploitation or on possession as power.[16]

Maraini's most recent prose, *Buio* (1999, *Darkness*, 2002), a collection of short stories, continues the discourse begun with *Isolina*: the human body as location for the sexual politics of power and violence that families and systems inflict upon the disempowered—this time, children. In a recent article for the *Times Literary Supplement*, "Dialects and Ecos: Italian Fiction Is in Good Shape," Peter Hainsworth studies the present literary scene in Italy, pointing out that "The most significant change that has occurred is that for the first time ever in Italian literature some of the most acclaimed writers are women." Of them, he continues, the only one who is "still pressing an overtly feminist agenda is Maraini" (14). Indeed, Maraini's course as a writer continues uninterrupted, as a natural consequence of her human vision: "For me 'feminism' is an awareness: a serious reflection on the concrete existential condition of women, and on the historical, social, political and cultural genesis of such conditions" (Santoro 13). Following Maraini's four decades of studying and writing about the condition of women with passion and compassion, perhaps her favourite author Samuel Beckett would say of her and the women she portrays what he wrote at the conclusion of *Company*: "Numb with the woes of your kind you raise none the less your head from off your hands and open your eyes" (80).

VFG, 2004

~

Notes

1   Maraini often travels outside of Italy and has visited Canada repeatedly, especially on the occasion of the International Festival of Authors at Harbourfront, in Toronto. In 1987 she visited with her noted companion of eighteen years, writer Alberto Moravia, who contributed an introduction to *The Holiday*. At Harbourfront Maraini read from what critics consider her "feminist manifesto," the novel *Woman at War*. On this occasion she was interviewed by Adele Freedman. See also details and schedule of the 1992 Festival in *The Toronto Star*, Sat. 3 October. Throughout this study translations are mine, unless otherwise indicated.

2   Maraini in *Contro Roma* (76-77). Unless otherwise indicated, in this afterword all translations from Italian to English are mine.

3   Dacia's father had to his credit a number of well-known scholarly publications in anthropology. In addition Maraini writes about her "paternal grandmother—a Polish woman with Irish citizenship who wrote travelogues—her paternal grandfather—a sculptor who wrote on art and aesthetics—and her maternal grandfather who published cookbooks and works of philosophy" (Lazzaro-Weis, 216).

4   Santoro 13.

5   In Centocelle, a depressed area of Rome, Maraini helped young women set up and run theatre groups with a view to encouraging the growth of "feminist culture in Italy" (Lepschy, 211). From her earliest plays—*Cuore di mamma* (Heart of a Mother), *La donna perfetta* (The Perfect Woman), and *Il cuore di una vergine* (The Heart of a Virgin)—to the more recent *Delitto* (Murder), and *Veronica, meretrice e scrittora* (*Veronica Franco, Courtesan and Poet*), Maraini addresses personal and social issues of central importance to

women and the nation: imprisonment, rape, illegal abortion, prostitution, dysfunctional family life, murder, as well as myths of the "Latin lover" as they appear in popular culture. The wide consideration that her large number of plays (over forty) commands is not possible in this overview on Maraini's prose works.

6 Unpublished English translation by Katharina Otto.

7 The introduction to the 3rd edition (1980) of *The Holiday* by Mondadori reviews the economic and social conditions of Italy's mid- to lower class, which Enrica inhabits. Italy's progressive economic improvements from the 1950s to the '60s mainly benefited the upper classes: "in universities [where] 9 percent of students come from working class families. In general improvements on life conditions (housing, sanitation, private transport, food), exclude many millions of citizens, entire underdeveloped regions of the North and South. Unions fight not only for salary increases but also for improved workers' conditions in factories: in 1960, 2,238,000 workers accumulated 46,289,000 strike hours. In 1961 the hours increased to 79,127,000 by 2,698,000 strikers. In 1960-61 the political climate, with the encouragement of the masses, marks the beginning of that alliance between centre and left … which was brought severely into question by the student and workers movement of 1968" (xv).

8 The title is rendered literally as By Heart (Lombardi), and From Memory (Pallotta). While "by heart" or "from memory" render the meaning that seems implied in the title ("to learn something by heart," "to repeat something from memory"), we nevertheless offer the title as Memory in order to better highlight the central idea of the novel that portrays the gradual disintegration of the relationship and the humanity of a man and a woman, husband and wife, resulting from their deliberate choice to live without memory—social, cultural, and personal memory.

9 *Il treno* 3, 266. Some of the novels of these first twenty years seem to bear stylistic relations to novels that trace the growth of an individual. But although Maraini's protagonists change in the course of the novels, Maraini criticism does not dwell on the question of *bildungsroman*, perhaps because Maraini's intent and purpose in writing was not really to trace the growth of an individual as such. That is, her works are less concerned with an "éducation sentimentale" (a maturing of emotions), than they are with a "prise de conscience," a woman's coming into a critical self-awareness and self-knowledge as a social and socialized human being. To this extent, Maraini's purpose is like that of many celebrated feminist writers: to show that women can win their freedom from historical, social, economic, and religious notions of their lives and roles as inert, as expiation, sacrifice, and subjection. Maraini presents to women alternatives that help to envision life as activity directed toward constructive activity. For an interesting study of Maraini's *Voci* (*Voices*) as "detective story and bildungs-

roman with a feminist perspective," see Ada Testaferri, "De-tecting *Voci*," in R. Diaconescu-Blumenfeld and Ada Testaferri, eds., 41-60.

10 Unpublished English translation by Katharina Otto.

11 In giving wide and persistent attention to violence against women, Maraini's literature echoes the central interest in the lesser as well as the more promi-nent novels by women in contemporary Italian literature: Sibilla Aleramo's *Una donna* (1906; translated as *Woman at Bay* by Maria H. Lansdale (New York: G.P. Putnam's, 1908, and by Rosalind Delmar as *A Woman* (Berkeley and Los Angeles: U of California P, 1980), and *Artemisia* by Anna Banti (1947; translated by Shirley D'Ardia Caracciolo [Lincoln: U of Nebraska P, 1988 and 1995]). Both works speak of a rape and its radical consequences leading the woman to a heightened and militant sense of self-awareness.

12 With *Isolina*, Maraini for the first time renders history central. This artistic device, finding in the fictitious or semi-fictitious past parallels to present real-ities, allows the artist freedom of expression while ensuring and safeguard-ing the attention and the intelligent interest of the reader. Italy's very first novel of the mid-nineteenth century, *The Betrothed* by Alessandro Manzoni, successfully uses history to distance the troubles of a divided and oppressed Italy, before unification, to the early seventeenth century when some of the same problems already existed.

13 The publisher Bompiani announced this novel as a *clamoroso giallo* (sensa-tional thriller). The newspapers reported that during the trial Isolina was viewed as a girl lacking high moral values and therefore responsible for her own misfortunes. Her officer lover, who was considered to be an hon-ourable man in every way, kept referring to Isolina as "light" and "little cow, monkey, scorpion." In mentioning these details, Lietta Tornabuoni comments: "His schizophrenia remains true today; how many men feel they are perfectly honest in their public selves, but are brutal and shameless in their manner of loving?" In her article on *Isolina*, the journalist goes on to quote Maraini: "Even today in rape trials, the mechanism used to discredit the victim is identical to the one used against poor Isolina, the girl cut to pieces" (3).

14 For a detailed understanding of Maraini's rewriting of the eighteenth cen-tury from a feminist perspective, see Marotti's essential study.

15 In the 1984 interview with Palestini, Maraini stated, "according to recent data out of every 10 readers at least 6 are female." Following the considerable suc-cess of her works after 1984, it is fair to suppose that through the 1990s and beyond at least half of her readers are male, and therefore her perspectives have broader resonances in Italy and abroad.

16 For an elaboration on this idea of friendship and a corollary quotation from Mary Wollstonecraft's 1792 treatise *Vindication of the Rights of Woman*, see Vera F. Golini, 217-18.

Works Cited

Aristotle. *De Partibus Animalium I and De Generatione Animalium I*. Trans. D.M. Balme. Oxford: Oxford UP, 1972.

Andelini, Serena. "Prolegomena for a Feminist Dramaturgy of the Feminine: An Interview with Dacia Maraini." *diacritics* 21.2-3 (1991): 148-60.

Bassnett, Susan E. "Towards a Theory of Women's Theatre." *Semiotics of Drama and Theatre: New Perspectives in the Theory of Drama and Theatre*. Ed. H. Schmid and A. Van Kesteren. Philadelphia: Benjamins, 1984. 445-66.

Beckett, Samuel. *Company*. London: John Calder, 1980.

Bellesia, Giovanna. "Variations on a Theme: Violence against Women in the Writings of Dacia Maraini." *The Pleasure of Writing. Critical Essays on Dacia Maraini*. Ed. R. Diaconescu-Blumenfeld and A. Testaferri. West Lafayette: Purdue UP, 2000. 121-34.

Bryden, Mary. *Women in Samuel Beckett's Prose and Drama*. London: Barnes & Noble, 1993.

Cambria, Adele. "Storia di gruppo in un esterno." *Minerva* July 1984: 45-46.

———. "Le confidenze si fanno romanzo." *Quotidiano donna* 17 April 1981.

Cixous, Hélène. "Difficult Joys." *The Body and the Text: Hélène Cixous, Reading and Teaching*. Ed. H. Wilcox, K. McWatters, A. Thompson, and L.R. Williams. Hemel Hempstead: Harvester Wheatsheaf, 1990. 5-30.

Fleischanderl, Karin. "Seefahrt in der Nußchale: Dacia Maraini und ihre literarischen Mütter." *Die Presse* 29 March 1986, IV.

Freedman, Adele. "Writing Enables Dacia Maraini to Burst out of Her Shell." *Globe and Mail* 3 March 1987, E1.

Golini, Vera F. "Italian Women in Search of Identity in Dacia Maraini's Novels." *International Women's Writing: New Landscapes of Identity*. Ed. Anne E. Brown and Marjanne Goozé. London: Greenwood P, 1995. 206-20.

Hainsworth, Peter. "Dialects and Ecos: Italian Fiction Is in Good Shape." *Times Literary Supplement* 2 May 2003: 14-15.

hooks, bell. Interview. "Feminist *Praxis* and the Politics of Literacy: A Conversation with bell hooks." *Women Writing Culture*. Ed. G.A. Olson and E. Hirsh. Albany: SUNY P, 1995. 105-37.

Irigaray, Luce. *This Sex Which Is Not One*. Trans. C. Porter & C. Burke. Ithaca: Cornell UP, 1977.

Lazzaro-Weis, Carol. "Dacia Maraini." *Italian Women Writers: A Bio-Bibliographical Sourcebook*. Ed. R. Russell. London: Greenwood P, 1994. 216-25.

Lepschy, A.L. "Drama, Realism, Identity and Reality on Stage." *Modern Italian Culture*. Ed. Z.G. Barański and R.J. West. Cambridge: Cambridge UP, 2001. 197-213.

Lombardi, Giancarlo. "*A memoria*: Charting a Cultural Map for Women's Transition from *Preistoria* to *Storia*." Ed. R. Diaconescu-Blumenfeld and A. Testaferri. 149-55.

Maraini, Dacia. *A memoria*. Milan: Bompiani, 1967.

————. *Isolina: la donna tagliata a pezzi*. Milan: Mondadori, 1985; Rizzoli, 1992.

————. *Mio marito*. Milan: Bompiani, 1968.

————. "Reflections on the Logical and Illogical Bodies of My Sexual Compatriots." Trans. R. Diaconescu-Blumenfeld in R. Diaconescu-Blumenfeld and A. Testaferri, eds. 21-38.

————. *The Age of Malaise*. Trans. Frances Frenaye. New York: Grove P, 1963.

————. *The Silent Duchess*. Trans. and Afterword, Anna Camaiti-Hostert. New York: Feminist P, 1998. 237-263.

————. *Woman at War*. Trans. M. Benetti and E. Spottiswood. London: Lighthouse, 1984.

Marotti, Maria O. "*La lunga vita di Marianna Ucrìa*: A Feminist Revisiting of the Eighteenth Century." Ed. R. Diaconescu-Blumenfeld and A. Testaferri. 165-78.

Palestini, Leandro. "Dacia Maraini, amore e miti del Sessantotto." *Provincia paese* 12 August 1984.

Pallotta, Augustus. "Dacia Maraini." *Italian Novelists since World War II, 1965-1995. Dictionary of World Biography*. Vol. 196. Washington: Bruccoli, Clark, Layman, 1999. 189-200.

Paris, Renzo. "Una pedagogia materna e dura dell'amore." *Paesesera*, Monday 30 July 1984: 11.

Piemontese, Felice, ed. *Autodizionario degli scrittori italiani*. Milan: Leonardo, 1990.

Poggioli, Renato. *The Theory of the Avant-Garde*. Trans. G. Fitzgerald. New York: Harper & Row, 1962.

Porta, Antonio. "Ricordi quel treno di gioventù?" *Il Corriere della sera*, Wednesday 7 July 1984: 14.

Santoro, Liberato. "Female Person Singular." *Irish Times*, Saturday 16 June 1984: 13.

Sumeli Weinberg, Grazia. "An Interview with Dacia Maraini," *Tydskrif vir Letterkunde* 27, 3 August 1989: 64-72.

————. *Invito alla lettura di Dacia Maraini*. Pretoria: U of South Africa P, 1993.

Tamburri, Anthony J. "Dacia Maraini's *Donna in guerra*: Victory or Defeat?" *Contemporary Women Writers in Italy: A Modern Renaissance*. Ed. Sante L. Aricò. Amherst: U Massachusetts P, 1990. 139-51.

Tornabuoni, Lietta. "Ho riscoperto Isolina, ragazza cancellata anche dalla cronaca." *La Stampa*, 23 March 1985: 1, *Tuttolibri Insert*.

∼

Appendixes

Interviews with Dacia Maraini

Anderlini, Serena. "Interview with Dacia Maraini: Prolegomena for a Feminist
Dramaturgy of the Feminine." *diacritics* 21 (1991): 148-160.

———. "Prolegomeni per una drammaturgia del femminile: Intervista a
Dacia Maraini." *Leggere Donna* 30 (1991) : 22-24 and 31 (1991):
24-27.

Arca, Antonia. *Intervista a Dacia Maraini*. Alghero: Apeus, 1990.

Bellezza, Dario. "Questo libro sulla memoria di una donna." *Paese sera*
22 April 1981. np.

Cambria, Adele. "Le confidenze si fanno romanzo." *Quotidiano donna*
17 April 1981. np.

Bruck, Edith. "Si vende per libera scelta la prostituta filosofa." *Il Messaggero*
21 June 1976.

Capozzi, Rocco. "Incontro con Dacia Maraini." *Homage to Moravia*.
Ed. R. Capozzi and Mario B. Mignone. Stony Brook, NY: Forum
Italicum Fililibrary, 1993. 57-61.

Ciambellotti, Edera. "Una stanza tutta per sé: Intorno a *L'età del malessere* di
Dacia Maraini," and "Parlando con Dacia Maraini: Intorno a *L'età
del malessere*." 0*Nel passato presente degli anni sessanta*. Urbino:
Montefeltro, 1981. 69-84.

Condorelli, Nella. "Dacia Maraini: quell'isola che è tra noi." *Noidonne*
March 1993: 68-69.

Debenedetti, Antonio. "Con Pasolini e altri amici in una cità amata e odiata."
Il Corriere della sera 15 July 1984. np.

———. "Donna guerriera." *Il Corriere della sera* 23 November 1975. np.

De Carli, Giovanna. "Due donne di provincia, anime innocenti in una
garconnière." *La Repubblica* 10 October 1979. np.

Freedman, Adele. "Writing Enables Maraini to Burst out of Her Shell."
Globe and Mail 3 March 1987, E1.

Gaglione, Paola, ed. *Il piacere di scrivere. Conversazione con Dacia Maraini.* Rome: Òmicron, 1995.

Garrone, Nicola. "Don Juan, seduttore sedotto dal potere." *La Repubblica* 29 November 1977. np.

―――. "Vergine e malmaritata, la sovrana non è felice." *La Repubblica* 18 December 1982. np.

Giustolisi, Livia. "Circo e teatro alla Maddalena, un musical di Dacia Maraini." *Paese sera* 19 February 1981. np.

Marinelli, Gioconda. *Dizionarietto quotidiano.* Milano: Rizzoli, 1997.

Martinoni, Renato. *Il palombaro delle acque profonde. Intervista a Dacia Maraini.* Balerna: Edizioni dell'ulivo, 1997.

Mitchell, Tony. "The Future Is Woman?" *Sydney Morning Herald* 18 May 1987. np.

Nakamura, Ryôji and René de Ceccatty. "La Nuit de Tempaku-Ryô: Entretien avec Dacia Maraini." *Europe: Revue Littéraire Mensuelle.* Vol. 693-94 (January-February 1987): 140-54.

Pansarella, Francesca. "Looking Back: Interview with Dacia Maraini." *New Observations* 69 (July-August 1989): 2-3.

Ravera, Lidia. "Siamo sempre state donne." *Il Corriere della sera* 7 April 1987. np.

Robinoy, Simonetta. "Prima delle femministe c'erano i sentimenti." *La Stampa* 4 August 1984. np.

Ruffilli, Paolo. "Tre domande a Dacia Maraini." *Il Resto del Carlino* 18 November 1975. np.

Santoro, Liberato. "Female Person Singular." *Irish Times* 16 June 1984. np.

Stampa, Carla. "Scrivo inebriandomi con il basilico." *Epoca* 2 May 1981. np.

Sumeli Weinberg, Grazia. "An Interview with Dacia Maraini." *Tydskrif vir Letterkunde* 27.3 (1989): 64-72.

―――. "An Interview with an Italian Feminist Writer." *Sojourner: The Women's Forum* 15.6 (1990): 21-23.

Testaferri, Ada. "Interview with an Italian Feminist Writer, Dacia Maraini." *Resources for Feminist Research* 16 (1987): 60-63.

Villa, Anna. "Una poesia immersa nella realtà." *Letteraria: incontri e commenti* 2 (1987): 4-5.

Wright, Simona. "Intervista a Dacia Maraini." *Italian Quarterly* 34 (1997): 71-91.

*B*ibliography of Maraini's Writings

Novels

La nave per Kobe. Diari giapponesi di mia madre. Milan: Rizzoli, 2001.

Dolce per sé. Milan: Rizzoli, 1997; Superpocket, 1999.

Voci. Milan: Rizzoli, 1994; Superbur, 1997; Superpocket, 1998.

Bagheria. Milan: Rizzoli, 1993; Superbur, 1996; Superpocket, 1997.

La lunga vita di Marianna Ucrìa. Milan: Rizzoli, 1990; Suprebur, 1992.
Isolina: la donna tagliata a pezzi. Milan: Mondadori, 1985; Rizzoli, 1992.
Il treno per Helsinki. Turin: Einaudi, 1984.
Lettere a Marina. Milan: Bompiani, 1981.
Donna in guerra. Turin: Einaudi, 1975; 2nd ed. 1984; Bur-La Scala, 1998.
Memorie di una ladra. Milan: Bompiani, 1972; Superbur, 1997.
A memoria. Milan: Bompiani, 1967. ʼ
L'età del malessere. Turin: Einaudi, 1963.
La vacanza. Milan: Lerici, 1962; Bompiani, 1976; Einaudi, 1998.

Short Story Collections

Buio. Milan: Rizzoli, 1999.
Nuovi racconti campani. Naples: Guida, 1997.
Mulino, Orlov e Il gatto che si crede una pantera. Rome: Stampa alternativa, 1995.
La ragazza con la treccia. Viviani, Edizione speciale, 1994.
L'uomo tatuato. Naples: Guida, 1990.
Mio marito. Milan: Bompiani, 1968; Rizzoli, 1999.

Essays, Interviews

Sicilia ricordata. Milan: Rizzoli, 2001.
Amata scrittura. Laboratorio di analisi, letture, proposte, e conversazioni. Milan: Rizzoli, 2001.
Un clandestino a bordo: le donne, la maternità negata, il corpo sognato. Milan: Rizzoli, 1996.
Cercando Emma. Milan: Rizzoli, 1993; Bur Supersaggi, 1996.
Il sommacco. Palermo: Flaccovio, 1993.
La bionda, la bruna e l'asino: con gli occhi di oggi sugli anni settanta e ottanta. Milan: Rizzoli, 1987.
Il bambino Alberto: Interviste. Milan: Bompiani, 1986.
Storia di Piera. Milan: Bompiani, 1980.
E tu chi eri? Interviste sull'infanzia. Milan: Bompiani, 1973; Rizzoli, 1998.

Theatre

Memorie di una cameriera. Milan: Rizzoli, 2001
Maria Stuarda e altre commedie. Milan: Rizzoli, 2001—includes *Mela, Donna Lionora Giacubina, Stravaganza, Un treno, una notte.*
Fare teatro. Milan: Rizzoli, 2000.
La casa tra due palme. Salerno: Sottotraccia, 1995.
Veronica, meretrice e scrittora. Milan: Bompiani, 1992; Rizzoli, 2001—includes *La terza moglie di Mayer, Camille.*
Erzbeth Báthory, Il geco, Norma '44. Rome: Editori & Associati, 1991.
Delitto. Lungro di Cosenza: Marco, 1990.
Stravaganza. Rome: Serarcangeli, 1987.

Lezioni d'amore e altre commedie. Milan: Bompiani, 1982—includes *Bianca Garofani, Fede o Della perversione matrimoniale, Felice Sciosciammocca, Mela, Reparto speciale antiterrorismo.*

I sogni di Clitennestra e altre commedie. Milan: Bompiani, 1981—includes *Due donne di provincia, Zena, Una casa di donne, Donna Lionora Giacubina, Maria Stuarda.*

Suor Juana. Turin: La Rosa, 1980.

Dialogo di una prostituta con un suo cliente. Padua: Mastrogiacomo, 1978.

Don Juan. Turin: Einaudi, 1976.

La donna perfetta, seguito da Il cuore di una vergine. Turin: Einaudi, 1975.

Fare teatro. Materiali, testi, interviste. Milan: Bompiani, 1974.

Viva l'Italia. Turin: Einaudi, 1973—includes the farces *La rosa serpentina indovina, Farsa popolare, Peppa e Carlino, Arruolamento, Farsa contadina, Crocifissa e Garibaldi.*

Il ricatto a teatro e altre commedie. Turin: Einaudi, 1970—includes *Recitare, La famiglia normale, Manifesto dal carcere.*

Cuore di mamma. Milan: Forum, 1969.

Poetry

Se amando troppo. Milan: Rizzoli, 1998.

Occhi di medusa: poesie. Calcata: Edizioni del Grano, 1992.

Viaggiando con passo di volpe: poesie, 1983-1991. Milan: Rizzoli, 1991.

Dimenticato di dimenticare. Turin: Einaudi, 1982.

Mangiami pure. Turin: Einaudi, 1978.

Donne mie. Turin: Einaudi, 1974.

Crudeltà all'aria aperta. Milan: Feltrinelli, 1966.

Children's Literature

La pecora Dolly. Milano: Fabbri editori, 2001.

Storie di cani per una bambina. Milan: Bompiani, 1996, 1998.

Selected Other

Dizionarietto quotidiano. Da "amare" a "zonzo": 229 voci raccolte da Gioconda Marinelli. Milan: Bompiani, 1997.

Joseph Conrad. *Il compagno segreto.* Trans. and introduction by Maraini. Milan: Rizzoli, 1996.

"Cinque donne d'acqua dolce." *Il pozzo segreto.* Ed. Maria Rosa Cutrufelli, Rosaria Guacci, and Marisa Rusconi. Florence: Giunti, 1993. 145-52.

Il sommacco: piccolo inventario dei teatri palermitani trovati e persi. Palermo: Flaccovio, 1993.

Nel segno della madre. With Anna Maria Mori. Milan: Frassinelli, 1992.

"Riflessioni sui corpi logici e illogici delle mie compagne di sesso." *La bionda, la bruna e l'asino: con gli occhi di oggi sugli anni settanta e ottanta.* Milan:

Rizzoli, 1987. v–xxx. Revised and translated into English, "Reflections on the Logical and Illogical Bodies of My Sexual Compatriots." *The Pleasure of Writing: Critical Essays on Dacia Maraini*. Ed. R. Diaconescu-Blumenfeld and A. Testaferri. West Lafayette, IN: Purdue UP, 2000. 21–38

"Suor Juana." Juana Inés de la Cruz. *Risposta a suor Filotea*. Ed. Angela Morino. Turin: La Rosa, 1980.

Introduzione. *Donne in poesia: antologia della poesia femminile in Italia dal dopoguerra a oggi*. Rome: Savelli, 1977.

La protesta poetica del Giappone. Antologia di cent'anni di poesia giapponese. Ed. with Michiko Norjiri. Rome: Officina, 1968.

Maraini's Filmography

(Most are not available for public screening.)

Lo scialle azzurro. 1980.
Giochi di latte. 1979.
La bella addormentata nel bosco. 1978.
Mio padre amore mio. 1976/1979.
Ritratti di donne africane. 1976.
Le ragazze di Capoverde. 1976.
Aborto: parlano le donne. 1976.
L'amore coniugale. 1970.

Films from Maraini's Prose Works

Voci from *Voci*. 2001. 110 minutes.
La lunga vita di Marianna Ucrìa from *La lunga vita di Marianna Ucrìa*. 1997. 120 mins.
Storia di Piera from *Storia di Piera*. 1983. 101 minutes.
Io sono mia from *Donna in guerra*. 1977. 100 minutes.
Teresa la ladra from *Memorie di una ladra*. 1973. 125 minutes.
Certo certissimo…anzi probabile from "Diario di una telefonista." 1969. 120 minutes.
L'età del malessere from *L'età del malessere*. 1968. 115 minutes.

Awards and Translations of Maraini's Prose Works

La vacanza (1962)
The Holiday. Trans. Stuart Hood. England: Weidenfeld & Nicolson, 1966.
Tage in augus. Trans. Herbert Schlüter. Germany: Aschehoug, 1963.
De vakantie. Trans. Jenny Tuin. Holland: Meulenhoff, 1962.

L'età del malessere (1963) Prize: Formentor 1963.
A idade ingrata. Trans. Fernanda Branco. Portugal: Circulo de Leitores, 1979.
Nebezpecné roky. Trans. Ján Proácka. Yugoslavia: Ján Proácka, 1965.

The Age of Discontent. Trans. Frances Frenaye. England: Weidenfeld & Nicolson, 1963.

The Age of Malaise. Trans. Frances Frenaye. USA: Grove Press, 1963.

Los años turbios. Trans. Jesus López Pacheco. Spain: Seix Barral, 1963.

Zeit des unbehagens. Trans. Werner Rebhuhn. Germany: Rowohlt, 1963, Rotbuch, 1965.

Olustenes år. Trans. Karin de Laval. Sweden: Bonniers, 1963.

Den svære alder. Trans. Cerl Johan Elmquist. Denmark: Gyldental, 1963.

Herämisen aika. Trans. Ull Jokinen. Finland: Otava, 1963.

Den urolige alder. Trans. Leo Stron. Norway: Gyldental, 1963.

(Available also in Japan, 1963; Greece: Am Oved, 1965; Holland: Mousault, 1963; France: Gallimard, 1963.)

A memoria (1967)

Nikto sa nepamäta. Trans. Ján Proácka. Yugoslavia: Ján Prohácka, 1969.

Memorie di una ladra (1972)

Spomeni na edna krala. Trans. Cetona Cioceva. Bulgaria: Danov, 1982.

Vagiles uzrasai. Trans. Dalia Lenkauskiene. Lithuania: Vagiles Uzasai, 1981.

Zapiski. Trans. Nicolai Tomascevskij. Russia: Progress, 1976.

Zapiski Terese Nume. Trans. N. Tomascevsko. Russia: Progress, 1976.

Teresa de dievegge. Trans. Mascha van Peype. Holland: Meulenhoff, 1975.

Teresa la voleuse. Trans. Paul Alexandre. France: Loisirs; Stock, 1974.

Spomeni malopridnice. Trans. Evelin Umek. Yugoslavia: Zalozba obzorja, 1974.

Memoirs of a Female Thief. Trans. Nina Rootes. London: Abelard-Schuman, 1973; Weidenfeld & Nicolson, 1974; Levittown, NY: Transatlantic Arts, 1974.

Memorias de una ladrona. Trans. Naldo Lombardi. Argentina: La Flor, 1973.

(Available also in Japan: Kadokava, 1976; in Germany: Piper, 1994; in China, 1997, trans. Sheen E. Mei.)

Donna in guerra (1975)

Kadin Savaşiyor. Trans. Semin Sayit. Turkey: Can Yayinlari, 1996.

Woman at War. Trans. M. Benetti and E. Spottiswood. USA: Italica Press, 1988.

Dagboek van en vrouw. Trans. Tineke van Dijk. Holland: Uitgeverij Contact, 1985.

Woman at War. Trans. M. Benetti and E. Spottiswood. England: Lighthouse Books, 1984.

Mulher em guerra. Trans. Maria F. Lusitano Leal. Portugal: Circulo de Leitores, 1983.

Femme en guerre. Trans. Michèle Causse. France: Des Femmes, 1977.

Lettere a Marina (1981)

Letters to Marina. Trans. D. Kitto and E. Spottiswood. England: Camden Press, 1987.

Oll treno per Helsinki (1984)
Zug nach Helsinki. Trans. Gudrun Jäger and Pieke Biermann. Germany:
Rotbuch, 1985; Rowohlt, 1992.
The Train. Trans. D. Kitto and E. Spottiswood. England: Camden Press, 1988.
De train naar Helsinki. Trans. Pietha de Voogd. Holland: Uitgeverij Contact,
1986.

Isolina: la donna tagliata a pezzi (1985) Prizes: Fregene 1985; Rapallo
1985
Isolina. Trans. Siân Williams. England: Peter Owen, 1993; Women's Press, 1995.
Isolina. Trans. Pieke Biermann. Germany: Rotbuch, 1995.
(Available also in Japan: Shobun-Sha, 1997; Spain: Luman, 1998.)

La lunga vita di Marianna Ucrìa (1990) Prizes: Supercampiello 1990;
Libro dell'Anno 1990; Calabria 1991; Apollo 1991; Quadrivio 1991; Marotta
1992
Lunga viata a Marianei Ucria. Trans. Gabriella Lungu. Romania: Univers, 2000.
Mykkä herttuatar. Trans. Sari Matero. Finland: Artemisia, 1998.
Marianna Ucrìa hosszú élete. Trans. Éva Székely. Hungary: Helikon Kiado, 1998.
The Silent Duchess. Trans. D. Kitto and E. Spottiswood. New York: Feminist
Press, 1998.
Die stumme Herzogin. Trans. Sabina Kienlechner. Germany: Piper, 1991;
Büchergide Gutenberg, 1995; Heyne bücher, 1997.
Niamata Ksercioghina. Trans. Rumiana Saraidarova. Russia: Xemus, 1996.
A longa vida de Marianna Ucrìa. Trans. Márcia Theóphilo. Portugal: Vega, 1996.
Dlugie zycie Marianny Ucrìa. Trans. Halina Karlova. Poland: Seria kieszonkowa,
1996.
Niamata chergozinia. Trans. Rumiana Saraidarova. Bulgaria: Chemus, 1996.
Niamata Ksercioghina. Trans. Rumiana Saraidarova. Russia: Xemus, 1996.
Den Stumma Hertiginnan. Trans. Ing-Britt Björklund. Sweden: Forum, 1994.
A longa vida de Marianna Ucrìa. Brazil: Mousault, 1994.
Marianna Ucria lange liv. Trans. Tommy Watz. Norway: Ascheoug, 1993.
The Silent Duchess. Trans. D. Kitto and E. Spottiswood. England: Peter Owen,
1992; Kingston, Canada: Quarry Press, 1992.
La vie silencieuse de Marianna Ucrìa. Trans. Donatella Saulmier. France:
Robert Laffont, 1992.
Die stumme Hertuginde. Trans. Nina Gross. Denmark: Forum, 1992.
La larga vida de Marianna Ucrìa. Trans. Attilio P. Malacrino. Spain: Seix Barral,
1991.
Een stille passie. Holland: Utgevenij Contact, 1991.
(Available also in Greece: Oceanida, 1991; Japan: Shobun-Sha, 1993; Poland:
PIW, 1996.)

Bagheria (1993) Prizes: Rapallo Carige 1993; Scanno 1993; Finalista Strega
1993; Joppolo, 1994

Bagheria. Trans. Teodosia Ghiannakopoyloy. Greece: Kastaniotis, 1997.
Bagheria. Trans. Nina Gross. Denmark: Forum, 1995.
Bagheria. Trans. Sabina Kienlechner. Germany: Piper, 1994.
Bagheria. Trans. D. Kitto and E. Spottiswood. England: Peter Owen, 1994.
(Available by the title of the Italian name of the protagonist, in Japan, 1995;
in Holland, 1995; in Israel, 1997.)

Cercando Emma (1993)

Searching for Emma. Trans. Vincent J. Bertolini. Chicago: U Chicago P, 1998.
Nachforschungen über Emma B. Trans. Sigrid Vagt. Germany: Piper, 1998.

Voci (1994) Prizes: Napoli 1995; Sibilla Aleramo 1995; Bancarella 1995;
Matilde Canossa 1996
Fonés. Trans. Antàios Krusostomides. Greece: Psichogios, 1997.
Voices. Trans. Dick Kitto and Elspeth Spottiswood. London: Serpent's Tail, 1997.
Golosa. Trans. A. Plesciakova. Russia: Raduga, 1997.
Voix. Trans. Alain Sarrabayrousse. France: Fayard, 1996.
Stimmen. Trans. Viktoria von Schirac. Germany: Piper, 1995.
Voces. Trans. Attilio P. Melacrino. Spain: Seix Barral, 1995.
Stemmen. Trans. Etta Maris. Holland: Uitgeverij Contact, 1995.
(Available also in Japan: Chuokoron-cha, 1996.)

Un clandestino a bordo (1996)

Stowaway on Board. Trans. Giovanna Bellesia and Victoria O. Polletti. Lafayette,
IN: Bordighera, 2000.

Dolce per sé (1997) Prizes: Un autore per l'Europa 1997; Vitaliano Brancati
1997; Città di Padova 1997; Internazionale Flaiano 1997
The Violin. Trans. D. Kitto and E. Spottiswood. England: Arcadia Books, 2001.
Liebe Flavia. Trans. Viktoria von Schirac. Germany: Büchergide Gutenberg,
1998.

Short Story Collections

Mio marito (1968; 1999)
Winterschlaf. Trans. Gurdrun Jäger. Germany: Rotbuch, 1984; Rowohlt, 1994.
Mio marido. Trans. Ana Godos. Argentina: Libreria Fausto, 1975.
My Husband. Trans. Vera F. Golini. Waterloo: Wilfrid Laurier University P, 2004.

Buio (1999) Prize: Strega, 1999
Darkness. Trans. Martha King. South Royalton, VT: Streetforth Press, 2002.
Karanlik. Trans. Semin Sayit. Turkey: Inkilap, 1999.

Critical Bibliography
of Maraini's Prose Works

Allen, Beverly, et al., eds. *The Defiant Muse: Italian Feminist Poems from the Middle Ages to the Present*. New York: Feminist P, 1986.

Bassnett, Susan. *Feminist Experiences: The Women's Movement in Four Cultures*. London: Allen & Unwin, 1986.

Birnbaum, Lucia Chiavola. *Liberazione della donna. Feminism in Italy*. Middletown, CT: Wesleyan UP, 1986.

Bono, Paola, and Sandra Kemp, eds. *Italian Feminist Thought: A Reader*. Oxford: Basil Blackwell, 1991.

Braidotti, Rosi. *Soggetto nomade: femminismo e crisi della modernità*. Rome: Donizelli, 1995.

Brooke, Gabriella. "Sicilian Philomelas: Marianna Ucrìa and the Muted Women of Her Time." *Gendering Italian Fiction. Feminist Revisions of Italian History*. Ed. Maria Ornella Marotti and Gabriella Brooke. Cranbury, NJ and London: Associated UP, 1999. 199-210.

Bruno, Giuliana and Maria Nadotti, eds. *Off Screen: Women and Film in Italy*. London: Routledge, 1998.

Cannon, JoAnne. "Rewriting the Female Destiny: Dacia Maraini's *La lunga vita di Marianna Ucrìa*." *Symposium* 49.2 (1995): 136-47.

Carini, Lucia. "Dacia Maraini: une force tranquille di féminisme." *La parole Métèque* 5 (1988): 9-11.

Cattaruzza, Claudio. *Dedica a Dacia Maraini*. Pordenone: ACP, 2000.

Cavallaro, Daniela. "*I sogni di Clitennestra*: The *Oresteia* according to Dacia Maraini." *Italica* 72 (1995): 340-55.

Dagnino, Pauline. "*Fra madre e marito*: The Mother/Daughter Relationship in Dacia Maraini's *Lettere a Marina*." *Visions and Revisions. Women in Italian Culture*. Ed. Mirna Cicioni and Nicole Prunster. Providence, RI: Berg, 1993. 183-98.

De Santi, Gualtiero. "La poesia d'amore in Italia, 1966-1983." *Testuale* 3 (1995): 11-35.

Diaconescu-Blumenfeld, Rodica, and Ada Testaferri, eds. *The Pleasure of Writing: Critical Essays on Dacia Maraini*. West Lafayette, IN: Purdue UP, 2000.

Di Pace-Jordan, Rosetta. Review of *Voci*. *World Literature Today* 69.2 (1995): 341.

Feinstein, Wiley. "Twentieth-Century Feminist Responses to Boccaccio's Alibech Story." *Romance Languages Annual* 6 (1989): 116-20.

Fernandez Torres, Alberto. "*María Estuardo* de Dacia Maraini: El rigor como método." *Insula* 38.437 (1983): 15.

Forti, Marco. "Dacia Maraini 'siciliana': romanzo storico familiare e memoria." *Nuova antologia* 547 (January-March 1995): 191-216; (April-June 1995): 136-59.

Forti-Lewis, Angelica. *Maschere, libretti e libertini: Il mito di Don Giovanni nel teatro europeo*. Rome: Bulzoni, 1992.

————. "Virginia Woolf, Dacia Maraini e *Una stanza per noi*: L'autocoscienza politica e il testo." *Rivista di studi italiani* 12 (1994): 29-47.

Frabotta, Biancamaria, ed. *Donne in poesia. Antologia della poesia femminile in Italia dal dopoguerra a oggi*. Rome: Savelli, 1976.

————. *Letteratura al femminile. Itinerari di letteratura a proposito di donne: storia, poesia, romanzo*. Rome: Savelli, 1980.

Gazzola Stacchini, Vanna, and Romano Luperini. *Letteratura e cultura dell'età presente*. Bari: Laterza, 1980.

Golini, Vera F. "Italian Women in Search of Identity in Dacia Maraini's Novels." *International Women's Writing: New Landscapes of Identity*. Ed. A.E. Brown and M.E. Goozé. Westport, CT: Greenwood P, 1995. 207-20.

Haffter, Peter. "Femminismo e seduzione nel *Don Juan* di Dacia Maraini." *Atti* (Terzo convegno dell'Associazione di Professori d'Italiano). Johannesburg: U Witwatersrand P, 1983. 382-93.

Kemp, Sandra, and Paola Bono, eds. *The Lonely Mirror: Italian Perspectives on Feminist Theory*. London: Routledge, 1993.

Lazzaro-Weis, Carol. "Dacia Maraini." *Italian Women Writers: A Bio-Bibliographical Sourcebook*. Ed. Rinaldina Russell. Westport, CT: Greenwood P, 1994. 216-25.

————. *From Margins to Mainstream: Feminism and Fictional Modes in Italian Women's Writing, 1969-1991*. Philadelphia: U Pennsylvania P, 1993.

————. "Gender and Genre in Italian Feminist Literature in the Seventies." *Italica* 65.4 (1988): 293-307.

————. "The Subject's Seduction: The Experience of Don Juan in Italian Feminist Fictions." *Annali d'italianistica* 7 (1989): 382-93.

Lister, Maureen. "Feminism alla milanese." *The Women's Review of Books* 8.9 (1991): 26.

Luti, Giorgio. *Narratori italiani del secondo Novecento. La vita, le opere, la critica*. Rome: Nuova Italia Scientifica, 1985. 193-229.

Maheux, Camille. "Connaissez-vous Dacia Maraini?" *Canadian Woman Studies* 5.1 (1983): 48-49.

Marotti, Maria Ornella. "Feminist Historians/Historical Fictions." *Italian Culture* 14 (1996): 147-59.

Marotti, Maria Ornella and Gabriella Brooke, eds. *Gendering Italian Fiction. Feminist Revisions of Italian History.* Cranbury, NJ and London: Associated UP, 1999.

Merry, Bruce. "Dacia Maraini: *La lunga vita di Marianna Ucrìa.*" *Pen: International Bulletin of Selected Books* 42.2 (1992): 33-35.

————. *Dacia Maraini and Her Place in Contemporary Italian Literature.* London: Berg, 1994.

————. *Women in Modern Italian Literature. Four Studies Based on the Work of Grazia Deledda, Alba De Céspedes, Natalia Ginzburg, and Dacia Maraini.* Townsville, AU: James Cook University of North Queensland, 1990. 193-229.

Milan Women's Bookstore Collective. *Sexual Difference: A Theory of Social-Symbolic Practice.* Trans. Teresa de Lauretis and Patricia Cicogna. Introductory essay by de Lauretis. Bloomington: Indiana UP, 1990.

Mitchell, Tony. "'Scrittura femminile': Writing the Female in the Plays of Dacia Maraini." *Theater Journal* 42 (1990): 332-49.

Montini, Ileana. *Parlare con Dacia Maraini.* Verona: Bertani, 1997.

Nozzoli, Anna. "La donna e il romanzo negli anni ottanta." *Rivista di vita cittadina.* Ed. Sergio Gengini. Empoli: Comune di Empoli, 1983. 45-53.

O'Healy, Áine. "Filming Female 'Autobiography.' Maraini, Ferreri, and Piera's Own Story." *Feminine Feminists. Cultural Practices.* Ed. Giovanna Miceli Jeffries. Minneapolis: U Minnesota P, 1994. 190-206.

Pallotta, Augustus. "Dacia Maraini: From Alienation to Feminism." *World Literature Today* 58.3 (1984): 359-62.

————, ed. "Dacia Maraini." *Dictionary of Literary Biography. Italian Novelists since World War II, 1965-1995.* Detroit: Gale Research, 1999. 189-200.

Panizza, Letizia, and Sharon Wood, eds. *A History of Women's Writing in Italy.* Cambridge: Cambridge UP, 2000.

Passione, Lina. *Sulle orme di Marianna Ucrìa.* Catania: CUECM, 1997.

Picchietti, Virginia. "Dacia Maraini." *Dictionary of Italian Literature.* Ed. Peter and Julia Bondanella. Westport, CT: Greenwood P, 1996. 358-61.

Picchione, John. "Poesia al femminile(?): rabbia, gioco, terapia." *Donna: Women in Italian Culture.* Ed. Ada Testaferri. U Toronto Italian Studies. Ottawa: Dovehouse, 1989. 59-70.

Pickering-Iazzi, Robin. "Designing Mothers: Images of Motherhood in Novels by Aleramo, Morante, Maraini, Fallaci." *Annali d'Italianistica* 7 (1989): 325-40.

Piemontese, Felice, ed. *Autodizionario degli scrittori italiani*. Milan: Leonardo, 1990.

Porta, Antonio. *Poesia degli anni settanta*. Milan: Feltrinelli, 1979.

Rasy, Elisabetta. *Le donne e la letteratura*. Rome: Riuniti, 1984.

Restivo, Angelo. *L'occhio e la parola*. Bagheria: Thule, 1997.

Riviello, Tonia Caterina. "The Motif of Entrapment in Elsa Morante's *L'isola di Arturo* and Dacia Maraini's *L'età del malessere.*" *Rivista di studi italiani* 8 (1990): 70-87.

Rosenthal, Margaret. *The Honest Courtesan: Veronica Franco, Citizen and Writer in Sixteenth-Century Venice*. Chicago: U Chicago P, 1992.

Rutter, Itala T.C. "Feminist Theory as Practice: Italian Feminism and the Work of Teresa De Lauretis and Dacia Maraini." *Women's Studies International Forum* 13.6 (1990): 565-75.

Santagostino, Giuseppina. "*La lunga vita di Marianna Ucrìa*, tessere sotto lo sguardo delle chimere." *Italica* 73.3 (1996): 410-28.

Sapegno, Maria Serena. "Oltre e dietro il pudore." *Conversazione con Dacia Maraini*. Ed. Paola Gaglione. Rome: Òmicron, 1995. 41-60.

Scattigno, Anna. "La retorica della debolezza: esperienza religiosa e percorsi di identità femminile." *Il femminile tra potenza e potere*. Rome: Arlem, 1995. 135-45.

Sumeli Weinberg, Grazia. "All'ombra del padre: La poesia di Dacia Maraini in *Crudeltà all'aria aperta.*" *Italica* 68 (1990): 453-65.

———. "Dacia Maraini e il teatro femminista come modello di trasgressione." *Italian Studies in Southern Africa* 3 (1989b): 20-31.

———. *Invito alla lettura di Dacia Maraini*. Pretoria: U South Africa P, 1993.

———. "Women's Theatre: Teatro la Maddalena and the Work of Dacia Maraini." *Western European Stages* 1.1 (1991): 27-30.

———. "Word and Commitment in the Works of Dacia Maraini." *DAI* 50.9 (March 1990): 2886A.

Tamburri, Anthony J. "Dacia Maraini's *Donna in guerra*: Victory or Defeat?" *Contemporary Women Writers in Italy: A Modern Renaissance*. Ed. Santo L. Aricò. Amherst: U Massachusetts P, 1990. 139-51.

Tian, Rienzo. "Dal carcere con rabbia." Review of *Manifesto dal carcere*. *Il Messaggero* 10 March 1971.

Valerio, Adriana, ed. *Donna potere e profezia*. Naples: D'Auria, 1995.

West, Rebecca. "Dacia Maraini." *An Encyclopedia of Continental Women Writers*. Ed. Katharina M. Wilson. New York: Garland, 1991. 775-76.

Wood, Sharon. *Italian Women's Writing: 1860-1994*. London: Athlone, 1995.

———. "The Language of the Body and Dacia Maraini's *La lunga vita di Marianna Ucrìa*: A Psychoanalytical Approach." *Journal of Gender Studies* (1993): 47-59.

———. "Women and Theatre in Italy: Natalia Ginzburg, Franca Rame, and Dacia Maraini." *Romance Languages Annual* 5 (1993): 343-48.

Wright, Simona. "Dacia Maraini, Charting the Female Experience in the Quest-Plot: *Marianna Ucrìa.*" *Italian Quarterly* 34 (1997): 59-70.

Zagarrio, Giuseppe. *Febbre, furore, fiele. Repertorio della poesia italiana contemporanea, 1979-1980.* Milan: Mursia, 1983.

~